"Not completely, no." Jonathon's deep voice poured warmth over her cold heart. "We share the blame and will face the consequences together, no matter how dire or life-altering."

He did not mention marriage, but he was thinking it. The evidence was there, in the grim twist of his lips and the stern set of his shoulders.

She'd dragged this man into a place he'd vowed never to go.

"Come." He tugged her toward the ballroom, toward their moment of reckoning. "Time to face the good people of Denver."

He guided her to the very edge of the French doors. A few more steps and they would cross over the threshold, into a future neither of them truly wanted. Jonathon for his reasons.

Fanny for hers.

She shot a glance at Jonathon from beneath her lashes. Even in the dense, flickering shadows, she recognized the resolve in his eyes, the willingness to do whatever was necessary to protect her from another scandal.

She could not let him compromise his future for hers.

Renee Ryan grew up in a Florida beach town where she learned to surf, sort of. With a degree from FSU, she explored career opportunities at a Florida theme park, a modeling agency and even taught high school economics. She currently lives with her husband in Nebraska, and many have mistaken their overweight cat for a small bear. You may contact Renee at reneeryan.com, on Facebook or on Twitter, @ReneeRyanBooks.

Books by Renee Ryan

Love Inspired Historical

Charity House

The Marshal Takes a Bride
Hannah's Beau
Loving Bella
The Lawman Claims His Bride
Charity House Courtship
The Outlaw's Redemption
Finally a Bride
His Most Suitable Bride
The Marriage Agreement

Journey West

Wagon Train Proposal

Love Inspired

Village Green

Claiming the Doctor's Heart

Visit the Author Profile page at Harlequin.com for more titles

RENEE RYAN

The Marriage Agreement

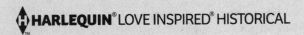

H HARLEQUIN® LOVE INSPIRED® HISTORICAL

LOVE INSPIRED BOOKS

Recycling programs for this product may not exist in your area.

ISBN-13: 978-0-373-28318-7

The Marriage Agreement

www.Harlequin.com

Printed in U.S.A.

For You formed my inward parts; You covered me in my mother's womb. I will praise You, for I am fearfully and wonderfully made; Marvelous are Your works, And that my soul knows very well.
—*Psalms* 139:13–14

For Cindy Kirk and Nancy Robards Thompson, the best plotting partners on the planet. Thank you for walking beside me throughout the process of writing this book and being willing to help me plot myself out of a corner far too many times to admit. I love you both!

Chapter One

The Hotel Dupree, Denver, Colorado 1896

Shadows sculpted the darkened ballroom as Fanny Mitchell awaited her employer's arrival. A happy sigh leaked out of her, echoing off the ornate walls. She loved this cavernous, oft overlooked room, loved it above all others in the hotel.

An expectant, almost dreamy silence hung in the air, as if Fanny was on the brink of something new and wonderful. Arms outstretched, she executed an uninhibited spin across the dance floor. Then stopped abruptly, frowning at her whimsy.

A quick tug on her sleeves, a readjustment of her skirt, and she was back to being the oh-so-proper guest-services manager of the finest hotel in Denver, Colorado.

Decorum restored, she continued her inspection at a more sedate pace. In four days, Mrs. Beatrix Singletary would hold her annual charity ball in this very room. Three hundred of Denver's most important residents were invited to attend, including most of Fanny's family. It would be the first time the widow held the event outside her home. Fanny suspected this change in venue was because Mrs. Singletary now owned one quarter of the Hotel Dupree.

As owner of the other three quarters, Fanny's employer wished to impress his new business partner with the efficiency of their hotel staff. Fanny would not let him down.

She would not let herself down. This was her chance to prove she was more than the gossips claimed, more than the labels others had attached to her since childhood.

By organizing this particular function, the largest and most anticipated of the year, Fanny would finally show the good people of Denver that she was worthy of their respect. That she hadn't jilted one of the most highly respected men in town on impulse, or because of some hidden flaw in her character.

Her decision had been well thought out and for all the right reasons.

Fanny moved to a nearby wall and pressed a switch on the raised panel. The recently installed Maria Theresa chandelier came alive with light.

The absurd fee to ship the exquisite fixture from Europe had been well worth the cost. Airy and delicate, the handblown glass and crystal rosettes twisted around the metal frame in such a way as to give the illusion of a floating waterfall.

Continuing her inspection, she made mental notes where to put tables, chairs and the myriad of flower arrangements she'd personally designed.

This was what she was born to do, taking an annual event people talked about for months and turning it into an even more spectacular occasion.

Why, then, did she experience a sudden burst of melancholy? Why this strange bout of dissatisfaction?

Fanny knew, of course.

She would soon celebrate her twenty-fifth birthday. Unlike her four married siblings, Fanny had no one special in her life.

There was still time for her own happily-ever-after. For now, she would focus on the many blessings the Lord had bestowed on her. She had siblings who adored her, parents who supported her unconditionally and a job she loved, working beside a man she greatly admired.

"Fanny," a deep, masculine voice called from behind her, the tone a mix of amusement and lazy drawl. "You've arrived ahead of me as usual."

She ignored a rush of anticipation and slowly pivoted around to face her employer. For one dreadful, wonderful moment, her heart lifted.

There he stood, framed in the doorway. Jonathon Hawkins. The intensely private, overly serious, wildly successful hotelier, whose rags to riches story inspired everyone he met, Fanny most of all.

He was so competent, so handsome. Tall, broad-shouldered, with a head of glossy, dark brown hair, he attracted more than his fair share of female attention.

He seemed oblivious to his effect on women. His mantra was business first, business always. Though she felt a sad heart tug over his resolve to remain unattached and childless, Fanny appreciated his single-minded focus.

That was, at any rate, her official stand on the matter.

His mouth curved in an easy half smile and a sudden dizziness struck her.

"Mr. Hawkins." She ordered her heartbeat to slow to a normal rate. "You'll be pleased to know I've secured—"

He lifted a hand to stop her. "You agreed to call me Jonathon."

Her breath snagged on a skittering rush of air. Of course. They'd been on a first-name basis for over a year.

She'd nearly forgotten in his absence, though he'd been gone but a week.

"I...yes, I..." *Get control of yourself, Fanny.* "Are you ready for our final walk-through, Jonathon?"

"I am, indeed." He pushed away from the door frame.

Here we go, she thought, silently bracing for the impact of his nearness.

As his long, purposeful strides ate up the distance between them, she noted how he moved with predatory grace. Jonathon Hawkins was a study in contradictions, a man who could be sophisticated and mannerly, or cunning and shrewd, depending on the situation.

He stopped, leaving a perfectly appropriate amount of space between them. *Always the gentleman*, she thought. She knew enough about his past to find that especially intriguing. And there went that sad little heart tug again.

"Shall we begin?" Under the bright glow of the chandelier, his eyes seemed to hold a thousand shades of blue.

She swallowed back a sigh. "Yes."

"After you." He gestured for her to take the lead.

For a dangerous moment, she couldn't make her feet work properly. Jonathon seemed different today, more intent, more focused. His silvery-blue eyes gleamed with intelligence and something else, something she knew better than to define.

Quickly breaking eye contact, she directed him to the far right corner of the ballroom. Their heels struck the freshly polished floor in perfect rhythm with one another.

"We'll set up banquet tables here and...over there." She made a sweeping gesture toward the opposite corner. "This will allow easy access to the food without obstructing the general flow of traffic to and from the dance floor."

He studied the two spaces. His eyes narrowed slightly, as if picturing the setup in his mind. "Excellent."

Pleased by his approval, she continued guiding him through the room, stopping at various points along the way to explain her ideas in greater detail. When they were once again standing in the spot where they'd begun, she drew in a deep breath. "Do you have any questions or concerns?"

"Not at the moment." He smiled down at her. "Thank you, Fanny. As always, you've thought of everything."

Had she? She turned in a slow circle, attempting to determine if there'd been a forgotten detail, something they were both missing. When nothing came to mind, she returned his smile. "I think we're ready."

"So it would seem."

A moment of silent understanding passed between them. His expression was so full of meaning, so unexpectedly affectionate, she thought he might lean in closer and…and…

She quickly looked away. "I hope Mrs. Singletary agrees."

That earned her a soft chuckle. "You've left nothing to chance. I'm confident your efforts will find favor with the illustrious Beatrix Singletary."

"Did I hear someone mention my name?" As if she'd been waiting for her cue, the widow materialized in the doorway, one hand on her hip, the other poised against her chin.

On anyone else, the pose would look ridiculous. Not on Mrs. Singletary. She was a woman with flair, always dressed impeccably in the latest fashion. A renowned beauty in her day, the widow had golden-brown hair that was a perfect foil for her fair complexion. Her face showed few signs that nearly four and a half decades had passed since her birth.

Fanny liked the woman. She especially appreciated the way she ran her vast fortune, and hoped to learn much from her now that she'd joined forces with Jonathon.

As was his custom, he stepped forward and greeted the widow by placing a light kiss to her extended hand. "It's always a pleasure to see you in the hotel, Mrs. Singletary."

"It's always a pleasure to be in the hotel, Mr. Hawkins."

Mouth tilted at an amused angle, he released her hand. "Would you prefer a walk-through of the ballroom now, or after we review the final guest list?"

"Now, of course. We did, after all, come here first."

One dark eyebrow shot up. "We?"

"My companion and I. Do come along, Philomena." A slight crease marred the widow's forehead as she glanced over her shoulder. "Lurking in the shadows is quite unseemly."

The young woman hurried forward.

Philomena Ferguson was, to Fanny's thinking, the most likable of the seven Ferguson sisters. With her remarkable hazel eyes, golden-brown hair and flawless complexion, she was also the most beautiful. Her pale green shirtwaist dress, cut in an A-line silhouette, only served to enhance her extraordinary looks.

Wondering if Jonathon noticed Philomena's undeniable charms, Fanny slid a glance at him. He was still looking at her. Not Philomena, *her.*

Fanny knew better than to read too much into his attentiveness. The one occasion she'd thought he might actually kiss her, or perhaps profess a personal interest in her, he'd taken the opportunity to explain the motivation behind his refusal to marry. Ever.

This time, when the heart tug came, she shoved it aside with a fast, determined swallow.

"Mr. Hawkins." Mrs. Singletary tapped his arm, the gesture sufficiently pulling his attention away from Fanny. "I believe you've met my companion."

"We are acquainted. Miss Ferguson." He cast a pleasant, if somewhat distant smile in Philomena's direction. "Lovely to see you again."

An attractive blush spread across her cheeks. "Thank you, Mr. Hawkins, and you as well."

As she bounced her gaze between the two, a speculative gleam lit Mrs. Singletary's eye.

That look put Fanny instantly on guard. It was no secret the widow considered herself an accomplished matchmaker. For good reason. Mrs. Singletary had proved herself quite skilled at ferreting out potential love matches. One of her most recent successes involved Fanny's childhood friend Molly Taylor Scott, who was now married to Fanny's brother, Garrett.

Thanks, also, to the widow's efforts, her sister was happily settled, as well—to Fanny's former fiancé. She was glad Callie and Reese had found one another. They'd married for love, which was the only reason for pledging lifelong vows, to Fanny's way of thinking. Marrying for anything less than an all-consuming love would be tantamount to imprisonment.

Mrs. Singletary's eyes sharpened over Jonathon and Philomena. Oh, no. Did the widow have her next match in mind?

"Well, then, Mr. Hawkins." A sly smile spread across the widow's lips. "Since you and my companion are already acquainted, I trust you have no objection to attending the opera with us tomorrow evening."

Fanny made a soft sound of protest in her throat, barely audible, but Jonathon must have caught it because he asked, "You have a concern?"

Think, Fanny, think.

"We're scheduled to, ah, review next month's bookings tomorrow afternoon." An endeavor that almost always went late. She started to say as much but stopped when she glanced at Mrs. Singletary's raised eyebrow. "However, we can certainly reschedule."

Jonathon frowned at her. "Reschedule? But we always—"

"Oh, excellent," Mrs. Singletary declared, cutting him off midsentence. "This is most excellent, indeed. You, Mr. Hawkins, are now perfectly free to join Philomena and me tomorrow evening."

His frown deepened. "Mrs. Singletary, I cannot attend the opera when I have a prior commitment here at the hotel."

"Miss Mitchell." Mrs. Singletary gave Fanny a pointed stare. "You don't mind, do you, dear, if Philomena and I steal your employer away for one evening?"

Actually, she minded a great deal. "Certainly not."

Jonathon opened his mouth, then shut it again as he considered the widow through narrowed eyes. "You seem very determined I join you."

"I am quite determined."

"Why?"

Undaunted by his suspicious tone, Mrs. Singletary gave a jaunty wave of her hand. "Considering the nature of our business relationship, I am determined we get to know one another on a more personal level. The opera is an excellent place to start."

Fanny shook her head at the widow's flimsy excuse. Surely Mrs. Singletary had figured out by now that *no one* knew Jonathon Hawkins on a personal level. He always held a portion of himself back, never letting anyone past the polished facade. It was that mysterious air that made him so attractive to women, and so confounding to Fanny.

"I appreciate the invitation," he said at last. "But I must decline."

He did not expand on his reasons.

A brief battle of wills ensued, but Mrs. Singletary gave in graciously after only a few seconds. "I suppose we will have to try for another time."

He smiled. Or maybe he didn't. Fanny wasn't sure what that twist of his lips meant. "Indeed we will," he said.

"Well, now." The widow clapped her hands together. "Shall we begin our tour of this lovely ballroom?"

Before anyone could respond, she linked her arm with Fanny's. "You will show me around, Miss Mitchell, seeing as the majority of the preparations have fallen upon your capable shoulders."

The widow all but dragged Fanny deeper into the ballroom, leaving Jonathon and Philomena together. Convenient.

At least neither of them seemed overly pleased to be in the other's company. Fanny found far more comfort in their mutual uneasiness than she should.

Did Jonathon have any idea what his business partner was plotting? Would it matter if he did? It was a well-known fact that once the widow set her sights on a particular match, there was no changing her mind.

Perhaps Fanny should warn him. Or...perhaps not. She was merely his employee. He'd made it painfully clear there would be nothing more than business between them. She had no claims on him, and she certainly wasn't interested in him romantically.

That was, at any rate, her official stand on the matter.

Jonathon had heard his share of disturbing tales concerning Mrs. Singletary's penchant for matchmaking.

He'd dismissed them out of hand. Beatrix Singletary was eccentric to be sure, but he'd never found cause to think her the meddling sort.

Until now.

The woman was actually pushing her companion on him, and she wasn't even attempting to be subtle. When next he had Mrs. Singletary's ear, he would inform her that her efforts were wasted on him.

Jonathon would never marry, nor father any children. He came from bad blood, from a long line of selfish men who'd destroyed the women in their lives.

He would not perpetuate the cycle. His newest project would become his legacy, a tangible way to help women rather than hurt them.

He clasped his hands behind his back and looked up at the ceiling, then across the ballroom, over to the doors leading to the terrace, anywhere but at the pretty young woman standing beside him.

Miss Ferguson was likable enough. She was perfectly suitable—for some other man.

"Mr. Hawkins, I apologize for my employer." Philomena shifted uncomfortably beside him. "She means well, I'm sure. But when Mrs. Singletary gets an idea in her head, she can be unrelenting in her desire to see it through to the end."

Pleased by the young woman's directness, Jonathon decided to be equally forthright in return. "Tenacity is an admirable trait. However, in this instance, Mrs. Singletary will be disappointed if she continues to push you and me together."

Relief filled the young woman's gaze. "I concur completely. You and I would never suit. A match between us would be the very worst of bad ideas."

Jonathon offered a sardonic tilt of his lips.

Her hand flew to her mouth. "Oh, Mr. Hawkins, please forgive my wayward tongue. I did not mean to insult you."

"I'm not offended, Miss Ferguson. I find your candor refreshing."

"Praise the Lord." She sighed. Then, clearly eager to move away from their discussion as quickly as possible, she looked out across the ballroom.

Jonathon followed the direction of her gaze and felt his gut take a slow, curling roll. Fanny was working her charms on Mrs. Singletary, directing the widow through the ballroom. Even dressed simply in a black, high-collared dress, Fanny exuded grace and elegance. Rather than detract, the lack of color in her clothing emphasized her natural beauty.

He watched, fascinated, as she pointed to the chandelier he'd had recently installed. Beneath the glow of a thousand flickering electric lights, her blue-green eyes sparkled with pleasure.

Jonathon blinked, unable to tear his gaze free of all that joy, all that beauty. He'd spent too many years surrounded by ugliness not to appreciate the way she'd scooped her silky blond curls in some sort of fancy twist atop her head. A few errant strands tumbled free, framing her exquisite oval face.

Fanny Mitchell was one of the Lord's greatest works of art.

She captivated him. In truth, she'd intrigued him from their first meeting. If any woman could entice him to reconsider his opinion on marriage, it would be Fanny Mitchell.

And yet, because he admired her so much, liked her even, she was the last woman he would consider pursuing romantically.

She'd become indispensable to him. *Here*, at the hotel. Her personal touches were everywhere. From the elegant yet inviting furniture in the lobby, to the specialty chocolates hand-delivered to the rooms each evening, to the list of Denver attractions provided to each guest at check-in.

As if sensing his gaze on her, she shot him a wink from over her shoulder. His mind emptied of all thought.

Footsteps sounded from the outer hallway, heralding someone's approach. Jonathon jerked his attention toward the doorway.

His assistant, Burke Galloway, hastened into the ballroom, a scowl on his face. Recognizing the look, Jonathon addressed Miss Ferguson directly. "Will you excuse me a moment?"

"Of course."

He approached his assistant, a tall, lean young man with dark hair and startling, pale blue eyes. "Is there a problem?"

Burke's mouth pressed into a grim line. "Joshua Greene is here to see you. I put him in your private office."

Everything in him went cold. "Which Joshua Greene, father or son?"

Neither man was welcome in the hotel.

"Son." Burke spoke in a hushed, hurried tone. "He refuses to leave the premises until he's spoken with you personally."

What business did his half brother have with him? Jaw tight, Jonathon returned to Miss Ferguson.

"I must bid you good-day, but I leave you in capable hands." He motioned Burke over. "Miss Ferguson, this is Mr. Galloway. Burke, please show the young woman around the ballroom while I address this other matter."

Burke's eyes filled with quiet appreciation. "With pleasure, sir."

Jonathon adopted a clipped, purposeful pace. He caught Fanny's eye before exiting the ballroom. She gave him a brief nod. The gesture confirmed that he'd left Mrs. Singletary in capable hands, as well.

Whatever he discovered during his meeting with Josh Greene, Jonathon knew one thing for certain. He had good men and women in his employ, people far more faithful to him than the father and half brother who'd dismissed him the one time he'd reached out for their help.

He'd come a long way since those dark, hopeless days of surviving alone on the backstreets of Denver by any means possible. He was a success in his own right now, on his own terms. He owed his family nothing.

After a final nod in Fanny's direction, Jonathon headed out of the ballroom, prepared for the confrontation ahead.

Chapter Two

Jonathon stood near the door, feet spread, hands clasped behind his back. He'd held the position for some time now, waiting for his half brother to stop pacing and state his business.

At seven years his senior, and their father's sole legitimate heir, Josh had been given all the advantages of a privileged birthright, including an education from the finest schools in the country. Yet the man had nothing to show for his life, other than a string of gambling debts and a miserable marriage.

Always the outward picture of propriety, Josh wore one of his hand-tailored suits. The tall, leanly muscled build, the dark, windswept hair and classically handsome features fooled many.

But Jonathon knew the truth. The outer trappings did not match the inner man.

Like recognizes like, he thought, a harsh reminder of the things he'd done to drag himself out of poverty. Though his choices had been about survival, at least at first, he would still have much to answer for when he faced the Lord. Sobering thought.

His brother finally paused, turned and studied him intently. Jonathon matched the rude regard with unflinching patience, a strategy he often adopted to ferret out a business opponent's underlying agenda.

Far stronger men than his brother had buckled under the calculated silence. Josh proved no more immune to the tactic than others before him.

"I need money," he blurted out.

With slow, deliberate movements, Jonathon unclasped his hands and balanced evenly on both feet. The irony of the situation was almost laughable.

I need money. Those were the exact same words Jonathon had uttered to his father twenty years ago in a final, desperate attempt to save his dying mother's life.

Resentment flared.

Jonathon struggled to contain the emotion, reminding himself he was no longer that helpless boy facing an uncertain future. He had power and wealth now.

He answered to no one but God.

"How much did you lose at the faro tables this time?"

Josh's mouth went flat. "I don't need the money for a gambling debt, I need it for—"

He broke off midsentence. His gaze darted around the room, landing nowhere in particular. "Do you mind if I sit?"

Not wanting to extend this conversation longer than necessary, Jonathon frowned at the request.

Without waiting for a response, Josh sat.

After settling in one of the wingback chairs facing away from the door, he rubbed an unsteady hand across his face. "Lily is with child."

Every muscle in Jonathon's back coiled and tightened. "Your wife's name is Amanda."

The other man sighed heavily. "Lily is my mistress."

Jonathon went very still. The son had followed in the father's footsteps. Inevitable, he supposed.

And he walked in all the sins of his father, which he had done before him...

Throat tight, Jonathon tried to empty his mind, but a distant memory shimmered to life. His mother, sitting in a tattered dress falling apart at the seams, tears running down her cheeks as she anxiously waited for the tall, distinguished man to return as he'd promised.

Even in her darkest days, when money had been scarce and she'd been forced to turn to prostitution to feed them both, Amelia Hawkins had continued hoping her lover would finally leave his wife.

That day had never come.

Jonathon had been too young back then, barely five, to remember much about the man whose visits had stopped so abruptly and left his mother in permanent despair. Only later, when he'd been sixteen, had he discovered that the venerable Judge Joshua Greene had been his mother's paramour. And Jonathon's father.

Josh's voice cut into his thoughts. "I need money to set Lily up in a small house of her own. I'll repay you, of course, when I'm able."

A spurt of anger ignited in Jonathon's chest. He moved to a spot behind his desk. Rather than sit, he remained standing, mostly to prove to himself he was still in control of his emotions. "Why come to me? Why not go to your father?"

Josh shook his head. "I can't. He warned me Lily would try to trap me with a child."

Trap him with a child? Jonathon had the presence of mind to pull out his chair before his legs collapsed beneath him. As if in a dream, he was transported back in time, to the terrifying nights he'd been banished to the alleyway behind the brothel.

Blinking rapidly, he heard his brother speaking, explaining his desire to keep his secret from his family. A part of Jonathon listened, taking it all in. The other part was unable to forget that he and this man shared the same blood. They came from the same, contemptible father.

He surfaced at the word *mistake*. "What did you say?"

"Father will never forgive me for making the same mistake he did."

Mistake. Jonathon had been Joshua Greene's greatest mistake. That's what the good, upstanding judge had told him on their first meeting.

"I'm not like Father. I won't turn my back on Lily. I won't let her fall into…" Josh glanced down. "You know."

"Do I?"

His brother's head snapped back up. "I should have known you wouldn't make this easy for me."

"And yet you came to me, anyway."

"All right, I'll say it." He rolled his shoulders as if trying to dislodge a heavy weight. "I don't want Lily to become a prostitute like…like your…mother."

Jonathon barely contained his rage. "And you think that makes you a good man?"

"It makes me better than our father."

Jonathon cleared his expression of all emotion. Inside, he burned. He briefly glanced at the small picture on his desk of his mother as a young woman. He knew a moment of pain, and the hollow feeling of remembered sorrow he'd tucked inside a dark corner of his soul.

Amelia Hawkins hadn't turned to prostitution lightly. She'd held out as long as she could, but had finally admitted defeat and taken a position in Mattie Silks's brothel. Jonathon had been seven at the time. The infamous madam had only agreed to take him in, as well, with the understanding that the customers must never find out about his existence.

Whenever his mother "entertained" he'd been locked outside, no matter the weather, left to run the streets. Out of necessity, he'd learned to take care of himself. He'd become a master at picking pockets and winning fights.

He would have continued down a similar path the rest of his life had it not been for Laney O'Connor, now Laney Dupree. She'd offered Jonathon a home at Charity House. She'd built the orphanage for kids like him, kids who weren't really orphans, whose mothers worked in brothels.

Jonathon shuddered, thinking of the things he'd done to survive prior to Laney's rescue, and the things he'd done after leaving Charity House to make his fortune.

Could God forgive so much sin? A preacher friend of his said yes. Like waves crashing to shore, the Lord's forgiveness was infinite and never ending. Jonathon had his doubts. The world was rarely fair.

And now, another woman had been lied to and compromised. Left to her own resources, she could very well travel the same path as Jonathon's mother. Joshua Greene's despicable legacy would live on into the next generation, and possibly the next. A never ending cycle.

Was it any wonder Jonathon never wanted to marry? Never wanted to bear children?

"I'll give you the money."

Saying nothing more, he opened the safe nestled beneath his desk, and pulled out a bundle of neatly stacked bills. The amount was more than enough to purchase a small, comfortable home for Josh's mistress and her innocent, unborn child.

Once the money was in his brother's hands, Jonathon rose. "If you'll excuse me, I have a hotel to run."

"Of course."

In silence, he escorted his brother to the exit. "I bid you good-day."

Josh started to speak.

Jonathon shut the door on his words with a resounding click. For several moments, he stared straight ahead, his gut roiling. In the unnatural stillness, he made a silent promise to himself. No woman would suffer because of his selfish actions.

The cycle of sin that ran in his family ended with him.

With their walk-through complete, Fanny escorted Mrs. Singletary and her companion back to the main lobby of the hotel. As they entered the skinny hallway leading out of the ballroom, Philomena fell back a step. The move put her directly beside Burke Galloway. Their footsteps slowed to match one another's, and their voices mingled in hushed tones.

Fanny wondered if the widow noticed the two were so obviously attracted to each other. She looked over at Mrs. Singletary, but the sight of Jonathon's office distracted her.

He rarely shut his door. The fact that he'd done so today warned Fanny something wasn't quite right. A terrible foreboding slipped through her.

Mrs. Singletary glanced at the closed door as well, a delicate frown knitting her brow. "It would appear Mr. Hawkins is still occupied with whatever concern called him away."

"I believe you are correct." Fanny's heart beat faster. She fought a sudden urge to go to Jonathon, to make sure he was all right.

But that would be overstepping her bounds. She continued leading Mrs. Singletary and the others down the hallway.

Once they were in the main lobby, Mrs. Singletary dug inside her sizable reticule and pulled out a stack of papers.

She handed them to Fanny. "Since it appears Mr. Hawkins will not be available for our meeting today, I am entrusting you with my final guest list for the ball."

Fanny scanned the top page, not really expecting any surprises. But when her gaze landed on a particular set of guests, her breath hitched in her throat. Judge and Mrs. Joshua Greene.

Joshua. Greene.

The man wasn't welcome in the Hotel Dupree. Short of exposing Jonathon's personal connection to the prominent judge, Fanny could say nothing to Mrs. Singletary.

She coerced air into her lungs, and adopted a breezy, nonchalant tone. "I will deliver your list to Mr. Hawkins as soon as possible. If he has any questions or concerns I'm certain he will contact you at once."

"That will be fine." Mrs. Singletary's gaze narrowed over her companion conversing softly with Mr. Galloway.

The widow sniffed in mild disapproval. Philomena didn't appear to notice her employer's reaction. She was entirely too absorbed in whatever Burke had pointed out to her in the lobby.

"Mr. Galloway, do come here." The widow spoke in a fast, impatient tone. "And you, as well, Philomena."

The two walked over as a single unit and faced Mrs. Singletary shoulder to shoulder.

Philomena spoke for them both. "Yes, Mrs. Singletary?"

The widow's gaze bounced between the two, a look of vexation in her eyes. "Mr. Galloway, would you please see that my carriage and driver are waiting for me out front?"

He gave her a pleasant smile. "I would be delighted."

"Yes, yes, off you go." She sent him away with a distracted flick of her wrist.

Philomena gazed after him with a wistful expression.

Mrs. Singletary studied the young woman closely, then pressed her lips into a tight, determined line. Fanny feared the widow still planned to push a match between Jonathon and Philomena.

"Hopeless," Fanny muttered under her breath.

"Did you say something, my dear?"

"No, Mrs. Singletary." Fanny lifted her chin. "Is there anything else I can do for you today?"

"Not a thing. Your commitment to detail is much appreciated, Miss Mitchell. I predict this year's ball will be spoken about long after the evening comes to a close."

"That is the plan."

"Yes, yes." The widow patted her hand. "I wish to raise quite a sizable amount of money for the new kitchen at Charity House."

Excitement spread through Fanny. "It's a worthy cause."

"Oh, indeed, it is."

They shared a smile. Fanny volunteered much of her free time at Charity House. She was even contemplating starting a program at the hotel to provide work experience for the older children. She wished she could do more. The orphanage had molded some of her favorite people into men and women of strong, moral character.

The widow continued speaking. "I understand the majority of your family will be in attendance at my ball."

Fanny's smile widened. It had been years since so many Mitchells were in one place at the same time. "I've reserved rooms for them here in the hotel. My parents will be staying in the bridal suite."

A gift from Jonathon. The dear, dear man.

Mrs. Singletary's expression turned somber and she reached out to touch Fanny's arm. "How is your mother managing these days?"

"Her asthma is much better." Or so her father had claimed the last time he'd come to town. The worry in his eyes had told a different story.

Her mother, always so full of life and energy, had contracted asthma recently, a chronic disease that usually showed up in childhood, but was not uncommon to reveal itself later in life. Although the doctor said Mary Mitchell's illness was manageable, Fanny still feared the worst.

Asthma was incurable. People had been known to die from a severe attack. Her mother suffered bouts regularly. Though hers were usually moderate in nature, stress brought on more severe symptoms. Fanny prayed the party didn't cause her any additional strain.

"I look forward to catching up with her while she's in town," Mrs. Singletary said. "Your mother has always been one of my very special friends."

"And you, hers."

"Walk us out, Miss Mitchell."

"Of course." Fanny led Mrs. Singletary and Philomena to the front steps of the hotel, then bade them farewell. Back in the lobby, she fingered the guest list. *This needs addressing immediately.* She cast a surreptitious glance toward Jonathon's office.

The door swung open and out walked the man himself.

Never one to put off an unpleasant situation, Fanny hurried over to meet him. Something in the way he held his shoulders caused her unspeakable concern.

Judge Greene forgotten, she touched her employer's

arm. It was barely a whisper of fingertips to sleeve, yet had the intended effect. Jonathon slowly looked down at her.

The moment their gazes merged, Fanny's breath backed up in her throat. His face was like a stone, but his eyes were hot with anguish.

She tightened her grip. "What's happened? Is something wrong with the hotel?"

"No, it's my…" His words trailed off and his gaze fastened on a spot somewhere far off in the distance.

Her hand fell away from his arm. However, her resolve to ease his distress remained firmly in place. "Perhaps you would care to take a short walk with me?"

She spoke in a mild tone, the way she would when making the same suggestion any other time. They often took walks together, mostly when Jonathon required her opinion about some issue in one of his hotels.

"A light snowfall has begun," she added, knowing it was his favorite time to be outdoors.

Hers, as well. There was nothing more wonderful than those precious moments when the world fell quiet beneath a blanket of fluffy white flakes.

Jonathon remained silent, his gaze unblinking.

"Come with me." She took his hand and pulled him toward the exit.

For several steps he obliged her. Just when she thought she had him agreeable to the idea of a brief stroll, he drew his hand free.

"Not right now, Fanny." His voice was hoarse and gravelly, not at all the smooth baritone she was used to hearing from him. "I have another matter that requires my immediate attention."

His deliberate vagueness put a wedge between them. She bit back a sigh. "I understand."

In truth, she understood far too well. He'd shut her out. It wasn't the first time and probably wouldn't be the last. Nevertheless, it stung to realize he didn't trust her, at least not enough to share what had put him in such a dark mood.

Without a word of explanation, he turned to go, then just as quickly pivoted back around to face her. "I'm not certain how long I'll be gone. I need you to see to any issues that may arise in my absence."

"You can count on me."

She didn't attempt to pry for additional information. He would reveal whatever was on his mind when he was ready. Or he wouldn't. It was a reminder of how little he trusted her concerning his life outside the hotel.

He's not for you.

But there was someone out there who was; she sensed it as surely as she knew her own name. She simply had to trust the Lord would lead her to her one true love in His time. Patience, faith—those were her greatest tools.

"I'll be here when you return," she said when Jonathon made no move to leave.

He reached up and touched her cheek. The gesture was brief, yet so full of tenderness she thought she might cry. Did the man realize how good he was beneath that polished, unflappable exterior he presented to the world?

He would make a wonderful husband, and an exceptional father, if only he would allow someone—anyone—to squeeze through the cracks and into his heart. She wanted that for him, desperately.

"I count on you always being here when I return, Fanny." His expression softened. "More than you can possibly know."

With relief, she heard the message beneath his words. Jonathon relied on her above all others.

The thought should have made her happy, but instead produced a small stab of pain in the vicinity of her heart. The sensation felt a lot like loss.

Chapter Three

Later that same afternoon, Fanny found one excuse after another to return to the hotel lobby. If she was called away, she took care of the matter quickly and then hurried back to her post behind the registration desk. She was probably overreacting, but she couldn't shake the notion that Jonathon needed her.

She knew the exact moment he reentered the hotel. Even if she hadn't been watching for him, the air actually changed. The atrium felt somehow smaller, his presence was that large and compelling. Everyone else in the building faded in comparison.

Or maybe that was Fanny's singular reaction to the man. None of the guests milling about seemed quite as captivated by Jonathon Hawkins as she.

Of course, she'd been watching for his return. Her concern had grown exponentially with each passing hour. Catching a glimpse of his face and the way he held his shoulders, she knew she'd been right to worry. He was still as distraught as when he'd left.

He hadn't seen her yet.

She took the opportunity to study him without interruption.

His steps were clipped, purposeful, a man in complete control of his domain. But his eyes. Oh, his eyes. Fanny had never seen that look of raw emotion in his gaze before.

Hurrying out from behind the registration desk, she cut into his direct line of vision.

His feet ground to a halt.

"Jonathon." Unable to mask her concern, Fanny spoke his name in a rush. *No good, no good.* That would only entice him to put up his guard.

She adopted a breezy, businesslike tone and began again. "Tell me what you need. Name it and it's done."

He looked at her oddly, then cracked a half smile. "I appreciate the offer, but everything's under control."

She frowned at the rasp in his voice. "Why don't I believe you?"

"Go back to work, Fanny." He shifted around her and continued on toward his office. Not sure why she couldn't leave him alone, she grabbed her coat from behind the registration desk and then hurried to catch up with him again.

His pace slowed.

She easily fell into step beside him.

He cast her a sidelong glance but didn't tell her to go away. *Progress.*

"You do realize, Jonathon, that you have *the look.*"

His footsteps stopped altogether. "What look?"

"Whenever something goes wrong in the hotel, a groove shows up right…there." She pointed to a spot in the middle of his forehead.

A strangled laugh rumbled out of his chest. "You know me well."

Not really. A mild glumness took hold of her. She didn't know him nearly as well as she wished, but enough to know how to lighten his mood.

She took his arm and steered him back in the direction he'd just come. "The snow is falling and you owe me a walk. I'm even prepared."

She gestured with her coat.

He stared down at her for an endless moment, so long, in fact, that she thought he might turn down her offer a second time in one day. But then he nodded and started for the exit with quick, even strides.

She had to break into a trot to keep up with him. Much to her relief, he slowed once they were outside.

They walked at a reasonable pace, falling into a companionable silence as they headed toward the heart of downtown Denver. The afternoon air was scented with fresh snow and a hint of pine. Fat, languid flakes floated softly around them, creating a surreal, almost wistful feel to the moment.

Fanny treasured these brisk walks with Jonathon, when it was just the two of them working out an issue in the hotel.

Although today she sensed the problem was more personal in nature. Something from his past?

She thought of what little she knew of his difficult childhood, so very different from her own. One of seven siblings, Fanny had been raised in a large, gregarious family on a ranch ten miles north of Denver. There'd always been plenty of food on the Mitchell table. Love and laughter had been abundant, as well, with the added bonus of parents who lived out their faith daily.

Fanny couldn't imagine the hardships Jonathon had endured. The thought made her stumble. He caught hold of her elbow, letting go only when she regained her balance.

"I failed to ask you earlier," he said, resuming his quick pace. "Did Mrs. Singletary have any questions about or concerns over the setup for her ball?"

"None. She seemed quite pleased with the preparations."

"Good to know." He drew to a stop.

Fanny followed suit.

Something quite wonderful passed between them.

"I appreciate you taking over in my absence with Mrs. Singletary." He plucked a snowflake off Fanny's shoulder, tossed it away with a flick of his fingers. "You always manage to make me look good. Thank you, Fanny."

"It's I who should thank you," she countered, meaning it with all her heart.

Prior to working at the hotel, she'd been caught up in the various roles others had assigned to her. The dutiful daughter. The adored sister. The accomplished beauty. She'd found favor wherever she went, had never taken a misstep and certainly never let anyone down.

Perhaps that was why her family had been confused and deeply concerned when she'd broken her engagement to Reese Bennett Jr., a man they had deemed her perfect match. Though her parents had been quick to support her decision, her behavior had set tongues wagging all over Denver. The ensuing scandal had been nearly impossible to bear.

Jonathon had come to her rescue, offering her the opportunity to manage the registration desk at his Chicago hotel. She'd leaped at the chance to leave town. Or rather, to escape the gossip.

Fanny wasn't particularly proud of her cowardice, but some good had come from her attempt to run away from the problem. She'd spent a lot of hours in her rented room in Chicago. After much prayer and soul-searching, she'd come to the realization that she was more than a pretty face, more than what others expected her to be.

Now, back in Denver once again, she would like to

think she'd found where she belonged. At the Hotel Dupree. She knew better, of course. She loved her job, but...

Something was missing. Her very own happy-ever-after that four of her six siblings had already found and were living out on a daily basis.

Gazing up into Jonathon's remarkable blue eyes, she felt a hopeless sense of longing spread through her. *He's not for you*, she reminded herself. *He doesn't want what you want.*

If only...

She knew better than to finish that thought.

As an uncharacteristic awkwardness spread between them, Fanny tried to think of something to say. She blurted out the first thing that came to mind. "Philomena looked rather lovely today, don't you agree?"

He cocked his head in a look of masculine confusion. "Mrs. Singletary always ensures her companion looks lovely."

So, he hadn't been especially taken by Philomena's considerable charms. Inappropriately pleased by the revelation, Fanny resumed walking, her steps considerably lighter.

They turned at the end of the block and retraced their route. In the past, this was usually when Jonathon revealed whatever was bothering him.

True to form, he blew out a slow hiss of air. "It confounds me how someone can just show up, unannounced, and expect to be given whatever he wants without consequences."

At the fire in his words, Fanny belatedly remembered the additional name on Mrs. Singletary's guest list. "Did Judge Greene contact you directly?"

Jonathon's face tightened at the question. "Are you saying he showed up at the hotel today, too?"

"No, I just assumed…" She shot a covert glance in his direction. "It's obvious something is troubling you. I thought it might be because Mrs. Singletary added your father to the guest list."

Jonathon stopped abruptly. "She what?"

Fanny sighed. "You didn't know."

"I did not."

She sighed again. She knew about Jonathon's personal connection to Joshua Greene only because the judge himself had told her. He'd misunderstood their relationship. Thinking they were more than business associates, he'd approached Fanny about setting up a meeting with his *son*. When Fanny had gotten over her shock and told Jonathon about the brazen request, he'd been furious. Not with her, with his father.

Her stomach dipped at the memory. "Would you like me to speak with Mrs. Singletary? I could explain the situation, you know, without actually explaining it."

For a moment, Jonathon's guard dropped and she saw the vulnerability that belonged to the boy he'd once been—the one who'd been summarily dismissed by his own father.

She thought he might share some of his pain with her, but his eyes became cool and distant. "Leave it alone," he said at last. "Mrs. Singletary is allowed to invite whomever she pleases to her charity ball."

They finished the rest of their walk in silence.

At the hotel entrance, Jonathon stopped Fanny from entering by moving directly in front of her. "Before we go in, I have a request."

She blinked up at him. "You know you can ask me anything."

"Have you secured an escort for Mrs. Singletary's ball?"

"I…no." She shook her head in confusion. "I have not."

"Good, don't."

"Is…" She cleared her throat, twice. "Is there a reason you wish for me to attend the ball alone?"

His lips curved into a sweet, almost tender smile. "You misunderstand. I don't wish for you to attend alone."

Oh. *Oh, my.* Her breath backed up in her lungs. "No?"

"I would like for you to attend with me." The intensity in his eyes made her legs wobble. "What do you say, Fanny? Will you allow me to escort you to the ball Friday evening?"

Her head told her to refuse. This man was her employer. He'd vowed never to marry. He didn't want children. No good would come from forgetting those very significant points of contention between them.

But then he took her hand.

She felt dizzy, too dizzy to think clearly. Surely that explained why she ignored caution. "Yes, Jonathon, I would very much like to attend the ball with you."

The following morning, Jonathon stood outside his office and tracked his gaze over the crowded hotel lobby. No matter what tactic he employed, he couldn't seem to concentrate on the scene in front of him. His mind kept returning to his conversation with Fanny after their walk.

He should *not* have asked her to Mrs. Singletary's ball. He knew that, but couldn't seem to regret doing so.

He enjoyed Fanny's company. Probably more than he should. Certainly more than their business association warranted. From very early on in their acquaintance, she'd made it clear what she wanted out of life—a satisfying job, marriage, children, a home of her own. Jonathon could give her only one of those things, the job.

But there were plenty of men who could give her the

rest, some of whom would be in attendance at the ball tomorrow evening.

Fanny, with her luminous smile and stunning face, would enchant each and every one of those potential suitors. She was unique. Special. The kind of woman a man wanted to cherish and protect, always.

Something unpleasant unfurled in Jonathon's chest at the thought of her sharing even one dance with someone, *anyone*, other than him.

Shifting his stance, he ground his back molars together so hard his neck ached. He forcibly relaxed his jaw and once again attempted to focus his attention on the hotel.

Again, his mind wandered back to Fanny and how badly he wanted her by his side tomorrow night. Facing his father would be…well, if not easier, certainly less challenging.

Guilt immediately reared up, producing a dull, burning pain in the back of his throat. Jonathon would not use Fanny as a shield between him and his father.

He should let her attend the ball alone. Yet he could not withdraw his invitation at this late date. He'd gotten himself in quite the quandary, with no simple way out.

He was spared from further reflection when his assistant, Burke Galloway, shouldered his way through the milling crowd.

"Mr. Hawkins, you'll be pleased to know we're nearly at 100 percent occupancy."

Jonathon pulled out his watch and checked the time. Not yet noon. He allowed himself a small smile of satisfaction. "Mrs. Singletary will be delighted so many of her party guests have taken rooms in the hotel."

"The discounted rate was a strong incentive."

"Indeed." The cut in price had been Fanny's idea, a

way to show off the newly renovated hotel to the locals. He made a mental note to increase her wages yet again.

"I have a few items we need to discuss." Burke eyed him with a questioning glance. "I trust now is a good time."

Jonathon nodded.

Burke retrieved a small notepad from an inside pocket of his jacket and proceeded to run through a series of problems that had arisen. When he'd finished, and Jonathon had given his decision on each matter, Burke flipped the page and addressed the final item scribbled in his book.

"As per your request, I've prepared the conference room on the second floor for your meeting with the Mitchell brothers this afternoon." He tapped the page absently with his fingertip. "Your attorney has already sent over five copies of the agreement, one for each person involved in the transaction and an additional copy to file with the county clerk's office once the sale goes through."

If *the sale goes through.*

Hunter, Logan and Garrett Mitchell still had to agree to sell Jonathon the parcel of land they jointly owned north of their family's ranch. He would pay whatever they asked, no matter how outrageous the price.

Turning the run-down train depot into a premier stop on the busy Union Pacific line wasn't just another business venture for him. It was a chance to set a new course for his future, a sort of redemption for the mistakes of his past.

Operating on the notion that the Mitchell brothers would be tough negotiators, he made one last request of his assistant. "Clear my calendar for the rest of the day, in case our meeting runs long."

"Of course." Burke made a notation on his notepad, then looked up. "We've covered everything on my list. Is there anything else you wish to review?"

"That's all for now."

"Very good." Burke left a few seconds later.

Jonathon returned his gaze to the lobby, his thoughts as disordered as the scene in front of him.

People came and went. Some hurried, others meandered. There was no pattern to their movement, yet the scene was a familiar one, replicated in every one of Jonathon's hotels, on any given day of the week.

After years of traveling from hotel to hotel, room to room, living out of a trunk or suitcase, Jonathon was ready to put down roots, deep and strong and lasting. His family would be the men and women he hired to work at the train depot, their changed lives his legacy.

If he happened to find himself lonely at times, it was the price he was willing to pay to break the chain of sin that plagued his family.

As if to test his resolve, he caught sight of Fanny out of the corner of his eye. *Beautiful.* That was the first thought that came to mind as Jonathon watched her move out from behind the registration desk.

She scanned the immediate area with a slightly narrowed gaze, probably looking for something out of place. Her earnest, blue-green eyes, starred with heavy, dark lashes, swept across the lobby, over the marble flooring, up to the glass atrium above her head.

The sunlight streaming through the windows slid over her in washes of yellow and gold, highlighting the variegated strands of blond hair piled atop her head.

Jonathon remembered the first time he'd seen her, standing in much the same place as she was now. He'd sensed the moment their gazes met that she was going to pose a problem for him. Not on a business level, but on a personal one.

He hadn't been wrong.

She caught him watching her. Smiling, she immediately changed direction. When she stopped beside him, his heart actually stuttered.

Up close, she was even more spectacular.

Her skin was flawless, her features almost doll-like. Pieces of hair had fallen free from her tidy coiffure. Since Jonathon rather liked the effect, he deemed it best not to point this out. No doubt she would reach up and tuck the wayward curls back in place.

"We have a busy few days ahead of us." She'd barely uttered the statement before a bellman, juggling several large pieces of luggage, staggered toward her. Deftly moving aside to let him pass, she added, "We're booked solid through Monday morning."

Not sure what he heard in her voice—worry, tension, mild agitation?—Jonathon raked his gaze over her face. She was definitely anxious about something. "Any concerns I should know about?"

She answered without hesitation. "No, of course not."

Highly unlikely, with every room booked for the next four nights. "None?" He lifted a single eyebrow. "Not one?"

Laughing softly, she shook her head. "Let me rephrase. Have problems presented themselves this morning? Yes, absolutely. Anything I, or my staff, can't handle? No."

"Good answer."

She flashed a smug grin. "I know."

He chuckled. She joined in.

A moment later her smile slipped, just a little, but enough that Jonathon noticed. He wondered at the cause but thought he probably knew. Her mother and father had arrived earlier this morning. "I trust your parents are settled in their room?"

"They are, yes." She angled her head to gaze up at him. "Thank you, Jonathon, for giving them the finest suite in the hotel. You have no idea how much I appreciate your thoughtfulness and generosity."

Something about her expression, so grateful, so overcome with emotion, made him stand a bit taller. He had a sudden urge to shield this woman from all the evil in this world, to slay every one of her dragons, real or perceived.

The need to protect Fanny, stronger than he'd felt for anyone before, wasn't entirely unexpected. Nor was it new. The sensation had been with him from the start of their association.

If she were a different woman, he a different man...

He shoved the thought aside. Fanny wanted marriage, children. Family. Jonathon knew nothing of those things. But he wanted her to have them. He wanted her to find happiness. With some other man?

No.

His mouth went dry as dust. He cleared his throat with a low growl. "How is your mother feeling?"

"She seemed well enough when I left her. Her color was good and she was breathing easily, but..."

Fanny's words trailed off and she snapped her mouth firmly shut.

"But...?" he prompted.

"But the ten-mile journey into town wore her out. She's putting up a brave front. I'm not in the least fooled by her false smiles. Thankfully, Dr. Shane is upstairs with her now, administering a breathing treatment." Gratitude returned to Fanny's gaze. "Thank you for making sure he was already here when she arrived."

Something that looked like affection, perhaps even admiration, replaced the gratitude.

How he wanted to be the man he saw in her eyes right now.

He cleared his throat again.

"I was happy to send for the doctor." Of course, Shane Bartlett wasn't just any doctor. He was the best in Denver. His connection to Charity House and his willingness to see patients regardless of their past—or current—lifestyles made him one of the few men Jonathon trusted. "I know how much your mother means to you."

Another, heavier sigh leaked out of Fanny's very pretty mouth. "I don't know what I'd do if one of her attacks becomes so severe she isn't able to recover."

The anguish in Fanny's voice was a sharp, tangible thing.

Jonathon was reminded of the day his own mother had taken ill. How well he understood the fear and pain Fanny fought to control.

Wanting to comfort her, he opened his mouth to say something, not precisely sure what, but a minor event playing out at the hotel's entrance captured his attention.

An expectant hush fell over the lobby as a stunning couple walked in with their sizable brood, plus one former, notorious madam Jonathon knew a bit too well. After all, she'd once owned the brothel where his mother had worked.

He had a lot of memories connected to Mattie Silks, not all of them good. But her appearance in his hotel wasn't the reason every muscle in his back knotted with tension.

Hunter Mitchell, the oldest of the Mitchell siblings, had arrived ahead of his brothers.

One down, two more yet to show.

Jonathon managed, just barely, to keep the anticipation from showing on his face. Unfortunately, none of his outward calm could temper his impatience to begin negotiations with the Mitchell brothers.

Soon, he told himself. If all went according to plan, his future would take a dramatic turn *very soon*.

Chapter Four

❧

Fanny knew a moment of quiet desperation as she watched her brother herd his family deeper into the hotel lobby. *That's what I want, Lord. That joy, that sense of belonging, a family of my own.*

She had to believe her time would come. For now, she would take a moment to enjoy the show. Hunter had brought his entire household to town, including his wife, all four of their children and, of course, his wife's mother, the incomparable Mattie Silks.

Laughter abounded among the group, while an entire team of bellmen wrestled the family's luggage onto a cart. Fanny's sister-in-law, Annabeth, attempted to oversee the process. Unfortunately, her mother added her own, very vocal "suggestions" on how to speed along the process. Mattie's input caused more mayhem, not less.

Hunter's oldest daughter, Sarah, skillfully pulled her younger siblings out of the fray. Unfortunately, Mattie added her assistance there as well, and pandemonium soon followed. The children quite literally ran circles around their grandmother.

Fanny thought she saw a brief twinkle of amusement dance in her brother's eyes before he quickly restored order with the gentle strength that had always defined him. Hunter looked good, she decided. His hair was a sun-kissed, sandy blond from the hours he spent outdoors on his ranch. His long-legged, leanly muscular cowboy swagger was replicated in all the Mitchell men.

Hunter had experienced some difficult years, including two spent in prison for manslaughter, but he'd overcome his past and was stronger for the challenges he'd once faced. She was proud to call him brother.

"Now, that's what I call an entrance," Jonathon muttered.

The look of amused horror on his face made her smile. "I should have warned you, the Mitchells never do anything by half measure."

"I was speaking about Mattie." His voice was infused with a touch of irony. "Watch. She's about to strike a pose. Ah, yes, there she goes."

As predicted, Mattie sauntered to a spot in the middle of the hotel lobby. With exaggerated slowness, she lifted her chin, thrust out a hip and then planted a fist on her waist.

The pose was so…completely Mattie. A snort of laughter erupted before Fanny could call it back. "You know the woman well."

"Too well," Jonathon muttered, his mouth now a little grim. "She's managed to draw almost every eye to her."

Gazes were, indeed, riveted in Mattie's direction. But Fanny suspected much of the interest was for the extraordinary-looking group as a whole. Even Hunter's children were beautiful.

A range of emotions swept through her. Fanny was excited to spend time with her family, but also determined to make the next few days count. When Mrs. Singletary's ball was over, all of Denver would see her differently. She would no longer be defined as that pretty Mitchell girl. Or that poor, misguided woman who'd jilted a prominent man in town.

She would prove she was a competent woman, capable of handling great responsibilities. When she walked through town next week, the whispers following in her wake would be not only accurate, but also complimentary.

Catching sight of her from across the room, Annabeth squealed in delight and waved enthusiastically.

The entire group changed direction, Annabeth leading the way with a waddle that bespoke her current condition. Judging by the size of her belly, Hunter's fifth child would be making an appearance in a few short months.

As Annabeth approached, smiling broadly, Fanny noticed that her sister-in-law glowed with good health and happiness. She was so very beautiful. The rich, caramel-colored skin and sleek dark hair she'd inherited from her Mexican father were the perfect foil for the pale blue eyes she'd gotten from Mattie.

Oddly, as Hunter and his family drew closer, Jonathon seemed to grow tenser. He shifted his stance slightly, then repositioned himself once again.

Interesting that while he appeared outwardly loose-limbed and relaxed, the lines around his mouth gave him away.

Fanny was given no more time to contemplate his strange behavior before she was hauled into her brother's strong arms and swung in fast, dizzying circles.

"Put me down, you big oaf."

He obliged, but only after two more heart-pounding spins.

Then, hands on her shoulders, Hunter studied her face with the narrow-eyed focus that had kept him alive during his rebellious years. She tried not to fidget under the inspection.

At last, he gave a quick nod of approval. "You look well, Fanny. Happy."

"I am well and happy." *Mostly.*

Angling his head, he paused, as if about to say something, then abruptly refocused his attention onto Jonathon.

They shook hands in a very businesslike manner.

"Have my brothers arrived?" Hunter asked.

"Not yet."

As Fanny watched the formal exchange between the two men, she had the distinct impression she'd missed something, something important. She opened her mouth to inquire, but they moved a few steps away and began speaking in low, hushed tones.

She couldn't quite make out what they said. She stepped closer. At the mention of a meeting—*what meeting?*—she leaned in a smidgen closer. She thought she caught Jonathon say her brother Garrett's name, but then Annabeth swooped in for a hug and that was the end of Fanny's eavesdropping.

She spent the next few minutes greeting the rest of Hunter's family. "Mattie, I do believe you look ten years younger than the last time I saw you."

The former madam responded to the compliment with a nonchalant wave of her hand. "It's all that fresh air."

The harried tone implied that fresh air was something to be avoided at all costs. Fanny wasn't fooled. The former madam was delighted with her decision to sell her brothel and move onto the ranch with her daughter, son-in-law and grandchildren.

Who would have thought Mattie Silks would turn into a doting grandmother?

"Hello, Aunt Fanny."

Fanny spun around at the sound of her name. "Sarah, look at you. You're all grown up."

The girl beamed. "I turn sixteen in four months, one week and five days. But who's counting?"

Fanny laughed. The sweet, pretty child with the dark hair and tawny eyes had become a confident, striking young woman. "Tell me how you've been."

Sarah did, in great detail, barely taking a breath. When she finally paused, Fanny took the opportunity to steer the conversation in a slightly different direction than the latest fashion for hats. "Are you excited about attending school in Boston next year?"

"I am. Very much. I thought Pa would never agree to let me go." She rolled her eyes in her father's direction. "He only relented when I promised to carry on your legacy at Miss Sinclair's Prestigious School for Girls."

Though she was flattered, and really quite touched, the last thing Fanny wanted was for her niece to follow in her footsteps. She'd been a model student at Miss Sinclair's, uncommonly obedient. That had been a mistake. When a young girl went away to school, she was supposed to spread her wings a little, to test her boundaries, to make mistakes and then learn from them.

Wanting to offer what advice she could on the matter, she touched her niece's arm, then decided it wasn't her place. Sarah should be allowed to find her own way, on her own terms. But still. "Let's talk more later, just the two of us."

Sarah's smile turned radiant. "I'd like that."

Fanny switched her attention to her sister-in-law's rounded belly. "How are you feeling?"

"Excited, impatient." Annabeth leaned in close. "Your

brother hovers like an old woman. Honestly, you'd think I'd never birthed a child before."

Despite her slightly miffed tone, Annabeth glanced over at Hunter. The way she looked at him, all dreamy-eyed and in love, told Fanny her sister-in-law adored every bit of the attention her husband bestowed on her.

A tinge of melancholy struck without warning. Would Fanny ever find that kind of love?

She certainly hoped so. And yet she wondered...

Was she even capable of having deep feelings for a man? She certainly hadn't felt anything more than friendship for Reese. What did that say about her?

Breaking away from the group, Hunter's youngest child toddled toward her. Happy for the distraction, she reached down to pick up her nephew. But the eighteen-month-old miniature copy of his father had a different plan in mind.

The little boy bypassed Fanny and went straight to Jonathon. "Up." He yanked on the crisp pant leg. "Up!"

Pausing midsentence, Jonathon looked down.

Christopher lifted his arms high in the air. "Up, up, up."

Chuckling, Jonathon obliged the child. The move was so natural, so casual, Fanny found herself staring at them in stunned silence. Christopher babbled away, while Jonathon responded as if he completely understood.

Fanny's heart gave a hard tug. Jonathon was so comfortable with the child, so patient and kind.

I will never father children.

His reasons for avoiding fatherhood made sense—at least to him. Not to Fanny. Yes, the Bible warned of the sins of the father, but Scripture also promised victory to those who broke the cycle.

Watching Jonathon with her nephew, knowing he'd

make a great father, she couldn't understand why he was so determined to avoid having children.

Releasing a heartfelt sigh, Annabeth linked her arm through Fanny's. "Johnny's very good with Christopher. Of course, I'm not surprised. He was the best big brother."

Fanny blinked at her sister-in-law in confusion. Then she remembered that Jonathon—or rather, *Johnny*—had lived in Mattie's brothel as a child. His path must have crossed Annabeth's often, probably even daily.

What else did she know about him?

Curiosity drove Fanny to pry. "What was he like as a boy?"

"Loyal, caring, a bit wild, but also protective of the other children. He…" Annabeth paused a moment, as if gathering her thoughts. "I guess you could say he kept a part of himself separate. He was friendly, but he didn't have a lot of friends."

He must have been so lonely, always watching out for others. *Oh, Jonathon, who watched out for you?* Fanny's heart hurt for the little boy he'd once been.

"That's not to say the other children didn't adore him. They did. Everyone looked up to him, even the girls." Annabeth laughed as if caught in a happy memory. "*Especially* the girls."

The boy Annabeth just described was much like the man he was today. Good. Kind. Distant. Fanny had more questions, lots more, but another commotion broke out at the hotel's entrance.

Her second oldest brother pushed into the lobby, his wife and three children in tow.

Her smile returned full force.

Logan and his family had arrived.

Later that afternoon, Jonathon stood in the conference room, impatiently biding his time. He wanted to begin negotiations at once, but the remaining Mitchell brother had only just arrived at the hotel. Coming straight off the train from Saint Louis, Garrett had promised to join them as soon as he helped his young wife get settled in their room.

That had been over thirty minutes ago.

Since Garrett's wife was with child as well, Jonathon figured getting her settled meant more than merely helping with the luggage. If the man was anything like his older brother, there was bound to be a good deal of husbandly smothering.

Jonathon felt a jolt of…something churn in his gut. Jealousy? Regret? Neither emotion had any place in today's meeting. He shoved the futile thoughts aside and attempted to get down to business.

Hunter stopped him midsentence. "We'll wait for Garrett. We make decisions as a family, or not at all."

Considering the nature of his relationship with own brother, Jonathon was both intrigued and baffled by the united front. He knew Hunter and Logan hadn't always been close. They'd actually been on opposite sides of the law for years and, according to some accounts, even enemies.

But now they were as close as any brothers Jonathon had run across. They even owned neighboring ranches connected to their parents' larger spread, which said a lot about their commitment to family.

At last, the door swung open and Garrett Mitchell entered the conference room in a rush.

"Sorry I'm late." The besotted smile on his face said otherwise. "Molly needed me to help her switch hats, and then we somehow got tangled up. The laughing began next, and well, here I am at last, better late than never."

"Save the excuses, little brother." Logan lifted his hand

in the air. "We all know you just wanted to spend extra time with Molly."

Garrett's grin widened. "Jealous?"

Logan snorted. "Have you seen my wife? She's always the most beautiful woman in the room."

"Unless, of course," Garrett countered, "*my wife* is in the room."

"Or mine," Hunter added.

Since Jonathon had known all three women in question before they'd met and married the Mitchell men, he kept his mouth shut on the matter. Each of their wives was special in her own way. Beautiful, smart, the very essence of goodness.

Jonathon nodded to Burke. His assistant shut the outer door to the conference room.

The brothers fell silent.

"Gentleman, if you will have a seat." Jonathon motioned them to the table in the middle of the room. "We'll begin."

They remained where they were, standing shoulder to shoulder. Three against one. Not the worst odds Jonathon had ever faced.

Normally, he enjoyed a tough negotiation, especially if pitted against a worthy opponent or, as in this particular case, several worthy opponents. However, the outcome of today's meeting was too important to indulge in the thrill that came from a proper battle.

Jonathon got straight to the point. "I recently acquired the property that runs along your northern border and—"

"So you're the anonymous Denver businessman who purchased Ebenezer Foley's ranch," Logan said, with the barest hint of bitterness.

Jonathon understood the man's frustration. It was no secret the Mitchell brothers had wanted the land. But

Ebenezer Foley had nursed a lifelong hatred for the entire family. He'd carried that animosity to the grave. On his deathbed, he'd instructed his son to sell his ranch to anyone but a Mitchell.

Mouth set in a grim line, Hunter crossed his arms over his chest. "You didn't ask us here merely to tell us you bought the land directly north of ours."

"No. I want to make an offer on the three hundred acres you jointly own that run along my southern border, including the dilapidated train depot. I'm willing to pay 10 percent above the going rate, as you will see in the offer my attorney drew up. Take a look."

He pointed to the files laid out on the conference table in a tidy row.

A silent message passed between the brothers before they stepped forward and opened the files with identical flicks of their wrists.

Hunter and Logan skimmed their gazes across the top page. Garrett Mitchell actually picked up the sale agreement and read through the legal document, page by page. It made sense he would take the time to consider the offer in its entirety, being an attorney who specialized in sales and acquisitions.

After a moment, Garrett looked up. "The asking price is more than fair, as are the other terms."

"Nevertheless." Hunter took a step back from the table. "We have one rule in our family when it comes to business. Mitchell land stays in Mitchell hands. We can't sell you the property."

Every muscle in Jonathon's back tightened and coiled. He forcibly relaxed his shoulders, then felt them bunch again. "Can't or won't?"

"Does it matter?"

No. He supposed it didn't.

Jonathon showed none of his reaction on his face, but inside he burned with frustration. To come so far...

"I'll pay an additional 10 percent per acre."

"Still no." Hunter said the words, but the other two men nodded in silent agreement.

And that, Jonathon realized, was the end of the negotiations. Five minutes, that's all it had taken.

The worst part, the very worst part, was that he respected the Mitchell brothers' reasons for not selling. *Mitchell land stays in Mitchell hands.*

There were other comparable properties near Denver. Two even had run-down train depots similar to the one on the Mitchell property. But none of the available parcels had a river running through the land. The natural water source made the Mitchell parcel ideal.

"You're a busy man," Hunter said. "Our decision is final. We won't take up any more of your time."

"I appreciate you hearing me out." Jonathon shook hands with each man. The oldest two brothers left the room almost immediately after that.

While Burke gathered up the files and followed them out, Garrett Mitchell hung back. "I'd like a quick word with you."

Eyebrows lifted, Jonathon gave a brief nod. "All right."

"Tell me your plan for the train depot. I know you have one or you wouldn't have mentioned it specifically in the contract."

Having worked with the young attorney before, Jonathon sensed the man's interest was genuine. Garrett Mitchell had a keen mind for business and a penchant for taking risks.

What harm could there be in sharing the basics of his idea? "My ultimate goal is to turn the stop into a premiere destination, with restaurants, shops, lodging and more."

Garrett rubbed his chin in thoughtful silence. "Entire towns have been built on less."

The other man's insight was spot on. "My hope is to create a community, not precisely a town, not at first, anyway. Rather a safe haven for my employees and their children."

He paused, thinking of his mother, of the desperation that had led her to make bad decisions out of terrible choices. "Each position will include a fair wage, on-the-job training, as well as room and board."

"If done right," Garrett mused, "the venture could bring you a great fortune."

"Money isn't the driving force behind the project." He went on to explain about the types of employees he would hire, mostly women like his mother.

"Ah, now I understand."

Jonathon believed Garrett Mitchell did, indeed, comprehend his motives. After all, the man was married to Molly, a woman whose mother had worked in Mattie's brothel, and whose older sister had adopted her when she was five.

"Let me speak to my brothers. Perhaps we can come to an arrangement."

Jonathon appreciated the gesture, but he needed to make one point perfectly clear. "I won't accept a lease, no matter how agreeable the terms."

"Understood." Now that their business was concluded, Jonathon expected the other man to take his leave.

Once again, this younger Mitchell brother surprised him. "Now that that's settled, tell me how my sister is faring in her new position here at the hotel."

Jonathon hesitated. He didn't feel right discussing Fanny with her brother. It felt like a betrayal to their friendship. "Why not ask her yourself?"

The other man shrugged. "I could. But she'll merely tell me she's doing fine."

True enough. "I can't speak for Fanny, but I can tell you she's doing an exceptional job. In truth, she's become indispensable to me." At her brother's lifted eyebrow, Jonathon added, "I mean, of course, *here*, at the hotel."

"Have a care, Hawkins." Garrett's eyes took on a hard edge. "Fanny has brothers who'll take on any man who tries to take advantage of her."

The warning was unnecessary. Jonathon would never hurt Fanny. If anyone dared to harm her or threaten her well-being, he would be first in line to deal with the rogue.

A knock came at the door and the very woman they were discussing appeared in the room. "Jonathon, we have a situation and…oh." Her eyes widened. "Garrett. I didn't realize you were involved in this afternoon's meeting."

"Didn't you?"

"No. I…" She tugged her bottom lip between her teeth. "I'm sorry, but I need to steal my boss away for a few minutes. We have a…situation." She gave Jonathon an apologetic grimace. "It's somewhat urgent."

"We'll talk out in the hall."

Before leaving the room, she tossed a sweet smile at her brother. "Good to see you, Garrett."

"You, too, Fanny. Been too long." He gave her a wry twist of his lips. "Great talking with you."

She laughed at his teasing tone. "Sorry I have to rush off. We'll catch up later?"

"Count on it."

The affection between the two was obvious. Clearly, the bond Jonathon had witnessed among the Mitchell brothers included the sisters, as well. For a brief period in his life he'd felt something similar with the other kids at Charity House, but that was a long time ago.

He followed Fanny out of the room, shut the door behind them. "You mentioned a situation?"

She puffed out a frustrated breath. "Mrs. Singletary has asked for extensive changes to the menu for tomorrow night."

"How extensive?"

"Ridiculously so, but before I send Philomena back with my carefully worded reply, I thought I'd better run it by you first."

She handed him a slip of paper with her neat handwriting scrolled across the page. The firm, yet oh-so-polite explanation as to why the hotel could not accommodate the widow's request was so perfectly phrased that Jonathon felt something move through him.

Admiration, to be sure, but something else, as well. Not quite affection, something stronger, something with an edge. "Fanny Mitchell, you are a marvel."

"You're not..." she took back the note "...upset that I'm holding firm against the widow's request?"

"On the contrary." He subdued the urge to kiss the top of her head. And then her temple. Perhaps even the tip of her nose. "I completely and thoroughly approve."

Chapter Five

The next morning, Fanny woke before dawn and went straight to work. Preparations for Mrs. Singletary's ball kept her busy all day, making it impossible to find a spare moment for herself. There hadn't even been time for a cup of tea with her mother.

Tonight, she promised herself, as she hurried back to the room she called home in the wing reserved for hotel staff. She would seek out both her parents later tonight, as well as visit with each of her siblings and their spouses. For now, she had to dress for the ball.

She slipped into her gown, buttoned up the bodice, tied the ribbons on her sleeves, then secured the last pin in her hair. Turning her attention to the writing desk, where she'd laid out her lists in a neat, tidy row, she couldn't help but think she'd forgotten something important.

Why did she have this nagging sense of doom, this foreboding that something terrible was going to happen at the ball this evening?

Nerves, she told herself, a simple case of nerves. Perfectly understandable, considering the importance of tonight's event.

The clock on her nightstand told her she had nearly

two hours before the first guests arrived. Plenty of time for another run-through of the ballroom, as long as she didn't fuss over her appearance.

Ironic, really, since most of her life she'd been lauded solely for her looks. Far too often she'd been touted as that lovely, charming Mitchell girl. Not a terrible reputation to have—quite pleasant, actually—but Fanny wanted to be seen as more than a pretty face.

Tonight the good people of Denver would meet a new Fanny Mitchell. A woman with substance and depth and a complex brain beneath the doll-like features.

With that in mind, she moved closer to her writing desk and reviewed her notes again. Working from top to bottom, left to right, she considered each item, one list at a time. Only after repeating the process twice over did she let out a sigh of relief.

The hotel was ready.

Was she?

Giving in to a moment of vanity—she *was* representing the Hotel Dupree, after all—she checked her reflection in the standing mirror by the window. The woman staring back at her looked refined and cultured, not frivolous and shallow. She supposed she looked pretty as well, not as striking as she had in the past, but not bland, either. The modern cut of her gown set off her trim figure, while the silvery-blue satin served as a perfect accompaniment to her pale blond hair. Best of all, the color of her dress was Jonathon's favorite.

A stirring of fascinated wonder settled Fanny's nerves, calming her ever so slightly. She still didn't know what had motivated his request to escort her to the ball. And yet hope surged. Why not use her time by his side to get to know him on a more personal level?

Her mood lighter than it had been in days, she gathered up her lists—all five of them—rushed out of the room and sped down the back stairwell. The noise level increased as she conquered each step. By the time she reached the first floor of the hotel she could no longer hear her footsteps.

The kitchen was a hive of activity. A sea of staff members hurried this way and that, carrying trays laden with food, moving with purpose and efficiency.

Fanny nodded in approval.

She entered the ballroom and paused a moment to catch her breath. Light blazed from the chandelier, wall sconces and candelabras placed strategically throughout the empty space. The floors gleamed. The gilded walls shone bright.

For days, Fanny had worried her decision to go with a simple color palette of green, gold and white was a mistake. Not so. Instead of overshadowing the crystal chandelier hanging from the high ceiling, the decorations enhanced the structure's unique artfulness.

Pleased by the overall effect, she floated through the room, her slippered feet soundless on the parquet flooring. A few mistakes caught her notice, mostly minor details, certainly nothing major. But still.

She could only hope Mrs. Singletary didn't notice that the ribbons on the candelabras were closer to ivory than gold. And that the cloths on the buffet tables had only three inches of lace hanging over the edge, instead of the requested four.

The stillness on the air was both soothing and yet disconcerting. A room this grand was meant to be full of laughter. Soon, hundreds of voices would clamor for supremacy, each trying to be heard above the loud din. Fanny would probably miss the quiet then.

She turned. And froze.

Her heart took an extra hard thump as she caught sight of the man standing just inside the ballroom. One shoulder propped against the wall, Jonathon watched her in silence, an unreadable expression in his gaze. A sense of déjà vu rocked her to the core. He'd stared at her like this once before, only a few days ago, and she'd found the experience just as unnerving now as then.

She scanned his face, seeing something quite wonderful in his eyes, something soft and approachable and solely for her. She was staring, she knew, but couldn't help herself. He'd never looked more handsome, or more accessible.

Her heart took a quick tumble.

She searched her mind for something to say. Anything would do, anything at all. "Jonathon, you haven't changed into your evening clothes."

Oh, excellent, Fanny, stating the obvious is always a marvelous way to show off your intelligence.

A slow smile spread across his lips. "Not to worry. The ball isn't for several hours yet, still plenty of time for me to transform into a suitable escort for a woman of your class and style."

What a kind thing to say, and spoken with such sincerity, too. Really, could the man be any more charming? Could she be any more touched by his compliment?

"You look perfectly fine just as you are," she whispered.

It was no empty remark. Even in ordinary, everyday business attire, Jonathon Hawkins exuded refined elegance.

Chuckling softly, he pushed away from the wall.

Now her heart raced so hard she worried one of her ribs would crack as a result.

Jonathon's eyes roamed her face, then lowered over

her gown. Appreciation filled his gaze. "You're wearing my favorite color."

"I...know." She swallowed back the catch in her throat. "I chose this dress specifically with you in mind."

Too late, she realized how her admission sounded, as if her sole purpose was to please him. She had not meant to reveal so much of herself.

He took a step forward. "I'm flattered."

He took another step.

And then *another*.

Fanny held steady, unmoving, anxious to see just how close he would come to her.

He stopped his approach.

For the span of three rib-cracking heartbeats they stared into each other's eyes.

She sighed. The sound came out far too tremulous.

"Relax, Fanny. You've checked and rechecked every item on your lists at least three times, probably more. Go and spend a moment with your—"

"How do you know I checked and rechecked my lists that often?"

"Because..." his expression softened "...I know you."

She fought off another sigh. There was a look of such tenderness about him that for a moment, a mere heartbeat, she ached for what they might have accomplished, together, were they two different people. What they could have been to one another if past circumstances weren't entered into the equation.

"We're ready for tonight, Fanny. *You're* ready."

She drew in a slow, slightly uneven breath. "I suppose you're right."

He took one more step. He stood so close now she could smell his scent, a pleasant mix of bergamot, masculine spice and...him.

Something unspoken hovered in the air between them, communicated in a language she should know but couldn't quite comprehend. If he lowered his head just a bit more...

"Go. Spend a few moments with your mother and father before the guests begin to arrive. I'll come get you there, once I've changed my clothes."

"I'd like that." She'd very much enjoy the chance to show him off to her parents.

He leaned in closer, closer. Fanny let her eyelids flutter shut. But then the sound of determined footsteps commandeering the hallway had her opening them again.

"That will be Mrs. Singletary," she said with a rush of air. The widow's purposeful gait was easy enough to decipher.

"No doubt you are correct." His lips tilted at an ironic angle, Jonathon shifted to face the doorway.

Mrs. Singletary materialized two seconds later, Philomena a full step behind her. Like Fanny, both women were already dressed for the ball. The widow looked quite striking in a gown made of black and glittering gold satin that spoke of her wealth and status in town.

Philomena's dress was slightly less elegant, but the pale green silk complemented her smooth complexion and pretty hazel eyes. She looked beautiful, excited.

"Ah, Mr. Hawkins, Miss Mitchell. The very people I wish to see." The widow moved to a spot directly between Jonathon and Fanny, forcing them to step back. "I have a concern about the timing of our request for donations."

She paused, eyed them both expectantly, as if waiting for one of them to respond.

Jonathon took the cue. "You foresee a problem?"

"Not a problem per se, I merely wish to switch the order of the night's events. In the past, I have presented the goodwill baskets at the end of the party. However, this evening I would prefer to do so earlier."

Though Fanny didn't think the timing truly mattered—the guests understood this was a charity event—Mrs. Singletary seemed to think this change was necessary. Important, even.

Jonathon inclined his head. "We'd be happy to accommodate your request."

Taking his lead, Fanny added, "I'll let the staff know of the change."

"Excellent." The widow glanced over her shoulder, clucked her tongue in frustration. "Whatever is that man doing here, when I specifically sent him on an errand outside the hotel?"

Curious as to the identity of *that man*, Fanny followed the direction of the widow's gaze. Burke Galloway stood in the doorway, conversing quietly with Philomena. Both looked caught in the moment, as if they were the only two people in the room.

"That girl is proving a most difficult challenge." Mrs. Singletary shook her head. "Most difficult, indeed."

Fanny bit back a smile, even as a quote from her favorite poet, Emily Dickinson, came to mind. *The heart wants what the heart wants—or else it does not care.*

It was clearly evident that a match between Philomena and Jonathon would not come to pass.

Surely, Jonathon was relieved.

Fanny cast a covert glance in his direction. His gaze was locked on her and that was *not* business in his eyes.

Something far more personal stared back at her. She had but one thought in response.

Oh, my.

Barely two hours after the first guests arrived, the ballroom overflowed with at least three hundred of Den-

ver's finest citizens. With the strains of a waltz floating on the air, and a rainbow of dancers whirling past,
Jonathon stood away from the main traffic area, Fanny
by his side.

He liked having her close, liked knowing they were
here, together, presenting a united front as representa-
tives of the hotel.

It seemed the entire female population of Denver had
gone all out for tonight's event. Dressed in formal gowns
made of colorful silks or satins, the women wore long,
white gloves, and jeweled adornments in their hair that
matched the stones glittering around their necks.

Fanny outshone every one of them, including the
women in her own family.

He watched her siblings laughing, joking with one another and generally having a good time. Their interac-
tion spoke of affection and easy familiarity. There was
an unmistakable connection between them, one that went
beyond words.

The Mitchells represented the very essence of family.

An icy numbness spread through Jonathon's chest.

What did he know of family? Nothing. No, that wasn't
entirely true. His mother had tried to give him a sense of
belonging. And, of course, Marc and Laney Dupree had
created a home for him at Charity House.

For nearly five years, they'd shown him unconditional
love. They'd stood by him, even when he'd made terrible
mistakes. It was Marc who'd retrieved him from jail the
night Jonathon had confronted Judge Greene at his home,
Laney who'd hugged away his pain and sense of betrayal.

Jonathon made a promise to seek them out tonight and
thank them for their love and acceptance.

He searched for them now, but was distracted when a

shrill, high-pitched female giggle sounded from the center of the dance floor.

One of the two oldest Ferguson sisters was making a spectacle of herself. Jonathon wasn't certain of her name. He always found it difficult to tell them apart. Unlike their younger sister, Philomena, the two oldest tended to behave in an inappropriate manner more often than not. Yet somehow they always managed to stay just on the right side of propriety.

Fanny released a chagrined sound from deep in her throat. "Penelope is in high spirits this evening. As is Phoebe, I'm afraid. I can't decide which of them is worse."

Jonathon divided his gaze between the two women in question. Both were shamelessly flirting with their dance partners. The sisters were so similar in appearance and behavior they were practically interchangeable.

"How do you tell them apart?" he wondered aloud.

"Years of practice." Fanny sighed again, then pointedly lifted her attention away from the Ferguson girls and to her own family. "My brothers are especially handsome this evening, their wives beyond beautiful. And Callie, oh, how she shines tonight. She's practically glowing."

Jonathon didn't disagree. "Your siblings seem happy."

"Marriage suits them." Fanny smiled. "Garrett once told me that when Mitchells fall in love they fall fast, hard and for keeps."

Emotion flashed in her eyes as she spoke. For a moment, she seemed very far away and very, very sad. As Jonathon watched Fanny, while she watched her siblings, a pang of remorse shot through him.

Was he making the correct decision about marriage? With the right woman, perhaps he *could* be a good husband. Perhaps, unlike his father and half brother, he wouldn't let down his wife. Perhaps the risk was worth the reward.

Another louder, shriller giggle rent the air.

"Poor Philomena," Fanny said, shaking her head. "To have such sisters."

Jonathon opened his mouth to agree when an older couple twirled past them. He studied the pair, the woman in particular. Fanny's resemblance to her mother was uncanny. They had the same tilt to their beautiful eyes, the same classic features, the same regal bearing.

"Your mother is quite lovely."

Fanny's eyes grew misty. "I'm so relieved to see her breathing easily."

He reached down to take Fanny's hand, and laced their fingers together. The connection was light, and was meant to offer her comfort. Yet it was Jonathon who experienced a moment of peace, of rightness.

This woman meant much to him, too much. He never wanted to lose her.

However, lose her he would.

Maybe not tomorrow, or next week, but one day, when some wise man offered her marriage, for all the right reasons.

As much as it would pain Jonathon to watch her fall in love with another man, he wouldn't stand in her way. Thankfully, the prospect of her leaving him—or rather, the hotel—was a problem for another day.

Tonight, Fanny was all his.

He gave her hand a gentle squeeze.

She returned the gesture, then angled her head to peer into his eyes. A small, secretive smile slid along her lips. His throat seized on a breath. Fanny Mitchell was the most beautiful woman he'd ever known.

For the rest of the evening, he promised himself, he

would avoid thinking of the future, forget memories of the past. All that mattered was this moment. This night.

This woman.

"Fanny, would you do me the honor of—"

Her sharp intake of air cut off the rest of his request.

He attempted to search her gaze for the cause of her distress, but she was no longer looking at him, rather at a spot just over his right shoulder.

A cold, deadening sensation filled his lungs.

Jonathon knew who stood behind him.

His father. He felt the man's presence in his gut, in the kick of antagonism that hit Jonathon square in the heart.

His grip on Fanny's hand tightened. He was probably squeezing a bit too hard. He couldn't help himself. She was his only lifeline in a sea of uncertain emotion.

Let her go, he told himself. Let. Her. Go.

He couldn't make his fingers cooperate, couldn't seem to distance himself from her.

Let her go.

Fanny was the one who pulled her hand free. The absence of their physical connection was like a punch, the pain that sharp and unexpected.

Instead of stepping away, she moved closer and secured her fingers around his arm. Her eyes filled with understanding and something even more disturbing. Sympathy.

He didn't want her sympathy. *Anything but that.*

He began to step away from her, to distance himself from what he saw in her eyes. She tightened her grip and smiled sweetly. "You know, Jonathon, it's long past time we took a turn around the dance floor."

Her voice came at him as if from a great distance, sounding tinny in his ears, waking a favorite memory he'd tucked deep in the back of his mind. Another evening. Another one of Mrs. Singletary's charity balls.

Fanny had stood at the edge of a similar dance floor, on the very night of her return from Chicago. Gossip had erupted the moment she'd stepped into the room. Speculation about her reasons for leaving town had been voiced in barely concealed whispers.

She'd held firm under the censure, alone, her posture unmoving, chin lifted in defiance, as courageous as a warrior. She'd been magnificent. Beautiful. Yet Jonathon had seen past the false bravado. He'd seen the nerves and vulnerability living beneath the calm facade.

He'd asked her to dance.

Later, when the waltz had come to an end, she'd thanked him for rescuing her from an uncomfortable moment.

Now *she* was rescuing *him*.

It seemed somehow fitting.

"I'd like nothing more than to dance with you, Fanny."

Taking charge of the moment, he directed her onto the floor and then pulled her into his arms.

Chapter Six

Although Fanny had initially suggested she and Jonathon join the flurry of dancers, she was pleased he'd taken the lead and guided her into the waltz. His father's hold on him was lessening, or so she hoped.

With the music vibrant around them, she settled into his embrace. They fitted well together, their feet gliding across the parquet floor in seamless harmony.

She'd known a moment of terrible distress when Judge Greene entered the ballroom. She'd recovered quickly, and had immediately taken charge of the situation.

Fanny was good at anticipating problems at the hotel, even better at dealing with situations before they became, well…problems. It was one of the reasons Jonathon valued her, why he kept giving her more and more responsibility.

Tonight, she'd been happy to put her skills to use for his sake.

Step by step, spin by spin, she could feel the tension draining out of him.

Beneath the flickering light of the chandelier, and the glow of a thousand candles, his features gradually lost their dark, turbulent edge. Jonathon was a man with many secrets and hidden pain harvested from a past no child should have to have suffered.

His present was proving no less harrowing, all because his father wished to acknowledge him publically. Not out of remorse for years lost, or guilt, or even sorrow for the harm he'd caused his son, but because Jonathon was a success now. His rags-to-riches story was legendary in Denver, almost mythical, and thus he was now worthy of Judge Greene's notice.

What a vile, hideous man.

Fanny caught a glimpse of him out of the corner of her eye. Tall and fit, with a shock of thick, white hair, he stood near the buffet table with his wife and family. The judge's features were distinguished and classically handsome, his face almost pretty. It seemed unfair that the man should look twenty years younger than his age.

His sins were supposed to show in his appearance, weren't they?

"He doesn't matter," she muttered.

To his credit, Jonathon didn't pretend to misunderstand who she meant. "No, he doesn't, not tonight."

Not ever, Fanny wanted to add, but Jonathon's hold around her waist tightened ever so slightly and he twirled her in a series of smooth, sure-footed spins.

The man was incredibly light on his feet.

"Where did you learn to dance so beautifully?"

"My mother taught me." His gaze darkened, filling with the shadows of some private memory. "She believed every gentleman should know how to waltz, her son most of all."

Proving his expertise went beyond the basics, he spun Fanny in a collection of complicated steps that had her gasping for air. "She instructed you well."

"Indeed."

They smiled at each other. More than a few interested gazes followed them through the next series of twirls. Fanny frowned at the words she caught from a gaggle of ladies on her left. *That's the girl who jilted Reese Bennett Jr.*

Whatever was she thinking?

Fanny could tell them, if they condescended to ask her directly. She would gladly explain that her worst fear was marrying a man she didn't love, or worse, who didn't love her. She couldn't imagine anything more awful than being trapped in a miserable, unhappy marriage.

Jonathon changed direction, backpedaling once, twice, spinning her around. And around. Her head whirled in the most delightful way, leaving her pleasantly breathless.

The whispers traveling in their wake were all but forgotten. She ignored everything—everyone—and focused solely on enjoying this moment, in this man's arms.

A man she admired above all others.

A man who'd made it perfectly clear he didn't want to marry, because of the paternal example he'd been given. The thought left her feeling glum. No. She refused to allow anything to ruin this waltz, this night.

Fanny's parents twirled past, catching her notice. She allowed their joy to fill her. They were both so beautiful, the handsome rancher and his stunning wife. Her mother was dressed in a midnight-blue gown several shades darker than her steel-blue eyes. Her entire being glowed as she smiled up at her husband.

Cyrus Mitchell's expression was incredibly tender as he gazed into his wife's eyes. The fear and worry was still there, but not as apparent tonight. Gone was the gruff rancher, and in his place, dressed in formal attire, was a besotted husband.

Fanny sighed. She adored her parents, and desperately

wanted what they had—a blessed, godly marriage filled with laughter, loyalty and, of course, love.

As if sensing her gaze on him, her father smiled over at her and winked. Fanny barely had time to return the gesture before Jonathon whirled her in the opposite direction.

Her heart lifted and sighed with pleasure.

He took her through another spin, then slowed their pace. The smile he gave her nearly buckled her knees. "Have I told you how beautiful you are tonight?"

"Yes, several times."

"It bears repeating."

She swallowed a nervous laugh. "You look quite handsome this evening yourself. Very elegant, very refined. I thoroughly approve of your attire."

The tension in his shoulders immediately returned.

What had she said to put him on guard once again?

"Clothing can change a man's appearance, but it cannot change his character."

What an odd thing to say. Surely he wasn't referring to himself. "I don't quite know what you mean."

His gaze connected with his father, who now stood just on the edge of the dance floor, watching them intently. "The inner man doesn't always match the outer trappings."

Ah, now she understood. "Don't compare yourself to your father," she ordered in a low, fierce tone. "You're nothing like him."

"You don't know that, Fanny."

"I know *you*. You're kind and generous and—"

"You wouldn't say that if you were privy to the things I've done in the past." Pain and self-recrimination inhabited his eyes as he spoke.

She wanted to weep for the little boy who'd done whatever necessary to survive, for the young man who'd made questionable choices to pull himself out of poverty. "The past should be left in the past where it belongs."

"Such innocence." The tenderness in his smile nearly broke her heart. "There are some things that can't be undone, Fanny, mistakes that can't be forgotten."

"You're wrong, Jonathon. That's the wonder of God's grace. He knows what we've done and loves us anyway."

Her partner opened his mouth to speak, probably to argue with her, but the music stopped.

Their steps slowly drew to a halt. By some unspoken agreement, they stayed linked in each other's arms, neither moving, neither speaking. One heartbeat passed, then another, by the third Jonathon took a deliberate step back and offered her his arm.

She accepted the silent invitation without question.

In strained silence, he escorted her off the dance floor. Fanny hated the sudden shift in the mood between them. A sense of awkwardness had returned to their relationship.

Experiencing a desperate urge to put matters right, she made a bold request. "Would you care to join me outside on the terrace for some fresh air?"

For several endless seconds, he simply stared at her. She could see the silent battle waging within him. "That would be unwise."

"Not if we stay in plain sight." She spoke in a rush, then forced herself to slow down, to speak calmly. "We won't be fully alone. People have been coming and going through the French doors all evening."

He glanced at the wall of glass doors lining the balcony. He drew in a slow, steady breath and then nodded in agreement.

They made their way across the ballroom without speaking.

He paused at the exit, dropped his gaze over her silk gown. "You aren't dressed for the weather."

"I can tolerate a few moments in the cold."

"That," he said, shaking his head, "I won't allow."

He shrugged out of his jacket and placed it around her shoulders. The gesture was so thoughtful, so…Jonathon.

Tears burned in her throat. He was such a good man, down to his very core, generous in both deed and spirit. If only he would see himself the way she did.

Blinking back a wave of emotion, she pulled the jacket's lapels together. Jonathon's warmth instantly enveloped her.

She walked with him onto the terrace, then lifted her gaze to the heavens. The air was cool on her face, refreshing after the stifling atmosphere of the ballroom.

Several other couples meandered past them. Others leaned on the balcony's railing. Caught up in their own conversations, none seemed to pay Fanny and Jonathon any notice.

She maneuvered past the bulk of the crowd, stopping at the edge of a tiny alcove at the end of the walkway. Though not completely hidden from sight, the small space afforded relative privacy.

Still, Jonathon took up a position at the railing.

Of course he would refuse to put her in a compromising position. Was it any wonder she admired this man?

Accepting the wisdom of the move, she joined him in the light, in full view of the ballroom, and anyone who cared to look. People *always* cared to look.

Something Fanny must keep in mind if she was to change the way society saw her.

Hard to do, when all she wanted was to be alone with the handsome, thoughtful, interesting man by her side.

Too late, Jonathon realized he'd made an error in judgment. He should never have agreed to escort Fanny outside. The intimacy of the moment was nearly too much to bear. Looking at her wrapped inside his jacket gave him all sorts of thoughts he shouldn't be entertaining.

She was a beautiful woman and he a man just hitting his prime, a man with a tainted past and a host of bad choices behind him.

He'd like to think he'd grown wiser in the past few years. Clearly, he hadn't. As evidenced by the fact that he was out on the terrace with Fanny.

Even if they stayed in the open, her reputation was at risk by simply being in his company. "Time to head back inside."

He reached for her hand.

She skillfully sidestepped him. "I have something to say."

Impatience slid through him. If they stayed away from the ballroom much longer, someone would come looking for them. "We can speak inside."

"Please, Jonathon. I'll be brief."

"All right." He made a grand show of putting a large amount of space between them. "I'm listening."

She gave him a mildly scolding look. "How am I supposed to talk to you when you've put a giant chasm between us?"

"Three feet is not a giant chasm."

"You're missing the point."

No, actually, *she* was missing the point. She, of all people, should know what was at stake if someone chose to misinterpret their little meeting out here on the terrace.

"Fanny, we can't stay out here much longer. Our absence will soon be noticed, if it hasn't been already."

"You're right, of course." She handed him back his coat but made no move to return to the ballroom. "I'm sorry Judge Greene showed up tonight."

Her words were steady, but her eyes spoke of her distress. So much sorrow, sorrow for him.

Had anyone ever cared for him that much? His mother, of course. Marc and Laney. A piteously small number of people, to be sure. "It's not your fault, Fanny. You didn't invite him."

"I didn't try to uninvite him, either."

She truly cared about him. The selfish part of Jonathon longed to bask in such favor. A dangerous prospect.

He had nothing to give her beyond material things. Fanny deserved more than pretty trinkets. And Jonathon wanted to give her more. But if he let down his guard, enough to explore the feelings he already had for her, there was no guarantee he wouldn't ultimately hurt her.

He couldn't risk causing her harm.

"You shouldn't be out here with me."

"Why not?"

"Your reputation—"

She cut him off with a delicate sniff. "My reputation was put into question long before you and I…"

Her words trail off, as if she wasn't sure what they were to one another.

He wasn't sure, either.

"Let's go back inside."

She remained rooted to the spot. "I haven't had my say."

"Then by all means carry on, but quickly."

"You aren't your father, nor are you going to turn out

like him. I have faith in you. You should have faith in yourself."

Her conviction shook Jonathon to the core. He hadn't expected this unwavering defense of his character. "What if you're wrong about me?"

"What if I'm right?"

For a dangerous moment, he allowed her certainty to sink past his cynicism, to permeate all the reasons he'd kept his distance from her.

"Yes, Jonathon, you started out life with the odds stacked against you. Of course you made mistakes, and a few bad choices. Haven't we all? What matters is who you are today, not who you once were."

She pulled his hand to her face, sighed into his palm.

Mesmerized, he could only stare. The smooth skin of her cheek felt like silk against his roughened hand.

He might not be able to give her what she wanted, what she needed, but he couldn't seem to walk away. He couldn't even pull his hand away from her face.

He stared at her, thinking…maybe. Maybe…

"Fanny." He said her name in a low growl. The sound came from deep within his soul, dangerous and full of warning. "Don't romanticize who I am beneath the fancy evening attire. You're looking at me from the goodness of your heart, not the reality of mine."

"You're wrong." She lifted her head. Her eyes were filled with warmth and affection.

His heart soared.

This woman could rescue me. He shoved away the reckless thought. "Don't look at me like that."

"I could make you happy."

Yes, he thought, she could. But he might very well destroy her in the process. She mattered too much to take the chance. "You want a conventional marriage. You want a happy, normal home full of children. And I want those things for you, too."

"But not with you."

The look of shattered dreams swimming in her eyes nearly brought him to his knees. "You know why."

"Why must you persist in thinking you'll become your father?" She practically hissed out the words, her tone fierce, her face a little ruthless. "Why? When evidence to the contrary is in everything you do?"

"Joshua Greene and I share the same blood."

"There are other examples in your life. Men who've mentored you. Marc Dupree, for instance. And, of course, there's the best example of all, our Heavenly Father."

There it was again, that unfailing faith in him. She couldn't know how badly he wanted to be the man she deserved.

In that instant, he allowed himself to believe in the impossible. "I like the man I see in your eyes."

He closed the distance between them, but still had the sense not to take her into his arms. A slight movement on his part, a shift on hers, and their lips would meet. He shouldn't kiss her. It would be the same as making a promise.

A promise he couldn't keep.

When clouds covered the moon, casting them in shadow, he didn't have the strength to push her away. The inevitability of this moment had been coming on for months.

There was still one small hope left. "Go back inside, Fanny, before I do something you'll regret."

Showing the stubborn streak he'd once admired, she stayed firmly rooted to the spot. "I'm perfectly happy right where I am."

A man could take only so much temptation.

Jonathon placed his hands on her shoulders, prayed for the strength to set her away from him.

"Leave me, Fanny." He gritted out the order through clenched teeth.

"Oh, Jonathon."

The way she said his name, so soft, so full of affection, he wanted to—

Suddenly, she cupped his face and pulled his head down to hers. At the same instant, he drew her against him. *Inevitable.* The word echoed in his mind.

The moment their lips touched, he was lost.

Inevitable.

By sheer willpower, he kept the kiss light, still on the edge of friendly, but barely. He tore his mouth free and lifted his head to stare into her eyes.

She blinked up at him in wonder. He'd done that to her. He'd put that dreamy look in her gaze. He was too much of a man not find satisfaction in that.

With his hands still on her shoulders, his breathing as unsteady as hers, he said, "We must get back."

She didn't argue the point. "Yes."

At the same time she lowered her hands from his face, he attempted to release his hold on her shoulders.

Only one of his hands came away. The other, or rather, his cuff link, was caught in her hair. He tugged as gently as possible. They remained connected.

He tugged again.

"Oh!" she cried out. "You…your sleeve…it's—"

"—stuck in your hair."

He reached up with his free hand.

Her instinctive flinch only managed to twine her hair more securely around his cuff link. "Hold still."

"I'm trying."

Additional clouds moved in, swallowing what was

left of the already meager light. Jonathon leaned in for a better look.

With his forehead practically pressed against Fanny's ear, he was finally able to discern that her hair had curled around his cuff link in a counterclockwise fashion. "I see the problem."

He slowly, carefully, unraveled each strand.

Just as he managed to pull his hand away, a female gasp sounded from behind him—followed by a distressingly familiar giggle.

He knew that sound. One of the silly Ferguson sisters stood at his back. The question was, how much had she seen?

The giggle turned into two, interspersed with titters, followed by overexcited, feverish whispering.

Both Ferguson sisters had come upon him and Fanny.

Jonathon told himself to remain calm. The shadows may have sufficiently hidden them from sight, or at least covered their identities.

Bracing himself for the worst, he gave Fanny an apologetic grimace, then pivoted to face the consequences of his actions.

His gaze fell on empty air.

Whoever had come upon them was now gone.

He turned back to Fanny. "I'm sorry."

Her lips quivered. "We are both to blame, I more than you, since I initiated our kiss."

Wishing he could take back the last half hour—not for his benefit but for hers—he refused to let her feel a moment of guilt.

"No, Fanny, the blame falls solely on my shoulders. I should not have escorted you outside. I should have at least insisted we return to the ballroom sooner."

She didn't immediately respond. With her finger tapping her chin in thoughtful reflection, she glanced to her right, then to her left. "You know, the Ferguson sisters may not have any idea who it was they interrupted. We may yet be safe."

"Perhaps," he agreed, although he didn't hold out much hope for that, especially since he and Fanny would be returning to the ballroom together. He would not allow her to face alone whatever censure awaited them. He would stand by her side and assume the bulk of the blame.

He feared his efforts wouldn't be enough. Fanny's reputation would soon be in tatters. At a time when she'd nearly broken free of the previous scandal, she would once again be the center of ugly gossip.

Mere days ago, Jonathon had promised himself his legacy would be different from his father's. He'd vowed no woman would suffer because of his actions. Now, because of his actions, the one woman he most wanted to protect was good and truly ruined.

As far as he was concerned, that didn't make him as bad as his father.

It made him worse.

Chapter Seven

Fanny held Jonathon's unwavering gaze with one of her own. As a matter of honor, she refused to be the first to look away. Because she watched him so attentively, she knew the precise moment their relationship took another critical turn. There was an invisible link between them now.

The anxiety roiling in her stomach calmed, then returned full force when Fanny thought of her mother. Mary Mitchell was just beginning to manage her devastating illness. Would another scandal attached to her daughter's name stifle her efforts? The doctor had warned that stress worsened the asthma attacks.

Something dark moved through Fanny, something that felt like guilt, or perhaps even shame. It appalled her to feel tears gathering in her eyes. She hadn't once thought of her mother when she'd convinced Jonathon to leave the ballroom, nor when she'd coaxed him farther along the terrace, and certainly not when she'd kissed him.

Jonathon had tried to send her back into the safety of the ballroom. Instead of heeding his warning, she'd dragged his head down to hers and melded their mouths together.

She was not innocent. She was not good. She'd earned every bit of the censure awaiting her in the ballroom.

To think, but a few hours ago, Fanny had convinced herself tonight would change the way people in town saw her. She'd certainly accomplished her objective. Clearly, she'd learned nothing from her past mistakes. Now others would suffer the consequences of her actions. Her mother. Jonathon. The rest of her family.

What have I done?

Another spurt of guilt squeezed the breath from her lungs. "I am completely at fault," she choked out between inhalations.

"Not completely, no." Jonathon's deep voice poured warmth over her cold heart. "We share the blame, and will face the consequences together, no matter how dire or life-altering."

He did not say marriage, but he was thinking it. The evidence was there, in the grim twist of his lips and the stern set of his shoulders.

She'd dragged this man to a place he'd vowed never to go.

What have I done?

"Come." He tugged her toward the ballroom. "Time to face the good people of Denver."

He guided her to the very edge of the French doors. A few more steps and they would cross over the threshold, into a future neither of them truly wanted.

The faint strains of a waltz floated out of the ballroom. One, two, three. One, two, three. The notes were simple in structure, but a mockery of the complex emotions pulling at her composure.

What have I done?

She shot a glance at Jonathon from beneath her lashes. Even in the dense, flickering shadows, she recognized the resolve in his eyes, the willingness to do whatever was necessary to protect her from another scandal.

She could not let him compromise his future for hers. "We should enter at separate times. Give the gossips less fodder to build their stories upon."

He lowered his gaze to meet hers.

"No, Fanny. We are in this together."

We are in this together. Jonathon Hawkins was proving to be a man of integrity—honorable, upright, noble. Was there any wonder she'd kissed him? And wanted to do so again?

For his sake, she once again grasped at a single thread of hope. "Perhaps Penelope and Phoebe didn't see us kiss. Perhaps they will only tell the tale of my hair stuck in your cuff."

The shake of his head said he didn't believe that any more than Fanny did. "More likely they will embellish what they saw with a decided lack of decorum. We'll find out soon enough."

He released her hand, moved in beside her, then offered her his arm in a gentlemanly gesture. Her throat seized shut.

What have I done?

If she walked inside the ballroom so thoroughly allied with him, there would be no turning back. For either of them.

"Take my arm, Fanny."

The request was kindness itself. Still, she hesitated. "I have weathered gossip before. I am not afraid to do so again."

"You are a strong woman, there is no doubt. However, you were not alone in the kiss we shared." His tone was resolute, but when he touched a fingertip to her cheek, the contact was gentle, a mere whisper of skin to skin.

"I was thoroughly present then, and I will not abandon you now."

Without pause, with one single, fluid motion, he scooped up her hand and placed it in the crook of his elbow.

They entered the ballroom side by side.

Every head turned in their direction. Significant glances were exchanged as people separated off into groups and began whispering over the music.

So the Ferguson sisters had done their worst.

Mrs. Singletary bustled through the crowd, her stride full of purpose. She met Fanny and Jonathon at the edge of the dance floor just as the final notes of the waltz played out.

"Ah, Mr. Hawkins, Miss Mitchell, there you are." She gave them each a pointed look, silently urging them to follow her lead. "I thank you for ensuring all is ready for the next portion of our evening."

Before either Jonathon or Fanny could respond, the widow positioned herself between them. The move was full of easy familiarity, as if they'd rehearsed this moment a thousand times over.

"Smile," she ordered under her breath.

Fanny managed a tentative smile, but feared she failed in her attempt to fully hide her nerves. A quick glance to her left and she saw that Jonathon had no such problem. His smile actually looked genuine.

Mrs. Singletary nodded to the staff lined up against the walls. With wicker baskets in hand, they took up strategic positions throughout the room.

The widow drew in a slow, dramatic breath, pulling every eye to her. An expectant hush fell over the room. "Mr. Hawkins, would you do the honor of calling for donations?"

"It would be my pleasure."

He asked for the crowd's attention. A ridiculously wasted effort, as all eyes were already on him. "As most of you know, Mrs. Singletary hosts her annual charity event to raise funds for one of her favorite causes in town."

As he spoke, he leveled a gaze over the assembled group, silently daring anyone to interrupt him.

No one dared.

Not even Fanny's brothers, who glared at Jonathon with the kind of disgust they reserved for poachers and horse thieves. Their wives held on to them with white-knuckle grips, as if holding them in place.

Ice lifted from Fanny's stomach, setting up residence in her lungs, stealing her ability to take a decent breath.

Jonathon continued his speech. "Tonight's proceeds will fund a long overdue remodel of the new kitchen at Charity House."

He went on to explain why the orphanage needed the upgrade, but Fanny was only half listening now. She circled her gaze around the room, stopping at various clusters of wide-eyed guests staring back at her.

She soon found Penelope and Phoebe. They stood among a group of their friends, looking smug, triumphant even, and completely unrepentant of the gossip they'd already spread.

Fanny leaned forward, counted to five silently in her head, putting a number to each second, then pointedly moved her gaze away from the troublemaking sisters.

She searched for her parents next, found them almost immediately.

No. *No!* Her father appeared to be supporting the bulk of her mother's weight. The once active, vibrant woman looked so small, so pale and vulnerable. Her breathing was coming too fast. Any moment she could suffer an asthma attack.

Fanny was the cause of her mother's distress. She'd given her reason to worry, the very thing Dr. Shane had warned against. Right then, in that moment, Fanny vowed to do anything, *everything*, to ensure Mary Mitchell suffered no setbacks because of her.

Jonathon's speech came to an end. "We thank you for your contributions to such a worthy cause."

Moderate applause broke out among the guests.

A single lift of Mrs. Singletary's chin and the hotel staff moved through the crowd, baskets extended. Despite the tension in the room, donations flowed in quickly.

The orchestra struck up a lively country reel. Some of the assembled men and women took to the dance floor, others resumed their private conversations.

Fanny didn't have to guess at the topic of their discussions.

She sighed. "Thank you, Mrs. Singletary. You quite literally saved the day."

"No, dear, I merely forestalled the inescapable." She patted Fanny's hand sympathetically, leveled a speculative glance over Jonathon. "The rest is up to the two of you."

She made to leave.

Fanny forestalled her departure a moment longer. "I'm sorry we ruined your ball."

"On the contrary." The widow fluttered her fingers. "I'm quite delighted with this turn of events. Tonight's ball will be talked about for months to come."

While that *had* been the intended goal, Fanny had hoped the talk would be for far different reasons than her scandalous behavior.

What have I done?

Her head grew light. Little spots played before her eyes. She swayed. Jonathon was by her side in an instant, hand at the small of her back, supporting her.

She lifted her gaze up to his. His attention was no longer on her, but trained at the back of the ballroom. Fanny swiveled her head in that direction, connected her gaze with Judge Greene. The odious man had the nerve to smile at her, the look far from polite.

Feeling suddenly unclean, she tore her gaze away.

Rising onto her toes, she caught sight of her father leading her mother to a chair. "I must go to my mother."

"I'll escort you." Jonathon shifted his hold to her arm.

They'd barely taken a step when Mrs. Singletary's voice halted their progress. "Brace yourself, Mr. Hawkins. Your moment of judgment is fast approaching."

Fanny nearly groaned aloud. Her brothers strode through the crowd, seemingly oblivious of the stares following them. Hunter led the charge, his menacing gait reminiscent of the ruthless gunslinger he'd once been.

Jonathon met the silent challenge with his own personal brand of grit. Not a blink. Not even a twitch. His eyes were as hard as Hunter's, and an equally threatening smile curved his lips.

Both men's dark pasts were evident in every fiber of their being. The two would be formidable foes under normal circumstances. These were *not* normal circumstances, Fanny realized with a jolt of terror. They must not fight over her.

She would not allow them to come to blows. With swift, sure steps, she hurried forward, slapped her palm on Hunter's chest. His feet pounded to a stop.

"Out of my way, Fanny." He glared hard at her hand. "This doesn't concern you."

She held her ground. "On the contrary, this is completely about me."

Logan and Garrett stood beside Hunter, flanking him, their eyes trained on Jonathon. He held their stares without flinching.

"You will not hurt Jonathon." She included all three of her brothers in the warning. "I will not allow it."

"Step aside, Fanny." This from Jonathon, spoken in a flat, unemotional tone. "Your brothers will have their say, and then I will have mine."

Jonathon's face was calm, almost stoic. She recognized that look, had seen it several times in the past year while working closely by his side. He would not tolerate her interference.

She would give him no other choice.

Just as she opened her mouth to explain her position, he shifted to stand in front of her, shielding her body with his, literally protecting her from her own brothers.

A sweet gesture, but unnecessary, especially when he was the one at the greatest risk.

She scrambled back around him. Again, he put himself between her and her brothers.

"This is ridiculous," she said. "You cannot think that I—"

She broke off, realizing the crowd was pressing in on their unhappy little group. Switching tactics, she carefully modulated her breathing and aligned her shoulders with Jonathon's.

"I can count on you to be reasonable?" She directed the question at her brothers. When none of them responded, she repeated herself.

They nodded, with very little enthusiasm. Nevertheless, she took them at their word. "I will hold you to your promise."

The next few moments passed in a blur.

Hunter officially requested to speak with Jonathon in private. Jonathon agreed, then suggested they continue their discussion in his office.

Fanny barely had time to blink after their retreating backs when Mrs. Singletary came up beside her. "Well, well, well, what I wouldn't give to be a witness to *that* conversation."

Fanny could not say the same.

The moment the men left the ballroom, Fanny was surrounded by her brothers' wives. They huddled around her, their physical presence and sympathetic smiles evidence of their unconditional love.

Each woman took a turn pulling Fanny into her arms. Annabeth spoke for the group, her words of encouragement reminding Fanny that she was not alone, never would be alone, and could turn to any of them in the next few weeks for whatever she needed.

"You can even move out to the ranch with Hunter and me," Annabeth assured her. "If it comes to that."

Fanny would never allow it to come to that.

More promises of a place to call home came from the others, then, at last, Fanny stood before her parents. Renewed panic stole her ability to take a decent breath. Her mother's face had gone white as the moon, her breathing labored, but not a full wheeze. Yet. "I'm so sorry, I didn't mean to—"

"Not now, Fanny." Her father laid a hand on her shoulder, cutting off the rest of her words. "Not here."

He was right, of course. Too many people closed in around them, prepared to spread pieces of conversation they overheard.

"Let's get you upstairs, Mary, my love." Her father helped her mother stand.

Fanny twisted her hands together. Oh, how she hated seeing her mother so dependent on assistance.

Proving she still had some spunk left in her, Mary Mitchell swatted at her husband's hand. "Cyrus, stop hovering like an old bird. I can walk on my own."

"Never said otherwise." Though he stepped back and let his wife leave the ballroom on her own steam, Fanny's father stayed close, hands poised to reach out if she lost her balance.

Lips pressed tightly together, Fanny trailed in her parents' wake.

At the elevator, her mother pulled to a stop. "Cyrus, you will join our sons and Mr. Hawkins, and ensure order is kept. Logic and good sense must rule the day."

"Now, Mary, you are my primary concern, I will see you settled in our room before—"

"I wish to speak to our daughter alone." She spoke with the no-nonsense tone that had kept her seven rambunctious children in line.

After a brief argument, Fanny's father admitted defeat. He turned to go, paused, then spun back around. His gaze was not unkind as it settled on Fanny. "You rarely take a misstep, my dear, but when you do, you make it a big one."

She could not argue the point. "Pa, please don't let the boys hurt Jonathon."

Her father looked at her steadily, with an ironic lift of his eyebrows. "I suspect the man can take care of himself."

"Please."

"Yes, yes, I will be the voice of reason."

"Thank you." As she watched her father disappear

around the corner, a flood of helplessness washed over her. Jonathon had promised to take his share of the blame.

What if he claimed all of it?

She would not put it past him. Her brothers would force his hand then, which must never happen. If only she knew what was being said behind that shut door. Perhaps she should—

The elevator whooshed open, reminding her of a far greater concern. She ushered her mother inside and told the attendant to take them to the ninth floor of the hotel.

By mutual agreement, Fanny and her mother kept silent on the journey to her parents' suite. Once inside, with her heart drumming wildly against her ribs, Fanny shouldered the door closed and then helped her mother to a small sofa.

The milky glow of the moon spilled in from the windows, creating a long, pale beacon across the blue-and-gold rug. Additional light from strategically placed lamps chased shadows into the far corners of the room.

Fanny sat beside her mother and took her hands.

For a moment, she simply studied the beloved face of the woman who'd raised her. There were new, deeper lines around her eyes and mouth, additional grooves across her forehead. But—Praise the Lord—her breathing sounded regular.

Relief had Fanny's eyes filling with tears. "Oh, Mother, I'm so sorry, I—"

"Hush, child, no apologies are necessary." Her mother pulled her into her arms and rocked her gently, in the same way she'd done when Fanny was a child.

The lack of condemnation was nearly her undoing. Several tears slipped free before she could call them back. She clung to her mother, praying for a composure she didn't feel.

In the next heartbeat, she squeezed her eyes tightly shut. A picture of Jonathon's face loomed in her mind. She shoved away the image. Enough stalling.

Sighing heavily, she set her mother back against the brocade cushions and said, "Pa was right. I've taken another misstep, far worse than the one before."

A broken engagement was nothing compared to kissing a man of some renown in the shadows. Her reputation was most definitely ruined. Her life would never be the same.

Jonathon's had permanently changed, as well.

"You know, Fanny." Her mother took her hand. "I have never put much stock in gossip. Why don't you tell me what really happened between you and your Mr. Hawkins?"

Fanny lifted her hands in a helpless gesture. "I don't know where to start."

"At the beginning, of course."

Yes, but where was the beginning? Long before tonight's kiss, she realized. Thus, Fanny told her mother about her relationship with Jonathon over the past year, highlighting how well they worked together. How much he trusted her, and she him. She spoke of their many walks, and felt a smile playing at her lips. "Jonathon and I prefer to stroll in the snow most often."

"You like him."

"I do. Oh, Mother, I do like him, so very much."

"He clearly likes you, as evidenced by his behavior this evening. He did, after all, kiss you under the moon and stars."

Fanny's heart sank, both at the romantic image her mother painted and the realization that the Ferguson sisters had witnessed everything.

"Jonathon behaved like a perfect gentleman. It was

only at my suggestion he escorted me out onto the terrace."

"I see."

"No, you don't." Why did her mother have to be so understanding, so accepting, so *wrong*? "Jonathon didn't take advantage of the situation, I did. *I* kissed *him*."

There, the truth was out at last. Unfortunately, she felt no better. Wasn't confession supposed to be the first step toward healing her soul?

Fanny felt only worse.

"You claim you initiated your kiss, yet Mr. Hawkins stood by your side during the call for donations, as if he'd been equally culpable."

"He is a kind, generous man. The very best I know."

"Perhaps marriage is the answer."

"No. Do not say such a thing." Fanny's pulse hammered in her ears. "Jonathon must not be forced to marry me."

"Perhaps he will want to marry you. The relationship you just described sounds far stronger than most marriages."

Fanny refused to allow a single spark of hope to flare into life. She liked Jonathon too much to trap him in an unwanted union. She would honor his reasons for remaining unattached. She owed him that. "I will never marry him."

"You may not have a choice, Fanny. The scandal may be too big for any other solution."

Fanny refused to despair. There were other ways to avoid scandal. She could return to the Chicago Hotel Dupree, or the one in Saint Louis, or even move to San Francisco. Except...

What if she moved away and her mother's asthma be-

came worse? What if she had a severe, life-threatening attack? Fanny couldn't bear the thought of being so far away.

Besides, running away didn't solve anything. She'd
learned that lesson well enough after the first scandal
attached to her name. No matter how ugly the whispers
became, no matter how hard her life grew, Fanny would
not run again.

She would face whatever ugly gossip was thrown her
way. She would stand sure, with courage and conviction.
She would not, under any inducement or threat, force
Jonathon into marriage.

Chapter Eight

When Jonathon was eight years old, and still new to the survival game, he'd picked the pocket of a man three times his size. To this day, he still remembered the fury in his quarry's eyes.

That same look was replicated in all but one of the four Mitchell men. Fanny's father simply observed the scene in cold, stark silence, arms crossed over his chest, expression inscrutable. With his back propped against the door, Cyrus Mitchell was either blocking the exit or allowing his sons to have their say before he intervened.

The three brothers stood shoulder to shoulder facing Jonathon. Their dark scowls and rigid stances indicated their mood. Even dressed in formal attire, each man projected intense, unyielding resolve to get answers.

Jonathon got straight to the point. "I will make this right for Fanny."

Unfortunately, the right thing by society's standards might very well be the wrong thing for her. A hard rock of remorse settled in the pit of his stomach. There could be no happy ending for Fanny. She wanted more than Jonathon had to offer. He wondered if she would grow to resent him one day.

How could she not?

She was all that was light and good and true. Jonathon was a mix of dark layers and murky complexities. He would ultimately let Fanny down.

Eyes hard, Hunter stalked up to him, going toe-to-toe, a move meant to antagonize. Jonathon strained to keep his hands loose by his sides. He no longer solved problems with his fists. He would not be induced into forgetting that he knew how to keep his temper in check.

"Tell me this, Hawkins." Hunter spat out his name as if tasting something foul. "Did you intentionally set out to ruin our sister? Was it part of some devious plan to get your hands on our land?"

A deep red haze fell over Jonathon's vision, momentarily blinding him. Of all the evils that could be laid at his feet, Hunter's indictment was the most insulting of all.

In a precise, cold tempo Jonathon ground out his response. "I would never use Fanny, or any woman, for my own personal gain."

The idea made him sick, a sensation that turned to a hot ball of revulsion in his gut. Using women was his father's modus operandi. Jonathon had thought himself better than the man who'd sired him.

Yet he'd followed in his father's footsteps and caused a woman's downfall. Not just any woman, either, but one he cared about above all others. Dark emotions pulled at him.

He clasped his hands behind his back.

"I'll marry Fanny as soon as we can make the arrangements." The instant the words left his mouth, he realized he'd made the decision long before this moment. He'd known what he would do even before he'd escorted her back inside the ballroom.

No turning back for either of them now.

Fanny would be trapped with him the rest of her life. Knowing she wanted things he couldn't give her, he felt his throat burn with self-recrimination. He wished there was another way, but there could be no other solution to save her reputation at this point.

The Ferguson sisters had made sure of that.

"Not so fast, Hawkins." Taking over for his brother, Logan shoved his face inches close to Jonathon's. "We haven't yet decided if you're worthy of marrying our sister."

Voice low and rough, Jonathon pointed out the obvious. "You would rather she face ruin?"

"That's not what I said."

"You would have her denied access to public businesses, her favorite shops, perhaps even her friends' parlors? You would have her whispered about on the streets, pointed out as a cautionary tale by mothers of young girls?"

"Of course that's not what we want." Logan bellowed louder this time. "But even you must agree. Marriage to a man such as yourself may be an equally devastating fate as the one you just described."

The insult hit home, a solid punch to his gut.

Jonathon blinked hard, his guilt a tangible thing, gnawing at him like tiny little rat claws. He'd made a terrible mistake out on that terrace, and now Fanny would suffer.

Still, resentment formed in the depths of his soul. All three of Fanny's brothers were married to women with similar backgrounds as his. "The circumstances of my birth—"

"Are not in question." Garrett dragged his older brother a few steps back, then took his place in front of Jonathon. "Our concern has nothing to do with who your mother was, or the childhood you endured. That sort of bias would make us hypocrites."

Indeed.

"It is the way you earned your fortune that gives us cause for concern," Hunter added, his mouth as flat and hard as before. "Your past is not exactly that of a godly man."

"Interesting argument," Jonathon said, leveling an ironic gaze over the other man, "coming from you."

Hunter inclined his head. "Point taken. However, my wife has suffered because of her connection to me. If she marries you, Fanny will also face unnecessary censure simply because she carries your name."

It was Jonathon's turn to incline his head. Fanny claimed she didn't care about his past, but polite society was not so forgiving. Oh, the good people of Denver loved his rags-to-riches story. That didn't mean they considered him one of them.

Beneath his outward control, Jonathon burned with regret. He'd had several opportunities to walk away from Fanny tonight. Instead, he'd given in to temptation. A single moment's indiscretion had brought life-altering consequences. Yet he wasn't sorry he'd kissed Fanny. He was only sorry she would have to marry a man such as him.

Her brothers flung more questions at him, most concerning his motives for throwing Fanny in the middle of another scandal. When the land deal came up once again, Jonathon chose his words very carefully. There could be no misunderstanding on this matter.

"For the entire time I was out on the terrace with Fanny, your land never once crossed my mind."

"And yet here we are, one day after turning down your offer, all but forced to welcome you into the family." Logan curled his lip. "Rather convenient, wouldn't you agree?"

"I would not."

More questions came at him, most about his motives, some concerning his intentions, his plans for the future.

Jonathon kept his responses clear and concise, even as his mind circled back to the same reality. If he acquired the piece of property from the Mitchell brothers now, his legacy would be forever tainted. And still he wanted to build something out of nothing. He wanted to create jobs for women like his mother, women with few choices available to them in the untamed West.

He did what he could now, gave many of them jobs at the hotel when a position came open, but it wasn't enough. Not nearly.

Cyrus Mitchell shoved away from the door and held up his hand to stop the questions.

Silence fell over the room.

"Boys, you have made your positions clear. I would now like a word with Mr. Hawkins alone."

The three brothers made no move to leave the room.

"Out."

His sons headed for the door. Before exiting, they each tossed a silent warning in Jonathon's direction. He acknowledged them with a single nod of his head.

Once just the two of them were left in the room, Jonathon focused his full attention on the older man. Cyrus Mitchell stared back at him with the eyes of a concerned father.

Jonathon cleared his throat. "I meant what I said, sir. I will do right by your daughter."

He wouldn't rest easy until Fanny's reputation was restored, if not completely, then as much as possible given the situation.

"I appreciate that." The other man shifted his stance. "This is your chance, Mr. Hawkins, to tell me what really happened out on that terrace between you and my daughter."

Jonathon hadn't expected an opportunity to explain himself. He kept his gaze as neutral as his tone. "We walked outside for some fresh air. We talked for several minutes. We kissed. We came back inside."

For several beats, the other man stared at him in stony silence, his face a landscape of hard planes and angles. "I sense you have glossed over several of the important details."

Perceptive man. "I provided the relevant information."

"Save for one key point. Do you care about my daughter?"

"I do."

The man's entire body seemed to relax, and Jonathon felt as though he'd passed a difficult test. But he knew that Cyrus Mitchell was not yet through with him. "Did you intentionally set out to ruin my daughter's reputation for a piece of land?"

"I did not."

Jonathon held steady while Fanny's father took his measure. "I believe you."

Unexpected relief nearly buckled his knees. The rest of the conversation would go easier now that this man knew where Jonathon stood. Or so he hoped. "Mr. Mitchell, I would like your permission to ask Fanny for her hand in marriage."

"You are asking for my blessing?"

"I am," Jonathon said without hesitation. "I would consider it an honor to call you my father-in-law."

A look of respect came and went in the older man's

eyes. "Don't get ahead of yourself, son. My daughter hasn't said yes yet."

With the faintest trace of amusement shadowing his mouth, Fanny's father opened the door and waited for Jonathon to join him on the threshold. "Fanny has a mind of her own and can be as stubborn as they come. You may be up against a tougher opponent than my sons."

Jonathon couldn't argue with the truth. "But if she does accept my proposal?"

"Then I will happily welcome you into the family."

By the time Fanny returned to the ballroom, the majority of the guests had left. A spattering of hangers-on milled about, perhaps hoping to see how the latest scandal would play out.

Fanny would like to know that herself.

She caught sight of Jonathon standing in the far corner of the room near the buffet tables, talking to Callie and Reese.

For a moment, Fanny studied her sister and brother-in-law. Marriage suited them both, but Callie positively glowed with happiness. Dressed in a delicate gown a lovely shade of green that matched her eyes, she kept smiling up at her husband, who seemed equally mesmerized with her.

The two were so obviously in love, Fanny's heart sighed with pleasure.

She wondered what people saw when they looked at her and Jonathon. Did they see two friends? Amicable business associates? Or something else entirely?

He caught her watching him and slowly, with casual effort, reached out his hand to her, as if asking her to join him while also giving her the opportunity to make the decision on her own.

She heeded his silent call and set out in his direction.

Whispers followed her as she made her way across the ballroom floor. She ignored them. Or rather, she *tried* to ignore them. Hard to do when speculation about her was so...profoundly...*vocal.*

She wanted to pretend she and Jonathon had done nothing wrong. But they *had* behaved inappropriately. The resulting scandal would not disappear easily. Fanny would give it her best effort, anyway.

Marriage was the obvious option, and one Fanny refused to entertain, even in the privacy of her own mind. Unfortunately, her mother's words came back to haunt her. *You may not have a choice.*

There was always a choice.

Finally, she arrived at her destination.

Jonathon took her hand, then laced their fingers together. The simple gesture gave her renewed strength.

She turned to her sister. Callie smiled at her, as did Reese, their unconditional support evident in their sympathetic gazes. Fanny was reminded of Mrs. Singletary's ball a year ago. They'd looked at her much the same way when she'd shown up unannounced, with no warning of her return to Denver.

Fanny still remembered her sister's shock at seeing her from across the room. She still remembered her own shock at seeing Callie with Reese.

Reese had taken Callie's hand and, together, they'd approached Fanny. By then, Jonathon had come to stand by her side. The four of them had exchanged awkward glances.

Just as she'd done that night a year ago, Callie broke the silence. "Well, here we are again."

It was the perfect thing to say to alleviate the tension, and Fanny finally found her smile.

She dared a glance in Jonathon's direction.

He stood silently beside her. He was so tall, strong and vigilant, ever watchful and protective of her. A little flutter took flight in her stomach.

Callie seized control of the moment, speaking of nothing in particular. Fanny was grateful for the easy conversation. Reese and Jonathon fell into their own side discussion, something about a contract negotiation that had gone bad. Apparently Reese had drawn up the initial agreement that had been summarily turned down.

The two men were of an equal height and build, their hair nearly the same color. Why had Fanny not noticed the similarities before?

Jonathon took advantage of a conversation lull. "Fanny, I'm afraid I have a handful of duties yet to tackle before the night is through. Will you join me?"

His gaze was so intense, so full of hidden meaning that she drew in a sharp breath. "Yes, of course."

They said their farewells to Callie and Reese.

As they strolled along the perimeter of the room an expectant hush fell over the remaining party guests. It was as if the entire room was poised in anticipation, eager to witness firsthand what she and Jonathon would do next.

Suddenly fatigued of the entire business of scandal, Fanny wanted nothing more than to retreat to her room and sleep for a solid week. There was still a very large issue that needed addressing first. "I hope my brothers weren't too hard on you."

"We'll talk about it later." He smiled at a cluster of guests passing by on their right.

Fanny waited until they were alone again, then asked, "Will you at least tell me if they were reasonable?"

"As reasonable as the situation warranted."

She opened her mouth to ask him to clarify. At the

same moment Mrs. Singletary hurried over to them, her skirts making a soft whooshing sound as she came to an abrupt halt. "I officially declare the evening a success."

Fanny nearly choked on her own breath.

Jonathon gave the widow a sardonic smirk. "I believe your definition of success, Mrs. Singletary, is at odds with mine."

"Now, Mr. Hawkins, there's no need to be distressed over tonight's doings. You simply need to reframe the evening's events from the proper perspective."

"And what perspective would you suggest?"

"The positive one, of course." She tapped him on the arm, as if scolding him for asking such a ridiculous question. "Not only did we raise a considerable amount of money for a very worthy cause, but tonight's ball will be remembered for a good long time to come."

"This is a true statement." Jonathon shot Fanny an apologetic grimace. "But for all the wrong reasons."

"On the contrary." The widow blessed them both with a self-satisfied smile. "The Lord has once again used me as His vessel to bring together two worthy people. My reputation as a successful matchmaker has been confirmed once again."

The woman certainly had nerve, Fanny thought, unable to hold silent any longer. "Mrs. Singletary, you cannot seriously think to take credit for...for our...our..."

She didn't quite know how to put the events of the evening into words.

"But of course I can take credit." The widow twirled her hand in the air. "You and Mr. Hawkins are well suited, and, I dare say, perfect for one another. I knew it all along."

Fanny shared a baffled look with Jonathon. "Might I remind you," she said, "that just three days ago you attempted to match Jonathon with your companion, Philomena."

The widow lifted a silk clad shoulder. "All part of the bigger plan, my dear. I am very good, am I not?"

"*Good* is not the first word that comes immediately to mind," Jonathon muttered.

She laughed, clearly delighted by his grumbled remark. "I believe, Mr. Hawkins, you have something important to ask Miss Mitchell. I shall leave you to it."

In a whirl of skirts, the widow exited the ballroom.

Fanny gaped after her. Surely she didn't mean what Fanny thought she meant.

Shaking his head, Jonathon pulled out his watch from his vest pocket and frowned. "It's later than I realized. The sun will be up soon."

"Very soon," Fanny agreed, glancing outside the wall of windows. The gray light of dawn had replaced the deep purple of night. Heavy mist rolled in off the mountains, slinking across the terrace floor.

"Come with me." Jonathon took her hand and towed her to the west corner of the room, where no one could see them. They might as well be completely alone. That wasn't what bothered her, though. He was entirely too serious for her peace of mind.

"Take a seat."

She reluctantly lowered herself onto the padded, straight-back chair nearest the terrace doors.

Fearful of what was about to come, she kept her gaze averted. She smoothed out her skirts with surprisingly shaky fingers.

"Fanny." He said her name in a whisper, the word a sweet caress. "You have no cause for nerves around me."

"I...I know." She balled her hands into fists to still

their trembling. This man was so familiar, and yet a complete stranger in so many ways.

He sat beside her. "We are in this together, you and I, and will face the future *together*."

Not daring to look him in the eyes, Fanny kept her gaze trained on the toes of her slippers. She didn't like where this was going, not one bit.

Jonathon closed his hand over hers. "There is only one option at our disposal."

Her heart dipped at the gravity in his tone. When she looked up, she went hot all over. "No, Jonathon, don't say anything else. Please," she pleaded. "Not another word."

He stood, then dropped to one knee.

"Fanny Mitchell. Will you…" His shoulders shifted, flexed, then went perfectly still. "Will you marry me?"

Chapter Nine

Jonathon's pulse roared in his ears. He told himself to remain coolheaded, as he would in the middle of any business transaction. Except this wasn't a business transaction. He'd just asked Fanny to marry him and she had yet to respond.

She simply stared at him in utter stillness, her hands balled into fists atop her lap.

The endless moment stretched into two. He ticked off the seconds in his head, willed her to give him an answer. Any response would do: *yes, no, could you repeat the question?*

She said nothing. She did, however, lower her head. The gesture caused a loose strand of hair to fall across her cheek. Absently, he reached up and tucked it behind her ear.

From his position on the floor, Jonathon had only a partial view of her face. He dipped his head for a better angle, immediately regretted the move. Her lovely features projected a loneliness and vulnerability he recognized. At the moment, the same emotions waged a war within his own soul.

In the halting silence that stretched from one minute

into two, he thought about the feel of her in his arms, not only when they'd been out on the dance floor but again on the terrace. He thought about their kiss, and the way she'd fitted perfectly in his arms, about what his life might be like with her as his wife.

Jonathon wasn't much of a dreamer. But right now, he let himself consider the impossible. Things he'd stopped believing in when he was still a boy. Things such as stability, a house of his own, someone to come home to every night. He could have all of that with Fanny, but only if she agreed to marry him.

"Fanny." He rested his palms on her knees, compelled her to look at him. "Will you marry me?" he asked again.

She lifted her head and considered him in the gray light of dawn. He worked at not reacting under her careful scrutiny.

Looking incredibly sad—an ominous sign of things to come—she scooted to her left and patted the chair beside her, a wordless invitation for him to join her.

He remained on bended knee, continued staring into her troubled eyes, waiting, watching, longing for a dream he'd relinquished years ago.

Her eyelashes fluttered and finally, *finally*, she spoke. "We both know you don't really want to marry me."

The words were wrapped inside a rough whisper. The tortured sound reminded him of sandpaper rubbing against splinters.

"Of course I want to marry you," he said, praying he sounded as sincere as he felt. "I wouldn't have asked otherwise."

Sorrow filled her face. And then—*Dear Lord, please, no*—tears gathered in her eyes. He climbed to his feet, drew her into his arms. "Don't cry. Fanny, please don't cry."

She stood stiffly in his embrace, her entire body taut with tension. He pressed her head gently to his shoulder and simply held her to him for several heartbeats.

Setting her away from him a moment later, he touched her cheek, wiped away the dampness with the pad of his thumb. "We can make a go of this, I know we can. I like you, and I believe you like me. We've conquered half the battle already."

She snuffled, swiped at her eyes, spoke again in that stark, hollow tone. "Marriage requires more than two people liking one another."

Considering her family dynamics, she would know better than he. After all, her parents had been happily married for over thirty years.

He switched tactics. "Let me protect you from ruin. Let me give you my name and shut down the gossip concerning your character."

"Oh, Jonathon." The sadness dug deeper in her gaze, sounded heavier in her voice. "I appreciate what you're trying to do. It's very noble of you to make me an offer of marriage. But you know as well as I that we will never work as a couple, not in the long run. We want different things."

Helpless in the face of her logic, he felt everything in him ache. He actually hurt from the inside out. "We may be able to come to a compromise that will satisfy us both."

She seemed to consider his suggestion. "What sort of marriage do you see us having? Be honest."

His first instinct was to tell her what she wanted to hear. But that wouldn't be fair to either of them. "We would have a marriage built on friendship, mutual admiration, loyalty and, of course, trust."

"You mean a marriage in name only."

"That's right."

He gave her a moment to process the meaning behind his words. Apparently, she needed more than one.

She simply gaped at him in stone cold silence.

"A marriage in name only." Utter disappointment threaded through her voice. "That is what you are proposing?"

He nodded, the muscles in his neck tensing. He knew what she was thinking. Yet she was forgetting an important factor. Him. Who his father was, the corrupted blood they shared. "I will not risk fathering a child."

She held his gaze for three endless seconds. Then slowly, carefully, she raised her chin a fraction higher. "Will you tell me why?"

"The men who share my blood have a history of hurting women. My father is especially guilty of this."

"That's not to say you will follow in his footsteps."

He shook his head at her innocence. "My half brother already has."

"You're not like either man. You are you, Jonathon."

"Precisely." She'd just made his argument for him. "I'm a prime example that mistakes happen."

Color drained from her face. "You are *not* a mistake," she all but growled at him. "You are a precious child of God. The Lord knew you before you were born. He knit you together in your mother's womb. Never believe otherwise, never."

He started to respond, but she wasn't finished making her point.

"Don't take my word for it, search Scripture yourself. Start at Psalm 139 and then move on to the first chapter of Jeremiah."

Jonathon blinked, not sure what to say to the fierce woman standing before him. Normally, he appreciated her keeping her opinions about God to herself. But for reasons Jonathon couldn't explain, her unshakable belief that he was something more than what he himself saw, spread warmth to the darkest places of his heart.

Cradling her face in his hands, he pressed their foreheads together and simply held on.

"You are a good man, Jonathon Hawkins." Her words grabbed something inside his chest and squeezed. "Don't ever let anyone make you believe otherwise, especially not that horrid man who fathered you."

Her words made Jonathon feel strong, keen on conquering the world and slaying her dragons with his bare hands.

Shrugging away the fanciful thought, he stuffed his hands in his pockets and rolled back on his heels. "We're not going to talk about me. You are my primary focus. I don't want to see you hurt, Fanny. Not when I have the power to prevent you from enduring another scandal."

"I'm afraid it's already done." She still sounded sad, as if she wanted something that could never be fully realized.

He knew the feeling.

That didn't mean he wasn't willing to try to make a marriage between them a success. "You haven't answered my question. Will you do me the honor of becoming my wife?"

Her eyes filled with tears once again.

He brushed them aside with his fingertips. The gesture seemed to make her even sadder.

"I cannot accept the type of union you are offering." She rose onto her toes and planted a tender kiss to his cheek. "No, Jonathon, I will not marry you."

Although he wasn't surprised by her answer, his heart took a hit. A part of him actually wanted her to say yes.

Not for propriety's sake, not to silence gossip, but simply because he wanted her in his life, wanted to face the future with her by his side.

This isn't about you, he reminded himself. If Fanny wouldn't accept his marriage proposal, then he would give her another option. "Then I'd like you to run my San Francisco hotel."

"You want me to…you wish to send me away?"

"No, I am offering you a job, a chance to start over in a new city, where no one knows you or has knowledge of your past."

She gathered in a sharp breath of air. "The San Francisco Hotel Dupree is still under construction."

"You would oversee the final building phase, and then take over operations once the hotel is up and running." He waited for his words to sink in, for her to understand what he was suggesting. "You would be the first female manager in the company."

"I'm flattered." She didn't sound flattered. She sounded insulted.

Somehow, he'd insulted her. That hadn't been his goal.

"It's a very generous offer. But one I can't accept."

"Why not?"

"If I run away again, I may never stop running. I must stand and face the consequences of my actions. Besides—" she gave a shrug "—a little gossip never killed anyone."

"Fanny, it's not *a little gossip.* Your very reputation is in question. Because of me, because of what I—"

"No, Jonathon. No more assigning blame, on either of our parts."

"If you will not go to San Francisco, then only one solution remains. Marry me, Fanny. It's the only way."

"I can't. Please don't ask me again." Choking on a gasp, she spun around and bolted from the room.

He called after her.

She didn't pause, didn't glance over her shoulder, didn't acknowledge him in any way.

With clipped strides, he set out after her, then stopped when she picked up her pace and disappeared around the corner.

Perhaps he should leave her alone with her thoughts for a while. She needed time to think, to process the situation before he proposed again. And, yes, despite her request, he would propose again, as many times as it took to convince her marrying him was the only way to save her reputation.

Still blinking after her, he caught the sound of masculine footsteps approaching from behind.

Instinct had his hands closing into fists. Forcing his fingers to relax, Jonathon exhaled slowly, turned and saw Hunter Mitchell.

Standing in the shadows of the empty ballroom, Fanny's brother looked as formidable as Jonathon had ever seen him. A very large, very lethal outlaw.

Jonathon remained unmoved. "I'm not in the mood for another lecture from one of Fanny's brothers."

"Good to know, since that's not why I'm here." Hunter shifted his stance. "I have a few things I'd like to say to you without my brothers or my father interrupting."

"All right."

"Not here, not where we can be overheard. Let's go outside." He cocked his head toward the hotel's exit.

Jonathon eyed the other man, considered, then decided what could it hurt to hear him out? "Follow me."

They left through the terrace doors and fell into step

with one another. Neither spoke as they worked their way through the shadows of the back alley.

The air was cool at this early hour, the streets all but empty of activity when they strode onto the main street beside the hotel.

Hunter broke his silence halfway down the block. "I can't understand why Fanny refused your marriage proposal."

Frustration washed over Jonathon. "How much of our conversation did you overhear?"

"Enough to know that Fanny turned you down."

Jonathon stopped walking, waited for Hunter to do the same. "I can't tolerate the thought of your sister weathering this scandal on her own."

"Nor can I." Hunter ran a hand over his face, the scratch of stubble rough against his palm. "The gossips will be harder on her than they will be on you. I don't think she understands what awaits her if she chooses to stay in town without the protection of your name."

"We live in an unfair world."

Hunter's mouth thinned to a line sharp as a blade. "My sister will be ostracized, denied access to most of the businesses in town. She'll be alone in this world but for our family."

"She'll also have me," Jonathon said. "I will not abandon her, I promise you that."

The other man acknowledged this with a solemn nod. "I know what it feels like to be shunned in this town."

So did Jonathon.

Throat tight, he glanced at the millinery shop on his left, one of the establishments that Fanny would be prevented from entering if she didn't accept his proposal. "I don't want her to suffer the humiliation of exclusion and unjust banishment."

"Nor do I."

"The only answer is marriage."

Hunter nodded. "We are full in agreement."

"Any ideas how I can convince Fanny to accept my proposal?"

"Just one." Hunter flashed a grin, his teeth a white slash against his tan face. "Woo her."

Fanny tossed and turned, and eventually gave up any thought of sleeping after an hour of trying. She had work to do, anyway. There were countless tasks that needed her attention. She welcomed the distraction from her thoughts, from the fact that Jonathon had asked her to marry him, and she'd said no.

Of course she'd said no.

The seemingly obvious solution to their problem— *marriage*—was no solution at all. She and Jonathon didn't want the same things out of life.

Regardless of his proposal, he didn't want to be married.

Fanny did.

He didn't want children.

She did.

The biggest tragedy was that she knew—*she knew!*— she would be good for him, and he for her. But without a true marriage, they would never build a lasting connection, one that would help them navigate the ups and downs of life.

Such a shame, really.

Frowning, she flopped onto her back, then kicked off the covers with a jerk of her foot.

Tears of misery formed in her eyes. She refused to give in to them. She must remember that Jonathon had made no declarations. He'd given no promises. He wanted to marry her only to protect her from scandal.

Did he not see how *good* he was, at the core? If only he would allow himself to let down his guard, he could be a loving husband. A wonderful father. A—

This line of thinking was getting her nowhere. She rolled out of bed and dressed for the day. Her movements were slow, her eyes gritty, her heart heavy. Streaks of morning sunlight filtered through the seams in the shut curtains. Considering her gray mood, Fanny kept them closed. She preferred the semidarkness.

She'd made quite a mess of her life. She would have to decide what to do next. Her mother would have wisdom to impart, but Fanny didn't want to risk upsetting her. No, she must come up with a solution on her own. Whenever she found herself indecisive, she turned to her Bible.

Proverbs especially had a way of putting matters into perspective, but nothing caught her eye this morning. She replaced her Bible on the nightstand and went to work.

She made her way directly to her office, avoiding the main hallways and staffing areas.

Stepping inside the tiny room where she spent most of her time, she shut the door, and found she wasn't alone.

"Mrs. Singletary?"

The widow looked up from her position behind Fanny's desk. "Ah, Miss Mitchell, I knew I could count on you to show up to work despite the events of last evening."

Fanny blinked in confusion. Mrs. Singletary was a partial owner of the hotel, but she'd never come to Fanny's office before today. She had to be making some point by sitting at Fanny's desk. Or perhaps the bold move was Mrs. Singletary being, well, Mrs. Singletary.

What was the widow up to now? "Did we have an appointment this morning?"

"No, dear, I merely stopped by to see how you were faring before I head upstairs to visit with your mother."

Fanny smoothed a hand over her hair. "I am well, thank you for asking."

Eyebrows raised, Mrs. Singletary stood and then began a slow perusal of Fanny's office. She moved through the room with a relaxed gait, idly touching random books on the shelving to her left, the stack of ledgers on her right. "Have you no news to share with me, Miss Mitchell?"

Affecting a bland expression, Fanny concentrated on the task of setting the ledgers on her desk in neat, organized rows. "I'm not sure I understand the question."

Mrs. Singletary paused in her inspection of an ink blotter, her eyes sparkling with a shrewd light. "Don't you, dear?"

"I'm afraid not." Fanny went to work on the pencils next, setting them side by side, their tips in a nice straight line.

"I see I'm going to have to be blunt." The widow sounded quite pleased with the prospect. "Did Mr. Hawkins propose to you after I left the ballroom last night?"

A sound of surprise slipped past Fanny's lips. She nearly said her relationship with Jonathon was none of Mrs. Singletary's business, but she didn't want to be rude. Besides, she rather liked the widow, when she wasn't being intrusive. "Yes, as a matter of fact, he did propose, and I told him—"

"Oh, excellent, this is most excellent news indeed." The woman clapped her hands together in a show of absolute pleasure. "Congratulations, Miss Mitchell. You must be over the moon with happiness."

"You don't understand, Mrs. Singletary. He asked, but I—"

The widow spoke right over her. "I'm assuming you

will want a short engagement. There will be very little time to plan your wedding. Let me be the first to offer you my assistance."

Speaking so fast Fanny couldn't keep up with half of what she said, the widow continued making plans without her.

"Of course, I will throw you and Mr. Hawkins an engagement party at my home next week, seeing as how I played such an important role in your romance." She winked. "We will invite everyone who is anyone in town, give them a good show."

The widow was like a runaway train. She had to be stopped. Fanny raised her voice. "Mrs. Singletary, I need you to listen to me before you say another word."

"Oh, well." She blinked, surprise evident in her wide-eyed gaze. "Yes, all right."

"An engagement party won't be necessary."

"Why ever not?"

"Because there is no engagement. I told Jonathon no."

Silence filled the room, a somber, dark curtain of gloom.

"Oh, dear." The widow fluttered a hand in front of her face, as if to fan away her distress. "I am quite confounded. Why would you turn the man down?"

Fanny could give many reasons, but decided to stick to the most simple, straightforward answer of the bunch. "He doesn't love me."

That, she realized, was not only the truth, but also a direct blow to the heart. If Fanny believed Jonathon loved her, really loved her, she might have accepted his proposal and hoped his stand on children would change in time.

"Of course Mr. Hawkins loves you. I have seen the truth of his feelings for you with my own eyes."

Fanny quelled the tinkle of hope that whispered through her battered heart. No good would come of wishing for something that would never come to pass. "I'm not sure what you saw in Jonathon, but I can assure you, Mrs. Singletary, it wasn't love. Affection, perhaps, but not love."

"Now, Miss Mitchell, when it comes to romance I am quite the expert." She gestured to herself with her thumb. "If I had to guess, I'd say Mr. Hawkins fell for you well over a year ago."

That couldn't be right. Just as Fanny opened her mouth to challenge the widow, a knock sounded on her door.

"Enter," she called out, with no small amount of relief.

The front desk manager stuck her head in the room. "Oh, forgive me, Miss Mitchell. I thought you were alone."

"No problem. What can I do for you, Rose?"

"A guest has made a special request I'm not authorized to grant on my own." She cut a glance at Mrs. Singletary. "But I can consult you on the matter another time."

"That won't be necessary. I'll come take care of it now."

With a smile she hoped registered a sincere apology, she said farewell to the widow and then hustled out of the room before Mrs. Singletary could protest.

Chapter Ten

Two days after Mrs. Singletary's ball, Jonathon sat at his desk, reviewing the latest report on the San Francisco project. A sense of accomplishment brought a smile to his face. Expenses were well within budget and construction was proceeding on schedule.

At this rate, the newest Hotel Dupree would welcome its first guest by midspring of next year. Jonathon calculated the months between now and then. He would attend the grand opening a married man, with his wife by his side, the two of them sharing in the ribbon cutting. It would be a good day, full of laughter and—

His smile slipped.

There was one large hitch in that plan. Her name was Fanny Mitchell. The woman was proving as stubborn as her father warned. She absolutely refused to allow Jonathon to court her, either by ensuring other people were always around her, or by avoiding him altogether.

How was he supposed to win Fanny over to the idea of marriage if he couldn't even get her alone?

Clearly, he needed to rethink his approach. Time was of the essence. The longer Fanny resisted his suit, the more her reputation would suffer. It was unacceptable.

He shoved away from his desk and got to his feet. Drumming his fingers against his thigh, he contemplated his next move. Now that he'd had time to consider spending the rest of his life with Fanny, he rather liked the idea. They were well suited in nearly every way that mattered.

They had a similar sense of humor, tackled problems with equal amounts of intellect and reason. In fact, they were so compatible they often finished each other's sentences.

They could—no, *they would*—have a satisfying marriage, once Jonathon convinced Fanny to say yes to his proposal.

Impatient to settle the matter, he left his office and strode toward the main lobby of the hotel. Fanny would be at the registration desk, supervising check-in and checkout.

Jonathon rounded the corner, stepped into the open-air atrium and came to a dead stop. The scene before him was worse than he'd imagined, and everything he'd hoped to avoid.

A chill navigated along the base of his spine.

In the four years he'd owned the Denver Hotel Dupree, he'd rarely seen a maddening crush like this one. By his calculation, only half the men and women were actually registered guests. The rest were here for a show, with him and Fanny in the starring roles.

Keeping his expression blank, his movements careful and controlled, he continued toward the registration desk.

The crowd didn't actually fall silent, yet there was a definite lull. He paused once again, reached up and pinched the bridge of his nose.

Conversations slowly resumed. From the bits he caught, Fanny's character was being put into far greater question than Jonathon's. Just as her brother had predicted, and Jonathon had feared.

A proper courtship was no longer an option.

At least Fanny seemed too absorbed in her work to notice the speculation thrown her way.

Eyebrows drawn together, she ran a fingertip along the registration book—top to bottom, left to right—her hand stopping at various points along the way to make marks and notations. Half her face was in shadow, the other half illuminated by a ray of sunlight streaming in from the skylight above her head.

She's so lovely, Jonathon thought, allowing himself a moment to watch her work. Head bent, she shoved a loose strand of hair off her face. She repeated the process twice more before giving up.

Jonathon couldn't look away, didn't want to look away. This wasn't the first time he'd stood in this exact spot, riveted. From nearly the first day of their acquaintance, he'd been irresistibly drawn to Fanny. Over the years, that fascination hadn't faded.

As though sensing his eyes on her, she lifted her head and looked over at him.

Their gazes locked, held.

The chattering grew frantic, a fast staccato of high-pitched whispers and suppositions. Every move Jonathon and Fanny made from this point forward would be discussed over pots of tea later that afternoon. In a few cases, the events would be reported truthfully. In most, they would be expanded upon, while in others, embellished to disastrous proportions.

He should not give the gossips additional fodder. Yet he couldn't seem to pry his gaze free of Fanny, nor did she seem to be able to look away from him. Seconds ticked by. Everything inside Jonathon settled. Doubt disappeared. He knew exactly what he wanted. Fanny. He wanted Fanny.

The woman understood him better than anyone else. She anticipated his preferences and made suggestions accordingly.

She must become his wife as soon as possible. Jonathon would allow no other outcome to prevail.

Just as he set out in her direction, she abandoned the registration desk and headed toward him. She moved purposely. She hadn't looked that willing to speak with him since the ball.

He paused in his own pursuit, overwhelmed by her fierce beauty. She'd arranged her hair loosely atop her head, with several strands cascading free. The tousled effect captivated him.

He swallowed, forced back a wave of attraction that went far beyond friendship. He'd meant what he'd told her. Their marriage would be in name only. It was the only way to ensure another generation escaped tragedy.

But he was getting ahead of himself.

Fanny still had to accept his proposal.

She closed the distance between them, careful to leave a respectable gap, proving she was fully aware of their audience.

They stared at one another. She looked unusually tired. Exhaustion etched across her features and there were purple bruises under her eyes, a visible sign she hadn't slept much since Mrs. Singletary's ball.

He desperately wanted to soothe away all her worries, to spirit her off and protect her from the cruel world. If only she would allow him that privilege.

"Good afternoon, Miss Mitchell."

"Good afternoon, Mr. Hawkins." She gave him a perfectly polite smile. It was a valiant effort to remain detached, but Jonathon recognized the nerves beneath her flat expression.

"As you may have noticed," she said, sighing, "the hotel is at full capacity, plus a wee bit more."

"The atrium has always been a favorite gathering spot for our guests." He glanced to his left, then his right, dropping a quelling look on the closest men and women in the process. "Plus a wee bit more."

Her lips twitched. Ah, now they were getting somewhere. He almost had her smiling.

Finished giving the nosy onlookers something to see, he extended his hand.

"It's a beautiful afternoon." He had no idea if this was true. He'd been inside all day. Nevertheless… "Come for a walk with me, Miss Mitchell."

Looking slightly caged, she took a step back, shook her head decisively. "That's a lovely offer, Mr. Hawkins, but I'm afraid I must decline. Duty calls."

"Duty can wait." Before she could protest yet again, he took her hand and guided her toward the exit.

For several steps she obliged him. But then she stopped and drew her hand free. "You do realize it's snowing."

Was it? He looked out the windows and saw that she was right. "So it is."

"We aren't dressed for the weather."

A problem easily remedied. "Get your coat and meet me back here in five minutes."

She hesitated, clearly pondering the wisdom of spending time alone with him.

Her reticence hit a nerve. He'd had enough of her avoidance.

"Get your coat, Fanny." He leaned in, his voice for her ears only. "You'll put me off no longer."

She opened her mouth, an argument clearly on the tip of her tongue, but the crowd pressed in and she simply sighed. "I'll be back shortly."

"As will I." Jonathon went to retrieve his own coat. He found his assistant waiting for him outside his office, shifting from foot to foot, his expression bleak.

"Is there a problem, Mr. Galloway?"

"Possibly." Eyes hooded, Burke consulted his notebook. "Judge Greene has asked for a private meeting with you as soon as possible."

Jonathon lifted his eyebrows. The timing of the request could not be by chance. "Did he mention the nature of his business?"

"No, sir."

Jonathon considered the request, his annoyance tempered by a jolt of curiosity.

"Tell Judge Greene I will see him this afternoon." Jonathon had resisted meeting with his father long enough.

Burke made a notation in his book. "What time should I tell him to arrive?"

"I'll meet with him in my office in one hour."

Jonathon would have preferred to spend the entire afternoon with Fanny, but until she accepted his marriage proposal, it was best to keep their public interactions to a minimum.

"I'll inform Judge Greene of your decision." Burke spared him one last glance before dashing off.

Precisely five minutes later, Jonathon joined Fanny at the bronze-encased glass doors leading to Stout Street.

Keeping silent, he ushered her out onto the sidewalk.

A blast of cold air slammed into them. Fanny burrowed deeper inside her coat, while he turned up his collar. They fell into step with one another, as they did on all their walks.

Rather than taking their usual route, Jonathon directed her down a side street, around the corner, along another street and finally into a small park.

Snowflakes fluttered from the sky, landing soundlessly at their feet. Jonathon brushed powdery crystals off a nearby wrought-iron bench. "Let's sit a minute."

He indicated the now snow-free seat angled beneath a large tree, its bare branches coated in ice. Sunlight danced off the white blanket around them in glittering sparks.

Fanny took her time lowering herself to the bench and then smoothing out her skirts. Once she was settled, Jonathon sat beside her. Her scent wrapped around him, a pleasant mix of wild orchid and mint. The air was clear enough that he easily heard the muffled slam of a door, the yapping of a dog. He tuned out the rest.

Turning slightly in his seat, he took Fanny's hand again and protectively cupped it within his. "You're so beautiful."

Pain flashed in her eyes. Instead of smiling at the compliment, she looked sadder than he'd ever seen her. For the first time in months, he couldn't interpret her thoughts.

Her expression suddenly changed. "My answer is no, Jonathon. I won't marry you."

Sweet, delightful woman. He should have known she wouldn't make this easy on him. Fair enough. Adopting a relaxed posture, he let go of her hand, leaned back against the bench and smiled. "I don't recall asking you to marry me."

"Oh." Her eyes widened. "You...I...*oh*."

What a wife she would make him. Unpredictable at times, bold at others, sweet. She was so familiar and yet there was still so much he didn't know about her.

A dull ache swirled in the pit of his stomach, a sensation that felt like longing, perhaps even yearning.

He would have liked more time to become better acquainted with her. It would have been pleasant to take his time learning her likes and dislikes, her favorite color and time of day. Was she a morning person or a night owl? Did she prefer chocolate or vanilla?

So much to uncover, so many layers to peel away.

"I want to know everything about you," he said in complete and total honesty.

Suddenly wary, she stared at him through narrowed eyes. "Why?"

He chuckled softly. "Because you're a fascinating woman. Let's start at the beginning. What was it like growing up on one of the largest cattle ranches north of Texas?"

She gave him an odd look, as if she didn't quite know what to make of him. "There was nothing really unique about my childhood." She shrugged. "It was like most others, I suppose."

Certainly not like his. "I can't speak to that. I've not been exposed to many families like yours."

"Oh, Jonathon." Everything about her softened, her eyes, her shoulders, her voice. "I'm sorry. I didn't mean to sound dismissive. I just…I don't understand why we're out here, sitting under a snow-covered tree, talking about my childhood."

He pulled her hand to his lips, letting go after making the briefest of contacts.

"We're getting to know one another outside our relationship at work." He gestured for her to continue. "You were telling me about your family."

"Oh, yes." She chewed on the fingertip of her glove, thought a moment, then smiled. "My parents raised the seven of us to pull our own weight. We worked hard, played harder, laughed a lot. When life got tough, we turned to God, and when things were good we praised Him for our blessings."

Jonathon nodded. None of what she said surprised him.

"With five brothers and one sister running around, I was never alone, never without someone to play with or talk to, or," she said with a laugh, "fight with. Somehow, everything seemed easier, better, because I had so many siblings."

"Sounds pretty incredible."

Her smile widened, while her eyes became wistful, a little distant, as if she'd gotten lost in her memories. "I had a happy childhood. I never questioned whether I was safe or cared for or loved."

"I take it you're an accomplished horsewoman."

"My father wouldn't have it any other way. I learned how to ride around the same time I learned to walk." As she tossed out amusing anecdotes, Jonathon was reminded of his time at Charity House with Marc and Laney Dupree.

He'd been happy and safe in their care. Although he hadn't been with them long, only four years, in that short amount of time Jonathon had enjoyed having a family, siblings included.

Perhaps he knew more about marriage and family than he realized.

But did he know enough to make Fanny a good husband, the kind she deserved?

Or would he eventually let her down, as the men who shared his blood did over and over again with the women in their lives?

The answer was painfully obvious. Fanny wanted a happy marriage like that of her parents. She also wanted a family of her own.

Jonathon could give only bits of those things, never the whole.

In the end, he would disappoint her. What was worse, he wondered. A ruined reputation that Fanny might never recover from fully? Or a childless marriage with a man who could give her only fragments of the life she wanted?

Neither was ideal.

He waited for her stories to end, then took her hand and walked with her back to the hotel. He didn't speak, but used the silence to organize his thoughts, to think through their options.

The things Jonathon wanted for himself must not be factored into his decision. He must act in Fanny's best interest.

It was the one gift he could still give her.

With their walk officially over, Fanny watched helplessly as Jonathon disappeared inside his office. She continued staring at his shut door, trying to pinpoint exactly when things had gone from bad to worse between them.

For a small portion of their time together in the park, she'd felt closer to him than ever before. As she'd talked about her childhood, she'd watched him visibly relax. He'd been approachable and attentive, until suddenly, he was neither.

One minute he was listening to her stories, smiling, eyes laughing, then, abruptly, his guard was up again.

A sigh leaked out of her. What had she done to change his behavior so dramatically?

As she thought back through the various stories she'd told, someone bumped into her, knocking her slightly off balance. She shifted to regain her balance. At the same moment, a pair of strong hands settled on her shoulders.

She looked up, sighed again. "Garrett, I didn't realize you were standing there."

He gave her a wry smile. "That's probably because you were staring at your boss's door so hard you practically bored a hole in the wood."

"I was just…that is, I was—"

"You don't have to explain yourself to me."

No, she didn't. When he continued watching her, his gaze running quickly over her face, she redirected the conversation in his direction. "How's Molly feeling this afternoon?"

"Exhausted and queasy. I left her resting in our room." He shook his head in wonder and awe. "I still can't believe we'll be welcoming our first child in less than five months."

The look of utter contentment in her brother's eyes sent a wave of yearning through Fanny. Garrett was going to be a father. She would soon have another niece or nephew to spoil.

Fanny had always believed children were a blessing straight from God. If she married Jonathon, she would never know that joy.

She sighed again.

"Fanny." Garrett took her arm and drew her toward a tiny alcove decorated with potted plants. "Tell me what I can do to make things easier for you. Name it and it's done."

Her brother meant well, she knew, but his soft voice and concerned expression only managed to annoy her.

She blew a wayward strand of hair off her face. "I love you for worrying about me. But, Garrett, I've suffered through gossip before."

"Not like this."

She shoved at the stubborn lock of hair. Why wouldn't

it stay tucked behind her ear? "The speculation and whispers certainly feel the same."

"The gossip is much worse and you know it."

She resisted another sigh. "Phoebe and Penelope Ferguson are prone to exaggeration. What happened between Jonathon and me was really quite innocent."

Garrett flicked his gaze over the crowded lobby, then shook his head in disgust. "In situations such as these, the truth hardly matters. The perception is that you and Hawkins—"

"I know what the gossips are saying."

He nodded. "Have you thought about your next step?"

In truth, she hadn't, not really. She'd been too busy pretending the problem would simply fade away. The interested stares from the men and women still milling about in the lobby dispelled that notion. She was going to have to make a decision about her future.

Garrett touched her arm, dragging her attention back to him. "Come live with Molly and me in Saint Louis."

The offer was so Garrett. Fanny wanted to hug him for his concern, for his readiness to rescue her. "I want to stick close to home, near Mother."

"Saint Louis is a train ride away."

"Still too far," she said, shaking her head. "Besides, running away isn't the answer, not this time."

"Was it the answer last time?"

"I believe so, yes." Closing her eyes, she drew in a careful breath, thought about the woman she'd once been. "I needed to go away and work out my convictions on my own. I had to find out who I was beneath the facade I presented to the world."

"Did you discover what you were looking for?"

"I'd like to think I did." She stared off into the distance, tapped her finger against her chin. "I know more about what I want out of life and, consequently, what I don't."

"How does Hawkins play into your future?"

Sometimes Garrett could be such a lawyer. Well, she wasn't a witness in a courtroom he could intimidate with his pointed questions. "That's between Jonathon and me."

"In other words, mind my own business?"

She managed a weak smile. "Something like that."

"For what it's worth, I believe Jonathon Hawkins is a good man."

"I agree." The very best of her acquaintance. If only he would embrace the person she knew him to be.

"Fanny." Garrett touched her arm again. "Tell me what I can do to make your sadness go away."

"I'm fine, really. I just have a lot on my mind."

"Then I'll leave you to your thoughts." He turned, then swung back around and tugged her into his arms. "I hate seeing you unhappy."

"I'm not unhappy." Chin lifted, eyes dry, she stepped out of his embrace. "I trust everything will work out eventually. The Lord already has the solution in place and will reveal the answer in His time."

"My offer still stands. You can come to Saint Louis anytime. The door is always open."

Though she knew she wouldn't accept his generosity, she appreciated the invitation. "Thank you, Garrett. I'll let you know what I plan to do about my future."

He glanced back at the crowd, scowled. "Make a decision soon, Fanny. Time is running out."

"I know."

He kissed her on the cheek and then was gone.

Alone again, she returned her attention to Jonathon's door, and she saw Judge Greene knock once and then enter a second later.

Fanny frowned.

What sort of business did Jonathon have with his father? Or was it the other way around? Was the judge the one who'd called for a meeting?

A protective instinct stole through her. She moved a step closer to Jonathon's office, thinking maybe she could catch part of their conversation.

Perhaps if she pressed her ear to the door—

She froze, horrified at the direction of her thoughts. Oh, the depths to which she'd sunk. Eavesdropping and lurking in shadows was completely, utterly beneath her.

Still, what could it hurt to move a step closer to Jonathon's office?

Chapter Eleven

Standing behind his desk, Jonathon stared in stunned silence at Joshua Greene, not quite believing the conversation he'd had thus far with the man who'd fathered him. Jonathon didn't know whether to laugh at the irony of the man's gall or slam his fist into that sanctimonious square jaw that looked entirely too much like his own.

Jonathon grasped for a calm that hovered just out of reach.

"Let me see if I understand you correctly." He chose his words carefully, keeping his expression blank. Greene didn't deserve a single reaction from him, not even a sneer. "You have come to congratulate me on ruining a young woman's reputation."

Two dark eyebrows lifted, haughty, arrogant arches over feral, ice-blue eyes. "You are intentionally twisting my words."

Maintaining his relaxed posture proved impossible. Jonathon stalked around his desk, stopping several feet from the cold statue who'd fathered him.

The other man stood his ground, unmoving, his gaze so direct it felt like a physical assault.

Jonathon couldn't hold back his sneer a moment longer. "By all means, Judge Greene, please, clarify your earlier statement."

"There's no need to use that antagonistic tone. I simply came here to commend you on your success. You have linked yourself with one of the most well-respected, prominent families in Colorado."

Anger and insult warred within him. Jonathon shoved down the volcanic emotions with a hard swallow. "You think I put a woman's entire future at risk for the sake of an alliance with her family? You think me that calculating?"

"Not calculating." The judge gave a nod of approval. "Merely shrewd."

"Shrewd." Jonathon repeated the word, hardly able to speak through his gritted teeth. This man, so distinguished on the outside, had a black heart, far uglier than he'd realized.

"I'm actually quite proud of your ingenuity," the judge continued. "And now, I believe the time has come for me to publically acknowledge our connection. If worded properly, the voters will find my honesty refreshing. They are already enamored with your climb out of poverty. Add in my heartfelt sorrow over a youthful indiscretion and I'll win over the hardest of hearts."

"Ah, now I understand. This is about your run for the United States Senate."

The man cocked his head in silent acknowledgment, completely unrepentant of his scheming agenda. "Cyrus Mitchell has withheld his support of my candidacy up to this point. However, if you step up and marry his daughter, and I then acknowledge you as my son, he will be forced to reconsider his position."

It was over, Jonathon thought. The last shred of hope

for reconciliation with the man who'd fathered him was good and truly gone.

Not once in his childhood had this man acknowledged his existence. Only now, when it served his own purpose, was the venerable judge willing to claim Jonathon as his son.

Casting a brittle, bitter grin in the judge's direction, he paced to the bookshelf, ran his finger along the binding of his Bible. Just this morning, he'd followed Fanny's suggestion and had read Psalm 139, specifically verse 13, a bold reminder that he had a Heavenly Father who loved him. Jonathon didn't need an earthly father's public acknowledgment.

Dropping his hand, he gave a nonchalant tug on his waistcoat, then faced Judge Greene once again.

"This conversation is over." He'd given the man too much of his time already, not only today, but in all the years he'd allowed him to take up residence in his thoughts. "You know the way out."

The judge made no move to leave the room. "You won't do better in a wife than Fanny Mitchell. Your tactic was really quite brilliant. You would have never secured her interest by conventional means."

The barb hit its mark, the message clear. He, the illegitimate son of a callous, calculating man and his prostitute mistress, didn't deserve a woman like Fanny.

"Consider yourself fortunate you are in a position to marry the girl."

"You mean," Jonathon scoffed, his blood icing over in his veins, "unlike the position you found yourself in when you ruined my mother's reputation?"

"Our situations are vastly different." The judge sniffed in disgust. "I already had a wife when I met Amelia Hawkins."

Jonathon knew better than to ask, yet he couldn't help himself. The words spilled out of his mouth before he could stop them. "Would you have married my mother had you been a free man?"

Greene held his stare, a hard, ruthless look in his eyes now. The world seemed to stop on its axis.

"I would not have married your mother under any circumstances. She was already compromised when I met her. She would never have made a man such as me a proper wife."

Jonathon thought of his half brother, the son so much like the father. The legitimate spawn of this self-serving man and his *proper* wife was, at this very minute, in the process of setting up his mistress in her own little house with Jonathon's money.

Did Judge Greene know what his heir was up to?

Would it matter if he did?

As if from a great distance, Jonathon heard the rest of Greene's words, heard him expanding on his mother's lack of pedigree. A part of him listened, taking it all in, realizing the true condition of this man's soul.

He is my father. I come from this ugliness.

But he also came from Amelia Hawkins.

He thought of the woman who'd given birth to him. Somewhere, deep down, he'd known she wasn't educated or refined or even proper. But she'd been unspeakably beautiful. Men of quality had sought her out over the other girls in Mattie's brothel. Looking back with the wisdom of age, Jonathon realized why. Amelia Hawkins's ethereal beauty had been her greatest attribute.

"…and so my advice would be to secure Miss Mitchell's hand in marriage as soon as possible."

Jonathon felt his jaw clench so hard he feared his back

teeth would crack from the pressure. He didn't need advice from this man.

Yet one truth could not be denied. If Jonathon didn't marry Fanny, if he abandoned her to her fate, he would be no better than the man who'd fathered him.

Though he couldn't give Fanny what she wanted—family, children—he could give her other things. Comfort, security, his complete devotion.

"We're through here." Jonathon laced finality in his words. "You will leave my office and my hotel at once."

"I'll go." His eyes full of the cunning he'd wrongfully attributed to Jonathon, Greene headed toward the door, then paused halfway through the room. "You should know I plan to release a statement in the *Denver Chronicle* about our connection, once you do the smart thing and marry the girl."

"I can't stop you from going to the newspaper." Jonathon maneuvered around the other man and set his hand on the doorknob. "But *you* should know that if asked about our connection, I will respond with complete and brutal honesty."

"Is that a threat?"

"It's a promise." Jonathon yanked open the door.

Fanny all but tumbled into his arms.

"Oh." She fought for balance, stumbled a step to her left before righting herself. "I was just about to knock, but I see you anticipated my arrival."

Jonathon eyed her closely, wondering why her gaze seemed unable to find a place to land. "Was there something you needed that couldn't wait?"

Her hands fluttered by her sides, then gripped one another at her waist.

"There's a…a problem with one of the guests. The situation must be addressed immediately." She cut a quick, furious glance at the other man in the room. "Judge Greene, I'm sure you understand."

"Indeed, Miss Mitchell, I understand perfectly." He gave her a charming smile, with a hint of smugness around the edges. "It's lovely to see you again."

Her scowl deepened. "I'm sorry I can't say the—"

"Fanny." Forestalling the rest of her response, Jonathon put a protective hand on her shoulder. "The judge was just leaving."

She turned her gaze to Jonathon, nodded slowly, then made a grand show of stepping aside to let the other man pass. "Please, Judge Greene, don't let us keep you."

Affection filled Jonathon's heart, warming him from the inside out. Righteous anger suited Fanny. Her face glowed.

Judge Greene paused at the threshold to stare into Fanny's eyes. "I'm sure we will see more of each other in the coming weeks, Miss Mitchell."

"I doubt that very much." Her smile was all teeth. "We rarely run in the same circles."

"An oversight I plan to remedy immediately." Having given his opinion on the matter, he ambled past her without another word.

As she gaped after his retreating back, Fanny's shoulders lifted in a noiseless sigh. "I don't like that man."

"That makes two of us."

Overcome with an emotion he couldn't name, Jonathon wanted to pull Fanny into his arms and kiss her soundly on the mouth. With the gentlest of touches, he instead reached up and tamed a stray wisp of hair behind her ear. "You mentioned a problem with a guest?"

"Oh, yes. It's…not precisely a problem. Just something I failed to mention earlier."

"Go on."

Her expression turned sheepish. "My parents have requested you dine with us this evening. They would like to eat somewhere other than here in the hotel."

"Any particular reason why? When we have a perfectly respectable restaurant on the first floor?"

She gave him a slow, appealing smile. "I believe my father mentioned something about the four of us needing a change of scenery."

Jonathon felt his own smile show itself at last.

"Well?" That stubborn strand of hair escaped once again. "Are you available to dine with my parents and me tonight?"

"My dear, sweet, beautiful Fanny." He tucked the curling wisp back in place. "Tonight, I'm all yours."

Not only tonight, he thought, but if he had his way, every night to come.

Fanny paused briefly at the entrance of the restaurant, her arm looped through Jonathon's. Her parents were a few steps ahead of them, suspended in a similar pose. All gazes turned in their direction and as soon as the whispering began, her mother let out a long, weary sigh.

Fanny's sentiments exactly.

Tonight was supposed to have been a break from the melodrama of the past few days. Apparently there was nowhere she and Jonathon could go in Denver to avoid the gossip. Now, her parents were at the center of the firestorm with them.

Would the stress be too much for her mother?

Fanny's heart endured a tight, panicky squeeze at the thought. But then she noted that her mother's breathing seemed to be coming at a normal rate.

Relieved, Fanny glanced around the restaurant. Rivaled only by the Hotel Dupree, the Brown Palace's rich, expensive decor was considered the height of fashion. The dining room was no exception. Bone china adorned every table. Engraved silverware and crystal goblets completed the elegant place settings.

Wondering what he thought of his competition, Fanny glanced up at Jonathon. His gaze gave nothing away.

Her first inclination was to ask him to escort her out of here, away from the whispers and pointed stares. But her mother seemed to be handling the situation with her usual grace and poise. Fanny would attempt to do the same.

Besides, if she was going to remain in Denver, then she had better get used to the unwanted attention.

At least tonight she didn't have to suffer alone. Jonathon and her parents stood with her. People continued watching them—especially the women—and by the look of their pinched, sour faces, directed mostly at Fanny, many would like to see her brought low.

"Is this a stupendously bad idea?" she asked in the barest of whispers.

Jonathon leaned his head a discreet inch closer. "We will know soon enough, perhaps even before the first course is served."

His response did nothing to dispel her concerns. But then he smiled. And the prospect of spending a few hours under the watchful stares of their fellow diners seemed slightly less awful.

"Smile, Fanny." Jonathon pulled her a shade closer. "I am certain we have nothing but a delightful evening ahead."

She wasn't nearly so confident, but managed a slight lift of her lips.

"Since you agree, let us enjoy ourselves fully." His soft tone and gentle expression instantly lightened her mood.

"I have it from a reliable source that the food in this restaurant is of the highest quality."

Since Fanny was the so-called reliable source, she could only laugh and shake her head. His responding wink made her think of happy futures and sweet kisses under the stars.

Out of the corner of her eye she watched her father pat her mother's arm, and the tender gesture spoke of their years together. Watching their easy intimacy, Fanny felt something move in her heart, a desire to have what they had. A bond that withstood life's hardships and grew stronger with time.

If only—

The maître d'hôtel appeared and directed them to their table. They were settled in their chairs with little fanfare, their orders taken quickly and efficiently.

To Fanny's surprise—and tremendous relief—the other diners lost interest in them halfway through the first course of their meal.

Jonathon and her father fell into an amiable discussion over the various investments they'd recently acquired. Fanny and her mother discussed far more important matters, specifically, the latest hat and clothing styles from Paris.

"You can never go wrong with the acquisition of property," she heard her father say. "Land is a finite commodity."

Jonathon agreed. And so began a lengthy discussion of their various individual real estate holdings.

As the evening progressed, the four of them fell into an easy rhythm. Conversation flowed effortlessly, skipping from one topic to the next, sometimes including everyone at the table, sometimes only two or three.

Fanny found herself falling silent more often than not,

preferring to watch Jonathon interact with her parents. He seemed perfectly at ease. Everything about the man appealed to her. She admired his sense of honor, his devotion to his employees, his patience while her father grilled him about his finances.

Personally, Fanny didn't care how much money Jonathon had made in recent years. She was more impressed with his work ethic and how he hired people other employers shunned. She really adored his face. Strong and handsome, each feature boldly sculpted. The overall impact was very masculine, very appealing.

She couldn't seem to take her eyes off him.

He looked in her direction and their gazes locked. Her breath caught in her throat. Her mind emptied of all coherent thought.

When he returned his attention to her father, the truth roared through her like a violent summer storm. Quick, fierce, life-changing.

She was lost, completely, hopelessly, irrevocably lost. Her brother Garrett had warned this would happen. His words came back to her with excruciating clarity. *When Mitchells fall in love, we fall fast, hard and forever.*

Fanny's heart twisted. She was in love with Jonathon. How could she have let this happen?

"Fanny?" Her mother's gaze grew serious. "Is something the matter? Are you feeling unwell?"

"No, I—I'm perfectly fine." But, of course, she wasn't fine.

Too much emotion spilled through her. Her arms felt unnaturally heavy and her pulse grew uneven.

"I just need to—" she touched her head, grateful to find that several stubborn locks had escaped their pins "—readjust my hair."

With her hands surprisingly steady, she set her napkin on the table and stood.

Jonathon was on his feet a half second later. "Let me escort you—"

"No. Stay." She managed a wan smile. "I'll only be a moment."

He reached for her.

Evading his touch, she forced her attention onto her parents. "Please, continue eating. I won't be long."

It took every ounce of control to walk through the dining room at a calm, sedate pace. She could feel countless eyes following her progress, Jonathon's most of all, but she kept her gaze trained on the ladies' washroom. Refuge was but a few feet away.

Slipping quickly inside, she shut the door and looked around for a place to sit. Several plush, navy blue stools stood in a row before individual mirrors encased in gilded frames. The room had an elegant, luxurious ambience that left her feeling empty.

Fanny took a seat before her legs gave way beneath her.

Needing something to do with her hands, she let down her hair and rearranged the loose curls in an easy, simple style. As she worked, she noted her drawn expression. She looked unusually fragile.

Why wouldn't she look fragile? She was in love with a man who wanted to marry her for all the wrong reasons.

There were worse fates, she knew. Yet, for a moment, she allowed herself to mourn what might have been, to regret what could never come to pass.

She would survive this. *She would.* All she had to do was hold firm to the reasons she must not marry Jonathon. Tears of regret pooled in her eyes. She ruthlessly blinked them away.

With stiff fingers, she stuck the last pin into her hair. Composure somewhat restored, she managed to stand.

And then, naturally, one of Denver's most determined gossips entered the ladies' washroom.

Fanny nearly groaned aloud.

Dressed in a pale pink evening gown, with yards upon yards of lace and too many ruffles for her plump figure, Mrs. Doris Goodwin strolled deeper into the room.

"Ah, Miss Mitchell, I see I have caught you alone."

Fanny tried not to bristle at the sugary-sweet tone. Clearly, catching her *alone* had been the woman's intention. "Good evening, Mrs. Goodwin. You are looking well."

"Why, thank you, dear. That is very kind of you to say."

The woman bustled past her, then made an elaborate show of checking her salt-and-pepper hair in the mirror. A ruse, no doubt, since she spent more time studying Fanny out of the corner of her eye than focusing on her own reflection.

Gaze narrowed, Fanny calculated how quickly she could slip out of the room without offending the other woman. All hope of a hasty retreat vanished when Mrs. Goodwin spun around and pinned her with a pointed gaze. "How are you faring since the scandal broke?"

Fanny searched for an appropriate answer but was unable to give one, so she simply shrugged.

"Oh, my, I've upset you." Looking unrepentant, she grasped Fanny's hands in a display of false concern. "Not to worry, dear, your shameful behavior will be forgotten once you are safely married. When should I expect an invitation to the wedding?"

"I... We haven't..." With great care, she withdrew her hands from the woman's clammy hold. "My parents will be wondering where I am. I must return to the dining room before they begin to worry."

Fanny tried very hard to escape, but the detestable woman called after her. "Your mother will never say this, so I will. It's time you faced some hard truths."

Despite knowing better than to engage the woman in conversation, Fanny turned back around. "Hard truths?"

"You must realize your attempt to snag a husband reeks of desperation. I'm afraid your reputation will never fully recover." She patted Fanny's arm in a patronizing manner. "For your mother's sake, I do hope you marry Mr. Hawkins very soon. It is your only hope of regaining a measure of respectability."

Fanny opened her mouth to say something scathing—really, the woman had overstepped her bounds—but then she remembered one of her mother's favorite Bible verses. *Let your conversation always be full of grace.*

She pressed her lips tightly together and boldly held the woman's stare. Mrs. Goodwin shifted uncomfortably from one foot to the other. Fanny felt as if she'd won the battle, but then the odious woman's gaze hooked on a spot just over her right shoulder.

"Oh, Mary, there you are. I was just having a nice conversation with your daughter."

"So I heard."

Her mother's labored breathing sent a jolt of fear through Fanny. She spun around and the panic dug deeper at the sight of Mary Mitchell's unnaturally pale face.

Fanny rushed forward, but her mother shrugged away her assistance.

"You've done your worst, Doris, now I'll ask you to leave."

Face pinched, the notorious gossip sniffed inelegantly,

and then stormed out of the room with a hard slam of the door.

The loud bang seemed to steal her mother's last breath, and she was forced to sit down.

Fanny sank to her knees. "Breathe, Mother. Yes, that's it. Slowly now. In and out. In…out."

When her mother's breathing failed to return to normal, Fanny jumped to her feet. "I'll get Father."

Her mother pressed trembling fingers to her throat. "I believe," she wheezed, "that would be…wise."

Chapter Twelve

Jonathon fetched the doctor himself. He escorted Shane through the back entrance of the Brown Palace, ignoring the curious stares from the hotel staff. Fortunately, management had been concerned enough over Mrs. Mitchell's health crisis to provide a room. Unfortunately, that room was on the fifth floor.

Neither man spoke as they entered the stairwell and commandeered the first of the five flights, far quicker than waiting for the elevator. The sound of their heels striking wood reverberated off the walls like hammers to nails.

Shane carried a medical bag in one hand, a breathing apparatus in the other. He wore what Jonathon thought of as his uniform—black pants, a crisp, white linen shirt and an intense expression. Jonathon had seen that same look in those steel blue eyes many times in his past. The most memorable, the night his mother died.

When they rounded the first corner and tackled the second flight of stairs, Shane broke his silence. "Tell me again what happened."

Jonathon pressed his lips tightly together. He'd already

relayed the story to Shane on the trip across town. "Mrs. Mitchell had a severe asthma attack."

The sharp planes of the other man's face stiffened. "That's not what I meant. I need you to describe the events leading up to the attack."

Keeping his eyes straight ahead, Jonathon tapped into his remaining stores of patience. "Fanny and I were dining with her parents in the restaurant downstairs. Near the end of the meal Fanny became noticeably upset and left the table with some excuse about fixing her hair. She wouldn't allow me to escort her, though I tried, and made a point of insisting—"

"Hold on," Shane interrupted. "Was Mrs. Mitchell's breathing normal up to this point?"

Jonathon thought a moment, then nodded. "As far as I could tell, she was fine. Her breathing only started coming quicker when Fanny didn't return to the table right away. She expressed a desire to check on her daughter. Her husband offered to go with her, but she rejected his support."

This was when the story got a little fuzzy, primarily because Fanny had been vague in her retelling. Jonathon had a good idea why.

"Apparently, Mrs. Mitchell arrived at the ladies' washroom in time to catch an unpleasant exchange between Fanny and another woman. I don't know what was said." Fanny claimed the conversation didn't matter. Jonathon suspected otherwise. "But the incident was the catalyst for Mrs. Mitchell's attack."

Jonathon had never witnessed an asthma attack before, but he'd watched his own mother gasping for air on her deathbed.

The memory materialized despite his efforts to hold it at bay. She would suck in a labored breath, pause for endless seconds and then choke out a wheeze. Just as he gave up hope that she would manage another breath, the pattern would begin all over again.

Shane had called it the death rattle.

Jonathon shuddered. There'd been nothing he could do. Tonight, he'd struggled with a similar sense of powerlessness.

"All right." Shane's voice came at him as if from a great distance. "That gives me a good idea what I'm dealing with."

"Will she survive?"

"I'll know more once I examine the patient."

Not the answer Jonathon wanted to hear, but he didn't press for more information. They'd arrived at the fifth floor. Reaching around Shane, he opened the door and motioned the other man into the hallway ahead of him.

Shane glanced back at him over his shoulder. "Which room is she in?"

"503."

He checked numbers on the closest doors, then set out down the long corridor. Jonathon fell in step beside him.

At their destination, Shane paused. "You'll want to wait here."

Not sure what he saw in the other man's eyes, Jonathon nodded. "Of course."

"I'll bring news as soon as I can."

"Appreciate that."

Features twisted in a frown, Shane entered the room and then shouldered the door closed.

Alone with nothing but his thoughts, Jonathon paced. The sound of his breathing filled the empty hallway, a mockery of what he'd witnessed tonight. He flexed his neck to relieve the knots that had formed there, then checked the time on his watch.

He'd felt this sense of helplessness during his mother's final hours. So many years had come and gone since that terrible night. Yet here he was, once again unable to ease a woman's suffering. When he'd watched Mrs. Mitchell struggling for air, when he'd felt Fanny's stark terror, it had become personal for him.

He stopped abruptly, leaned a shoulder against the wall and lowered his head in prayer. *Lord, heal Mrs. Mitchell. Give her relief from the pain. Please, help her find her breath again.*

The door to room 503 swung open.

Shane joined Jonathon in the hallway. His dark, rumpled hair had a wild look, as though he'd run his fingers through it so many times that the ends now stuck out permanently.

A lump rose in Jonathon's throat. He pushed it down with a hard, silent swallow. "How is she?"

Rubbing a hand over his face, Shane rolled tired eyes to him. "She's resting."

"Will…" Vicious fear clogged in his throat, stealing the words out of his mouth. He swallowed again, started over. "Will she recover?"

Shane speared splayed fingers through his hair. "She's had a life-threatening attack. I believe the worst is over, but I'm afraid she still has a long, agonizing night ahead."

Memories of his mother's long, agonizing nights swam in Jonathon's head. Amelia Hawkins had died of tuberculosis, another terrible lung disease. Her final days had been excruciating and painful.

But that had been years ago. Surely modern medicine had made strides since then. "Is there no medication you can give her? Don't you have something in that black bag of yours that will relieve the pressure in her lungs?"

"I've done what I can." A line of consternation drew

Shane's eyebrows together. "There's no cure for asthma. I can only relieve the symptoms as best I can."

That wasn't the answer Jonathon wanted. "Tell me what I can do to help avoid another one of these attacks."

Shane studied his face for an endless moment. The look in his eyes warned Jonathon he wasn't going to like what he heard.

"I've known you for some time, since you were a boy living at Charity House, so I'm going to be frank."

Jonathon waited for the rest.

"Tonight's attack was triggered by stress. Mrs. Mitchell is the kind of mother who loves her children and worries about their welfare, at the expense of her own. If you truly want to prevent another episode, then do whatever you must to shut down the gossip concerning her daughter."

"Understood." Conviction sounded in his voice, spread deep into his soul. The situation between him and Fanny had become a matter of life and death.

"I trust you'll make the right decision." Shane gripped him on the shoulder. "You're a good man, Johnny."

Johnny. No one had called him that since childhood.

Giving him a tight smile, Shane dropped his hand. "I need to get back to my patient now."

After watching the doctor return to the room and shut the door behind him, Jonathon went back to pacing and praying, praying and pacing.

Ten minutes later, the door swung open again. This time, Fanny stepped out into the hallway.

Jonathon strode over to her. Taking note of the worry creasing her brow, he opened his arms in silent invitation.

She launched herself into his embrace.

"Oh, Jonathon." She said his name in a low, aching tone. "I've never been so scared in all my life."

"I know, baby." He tightened his hold.

"She's breathing easier now."

"Praise God for that." Watching Mrs. Mitchell struggling to breathe earlier tonight had been living torture.

Fanny shifted in his arms and glanced up.

At the look of sorrow in her eyes, a dozen simultaneous thoughts shuffled through his mind, pinpointing to one clear course of action. Ease this woman's pain.

This wasn't the way he wanted to propose to her again. He'd had plans of courting her properly, with flowers, unexpected gifts, gentle kisses, the whole romantic package. There would be time for all that later.

For now, he started with a simple apology. "I'm sorry, Fanny. I'm sorry your mother suffered because of something I did."

"You mean something *we* did together. Oh, Jonathon." She pressed her cheek to his shoulder. "You realize what this means, don't you?"

"I do." He ran his hand over her hair. "We'll make it work. I promise we'll figure out a way that will benefit all parties involved."

As if she didn't hear him, she continued speaking into his shirt. "San Francisco isn't so very far away. I can come home several times a year."

"No, Fanny, you don't need to leave Denver." He set her away from him, looked her straight in the eye. "You can stay in town, if you marry me."

She blinked. "You...you're proposing again?"

"I am, and by the shock in your eyes, I'm making a terrible hash of it. Let's try this again." He took her hand, brought it to his lips, then pressed her palm to his chest. "Fanny Mitchell, will you marry me?"

"You don't have to do this." She swiped at her eyes. "I know how you feel about marriage, and I—"

"Will you marry me?"

She dragged her bottom lip between her teeth. "You are sure this is what you want?"

More sure than he'd been about anything in his life, he repeated the question a third time. "Will you marry me?"

He saw her mind working, saw the moment when she quit fighting the inevitable. For the rest of his life, he would remember the look in her gaze when she became his wife, all but for the ceremony.

"Yes, Jonathon." She rose on her toes and placed a soft, tender kiss to his lips. "I will marry you."

Over the course of the following week, Fanny's life changed dramatically. Her brothers and their families left Denver and returned to their lives, while her parents remained in town, primarily so Dr. Shane could monitor her mother's health.

Fanny liked having her parents close by. It was a pleasure planning her wedding with their input.

Sitting behind her desk, she opened the writing tablet beneath her hand, then reached for the stack of RSVPs. One by one, she checked the responses against the master list of wedding guests.

The news of her impending marriage had not brought a complete end to the gossip, but enough that Fanny no longer worried about her mother's health. In fact, Mary Mitchell hadn't suffered a single relapse since Fanny's engagement became public. Physical proof she'd done the right thing by accepting Jonathon's proposal.

In one short week, she would recite wedding vows with him and become his wife. A little jolt of excitement raced through her. In the days since she'd accepted Jonathon's proposal, he'd made no mention of conditions on their marriage.

Dare she hope he'd changed his mind? Dare she hope he wanted true love and, maybe, one day…children?

It would be foolish to allow her mind to chase down that rabbit trail. One step at a time, she told herself.

She would enjoy being engaged to Jonathon. She had faith the rest would work itself out in time.

Claiming a key role in their romance, Mrs. Singletary was enjoying many accolades for her continued success as a matchmaker. Tomorrow evening, when she hosted Fanny and Jonathon's engagement party, the widow would remind everyone in attendance of her skillful maneuverings on their behalf.

Checking the time on the clock perched above her small fireplace, Fanny yelped. Five minutes past three.

She was late for tea with her mother and sister.

After a quick check of her hair, she hurried through the lobby. She passed a familiar woman and her two teenage daughters. All three were dressed in various shades of blue, their beautiful, expensive gowns cut in a popular style, with the requisite form-fitting bodices and A-line skirts.

The three halted when they saw her.

Fanny smiled. Only one returned the gesture, the youngest.

Fanny refused to be daunted. "Good morning, Mrs. Wainwright." She glanced from mother to daughters. "Sylvia, Carly, lovely to see you both."

The older woman sniffed in disdain. "Girls, do not respond." She herded her daughters away from Fanny, giving her a ridiculously wide berth. "We do not speak to women *like her*."

Mortified at the implication of the words, Fanny found her footsteps faltering.

Did Mrs. Wainwright think she had no feelings? Did she not care that it hurt to be snubbed so profoundly? Of course it hurt. But after facing the very real prospect of losing her mother, Fanny recognized the value of putting moments such as these in perspective.

Once she married Jonathon, much of the censure would disappear, but some would never go away. There wasn't much she could do about that, except hold her head high and pray her mother didn't suffer because of the gossip.

Shaking her head, Fanny continued on to her destination.

The maître d'hôtel welcomed her with a large smile. "Miss Mitchell. Your sister and mother are already at the table you reserved for the afternoon."

"Thank you, Mr. Griffin. I'll find them."

With a critical eye, she took a quick inventory of the restaurant. She noted the details others would miss. The white table linens were clean and pressed, with perfectly placed pleats hanging down the sides. The silverware was dainty and feminine, specifically purchased to use solely at afternoon tea.

Fanny's gaze landed on her mother and sister, who sat at a table near the fireplace. Beneath the golden light, Callie glowed. Her mother looked equally healthy and happy.

Callie caught sight of her first and gave a quick, jaunty wave above her head. Returning the gesture, Fanny hurried to the table.

"Hello, Mother." She leaned over and kissed the beloved cheek. "How are you feeling this afternoon?"

"Like my old self. The daily breathing treatments Dr. Shane is administering are working wonders. I haven't wheezed in nearly a week."

Fanny's heart soared. "Are you certain? You're not—"

"Now, Fanny. We are here to celebrate your engagement to a kind, wonderful man I am growing more and more fond of by the day."

"I like him, too." Beaming at her, Callie poured Fanny a cup of tea. "He makes you happy, which makes him pretty wonderful in my eyes."

Laughing, Fanny took a sip of tea while she eyed her sister over the cup's rim. Speaking of happy...

"Marriage suits you, Cal."

Her sister laughed, clearly delighted by the compliment. "Oh, Fanny, I never expected to find such joy in my life. But Reese is the best thing that ever happened to me. I fall in love with him more every day."

"It shows."

"While we're celebrating, your sister has news," her mother said, smiling at Callie. "Tell her, dear."

A delicate frown marred Callie's pretty face. "Now's not the time, Mother."

"Of course it's the time."

Wondering at the odd mood that had descended over the table, Fanny looked from one woman to the other. "Tell me what? What's going on with you, Callie?"

"Nothing that can't wait." Callie lowered her head, looking incredibly uncomfortable and far too much like the old Callie, the one who didn't like to be the center of attention.

"Tell me your news." Fanny reached over and touched her sister's hand. "Please."

"All right, I...we..." Her cheeks turned a becoming shade of pink. "Reese and I are going to have a baby."

A baby. Fanny stared at her sister. *A baby.* Callie and Reese were officially starting their family. No wonder Callie glowed. She was with child.

Fanny blinked as the news settled over her, as reality gripped her heart and squeezed. Hard.

I will never have news such as this to share.

For a terrible, awful moment, she didn't know what to say, how to feel.

Happy. She was supposed to be happy for her sister. *Of course* she was happy for Callie.

"Oh, Callie, that's marvelous news."

Will that ever be me? Will I ever know that joy?

She squeezed her sister's hand. "You're going to make a wonderful mother."

Happy tears sprang into Callie's eyes.

Fanny's filled as well, and she had a moment, a brief, terrifying moment, when she felt a surge of crippling jealousy. She wanted what Callie had. She wanted a husband who adored her, who wanted her to bear his children.

If only Jonathon would…

No. She would not allow her mind to formulate the rest of that thought. She'd made her choices and would live with them. "How did Reese take the news?"

"He picked me up and twirled me around and around until we were both dizzy. Then—" she giggled "—he called his father into the room and told him the news. A lot of hugs with me and backslapping between the men followed."

Laughing softly, she shook her head, her expression filling with fond affection over the memory. It was the same look Callie got in her eyes whenever she spoke of her husband.

A happy ending to what could have been a disaster. Fanny had been right to jilt Reese. She'd also been right to leave town. Her absence had given her sister the opportunity to fall in love with the man she was meant to be with for all eternity.

"I'm so happy for you, Cal." Her vision blurred, her eyes turned misty. "You and Reese belong together."

As if sensing her shift in mood, Fanny's mother reached over and patted her hand. "I'm confident your marriage will bring you equal happiness and joy."

"You're right, of course." She said the words for her mother's benefit. But, oh, the mess she'd created. One impulsive kiss under the moonlight, and she'd changed several lives forever, Jonathon's most of all.

Thinking of him now, of the situation she'd put them both in, Fanny could barely hold back her grief. One rogue tear wiggled to the edge of her lashes and slipped down the side of her face.

No. No more crying. She would not regret her decision. She only regretted that her behavior had affected others.

"We've already discussed baby names," Callie said, blissfully unaware of Fanny's battle to contain her rioting emotions.

Happy for the distraction, Fanny focused once again on her sister. "Any you'd like to share?"

"If it's a boy, Reese, of course."

"Of course," she said, then laughingly added, "Reese Bennett III is a most regal name, indeed."

"And if it's a girl?" her mother asked.

"We plan to name her Fanny," Callie said, her eyes shining with quiet affection, "after the best sister a woman ever had."

Fanny could hold back the tears no longer. She let them fall freely down her cheeks.

Over sandwiches and cookies, they discussed her future namesake because, according to Callie, she was surely carrying a girl.

Fanny allowed herself to get swept away in her sister's joy. By the time she returned to work, her mood was restored.

She was helping behind the registration desk when

Jonathon appeared by her side. He'd been doing that a lot, showing up unexpectedly, taking her on long walks, where they discussed themselves, their childhoods, their likes and dislikes.

"Did you have a nice visit with your mother and sister?"

She smiled. "I did."

"I'm glad." Their gazes stayed connected for longer than usual.

Jonathon looked especially handsome this afternoon, his blue-gray eyes full of masculine interest. It was then that Fanny realized what he was doing. He was officially courting her, attempting to win her affection.

What he didn't seem to know was that the battle had been decided long ago.

Her heart already belonged to him.

Chapter Thirteen

The night of their engagement party, Jonathon settled on the cushioned seat across from Fanny in their hired coach. Due to a last-minute issue with the kitchen equipment, they'd left the hotel a half hour later than planned. He'd sent Fanny's parents ahead so they could alert Mrs. Singletary of the delay.

Now, as their carriage bounced over ruts and divots in the Denver streets, Jonathon took the opportunity to study his fiancée. His heart pounded with uneasiness. Something was wrong.

Fanny wasn't herself.

In truth, she hadn't been herself for several days. Nothing was amiss at the hotel. That meant whatever was bothering her was personal. He studied her a moment longer in the semidarkness.

A sliver of moon provided him enough light to see that her lips were tilted at a worried angle and her gloved fingers were threaded together primly in her lap. He'd seen her adopt the pose before. That, coupled with her unnatural silence, convinced Jonathon she was upset.

He leaned forward. "What's troubling you, Fanny? Is it your mother's health?"

Not quite meeting his eyes, she readjusted her position so that their knees wouldn't touch. "No, she's quite well."

He felt a moment of relief.

"Then what's wrong?" He sat back and employed a relaxed posture, hoping to put her at ease. "Whatever it is, you know you can tell me."

She lifted her chin at that stubborn angle he was growing to recognize as a precursor to trouble. "If you must know, I've been thinking about us."

Several responses came to mind, none of which he voiced aloud. "In what way?"

"It's…we need to…" She lowered her head and stared at her lap. "We need to make our engagement look real."

"It *is* real."

Head still bent, she muttered something that sounded suspiciously like *not real enough*. Whatever that meant.

"Fanny." He placed a knuckle beneath her chin and applied gentle pressure until her gaze met his. "What's happened to make you so distraught?"

She closed her eyes and gave a slight, shuddering sigh before opening them again. "Since the official announcement of our engagement ran in the *Denver Chronicle*, my mother's health has shown rapid improvement."

"That's a good thing."

"Yes, but I fear it won't last."

"What makes you convinced she'll have a relapse?"

"I discovered recently that the gossip about us hasn't actually faded. It's merely shifted in a new direction." Gaze troubled, Fanny glanced out the small carriage window. "If what people are saying gets back to my mother, I'm afraid she'll suffer another life-threatening asthma attack."

"The talk about us is still that significant?"

Not quite meeting his eyes, Fanny lifted a shoulder.

He said her name again, softer this time, wishing he could soothe away her concerns with nothing but his voice. "Once we are married, the gossip will go away, if not completely, then nearly so."

"You can't know that for certain."

No, he supposed not. "You have evidence to the contrary?"

She snapped her gaze back to his. "Don't you know what they're saying about us?"

Her frustration filled the tiny, enclosed space of the carriage, wrapping around Jonathon as if it were a living, breathing thing. "Has someone said something to you? Did they approach you in the hotel? If that's the case, I'll make sure they are denied permanent access. Give me a name."

Sighing again, she gave a weary shake of her head. "It doesn't matter who started the rumors. The point is that people are openly questioning our motives for marrying. Some claim it's a desperate attempt to quash gossip."

Two simultaneous reactions shot through him, one of impatience, the other of fury. "If you tell me who started this latest rumor, then I'll—"

"What? What will you do, Jonathon? Tell them to stop?"

"If it'll make a difference, yes."

"You know it won't."

He frowned. She was probably right, but he wasn't willing to concede fully. "You are proposing that we combat this latest spin of the gossip mill by making our engagement look real?"

"I know how it sounds," she admitted, twisting her hands over and over again in her lap. "As though I'm asking you to put on a show for the benefit of others."

For all intents and purposes, that was exactly what

she was asking of him. She'd clearly put a lot of thought into this, but she'd missed a key element in the argument.

"Our engagement is real, Fanny." He moved to her side of the carriage. The seat dipped and squeaked under his added weight. "In less than a week, we will pledge our lives to one another before God."

"I realize that." And yet she worried her bottom lip between her teeth, as if she feared their wedding wouldn't come to pass.

The carriage hit a bump and she lurched forward. Jonathon pulled her against him to prevent her from falling to the floor.

With her wrapped in his arms, and the pleasing scent of her hair in his nose, he set his chin atop her head and spoke the truth from his heart. "I will honor our wedding vows, always, and will remain loyal to you until the day I die."

Her shoulders rose and fell with a wordless sigh. "I will do the same."

"But you would feel better if the skeptics believed that ours is a love match."

Misery rolled off her in waves. "Don't you see, Jonathon? It's the surest way to end the speculation for good."

Setting her away from him, he returned to his side of the carriage and considered her request. There were a dozen reasons why showing the world how much he cared for this woman was a bad idea. The most powerful one being he was already half in love with her. Allowing his affection free rein might very well send him over the edge.

Then where would they be?

Headed straight for heartbreak, both of them.

As if sensing where his thoughts had gone, Fanny smiled at him. It was a lovely display of fortitude. However, it fell flat enough for him to see past the false bravado.

"You only have to pretend you are in love with me when we are in public. I wouldn't expect you to continue the pretense when we are alone."

Her voice sounded as tormented as she looked. Jonathon's heart lurched in his chest. He'd hurt her. They weren't even married and he'd already let her down.

The thought barely had time to settle over him when the carriage pulled to a grinding stop outside of Mrs. Singletary's house.

Jonathon did not reach for the door handle.

He continued staring at Fanny, consumed with an emotion he couldn't name. The sensation reminded him of grief, as if he'd just lost something very precious before he'd ever fully had it in his grasp.

"Say something," she whispered.

"I'll do it. I will play the besotted suitor tonight, and every night until our wedding." The promise had disaster written all over it. Jonathon would be in love with Fanny before the week was out, and then it would be that much harder to keep their marriage in name only. Especially if she looked at him the way she was now, with a mixture of adoration and tempered hope.

"You...you will? You will pretend to be in love with me?"

Lord, help us both. "Consider it done."

Happiness bloomed in her eyes, then immediately vanished behind a scowl. Even in the muted light, he could see her mind working at double its normal rate.

"Don't look so worried, sweetheart." He took her hand and dragged it to his heart. "Tonight is supposed to be a celebration. We're going to have a grand time at our party."

Without waiting for her response, and praying he was right, he wrenched open the door and helped her out of the carriage.

They entered Mrs. Singletary's house just as a large grandfather clock struck the bottom of the hour.

The widow's butler met them in the foyer.

Threads of silver encroached on the few strands of red left in the bushy head of hair. But the broad, welcoming smile erased at least ten years from the heavily lined face.

"Mr. Hawkins, Miss Mitchell." Back ramrod straight, he took their coats with the efficient movements that came from decades of practice. "The other guests are gathered in the blue parlor on the second floor."

"Thank you, Winston, we know the way."

Taking Fanny's arm, Jonathon guided her toward the sweeping stairwell that wound along the southern wall of the cavernous foyer.

Fanny paused at the foot of the steps to study a portrait of Mrs. Singletary and her now deceased husband.

Jonathon considered the painting, as well.

"My sister discovered in her time as Mrs. Singletary's companion that the widow's marriage was one for the ages," Fanny murmured.

Jonathon didn't doubt this. The people in the portrait were the picture of happiness. "I heard they married young."

A wistful smile played at the corner of Fanny's lips. "She was barely seventeen, he but nineteen. Sadly, Mr. Singletary died fifteen years later."

Jonathon did a quick calculation in his head. Mrs. Singletary had been a widow for nearly thirteen years. That was a long time to grow comfortable in her circumstances. Yet was she? She seemed to still believe in fairy-tale endings, as evidenced by her penchant for matchmaking.

"Perhaps," he mused aloud, "it's time the widow quit meddling in other people's lives and made a match for herself."

Fanny smiled at the suggestion. "Callie recently intimated that Reese's father is campaigning to win Mrs. Singletary's heart, but the widow is proving most stubborn on the matter."

Chuckling softly, Jonathon shook his head at the image of Mrs. Singletary and Reese Bennett Sr. as a couple. "Your sister is an endless source of information."

Fanny joined in his laughter. "So it would seem, at least where Mrs. Singletary is concerned."

Appreciating the light mood between them, Jonathon took Fanny's hand and guided her up the stairs. At the second floor landing, they worked their way toward the blue parlor.

The sound of laughter spilled out into the corridor, a clear indication that nearly all forty invited guests had arrived.

As if by silent agreement, Fanny and Jonathon both halted several feet away from the room. Practicing his role as besotted suitor, he dropped a look of adoration onto his lovely fiancée.

Her answering smile sent his pulse roaring in his ears. "Are you ready?"

She nodded, the gesture loosening several curls from their pins. Unable to resist, he reached up and tamed the stray wisps of hair. At the feel of the silken strands between his fingers, resolve filled him. After tonight, everyone in Mrs. Singletary's home would know his engagement to Fanny was real, including Fanny herself.

* * *

Caught by Jonathon's stare, Fanny couldn't take a single easy breath. He was looking at her with such open affection her heart tripped over itself. She wanted to bask in the moment, but they were already late to their own party. After several failed attempts, she managed to tear her gaze free and then leaned forward just enough to get a glimpse inside the blue parlor.

None of the occupants had noticed their arrival.

Fanny took a quick inventory of the guests already in attendance. Her eyes landed on one in particular, a lone gentleman who'd evidently come without his wife. Something hot and ugly filled her. "What is *he* doing here?"

Jonathon followed the direction of her gaze. His shoulders visibly stiffened. "I'd like to know that, myself."

Judge Greene had not been included on the guest list for tonight. Yet there he was, conversing with—of all people—Fanny's parents.

The rush of fury had a growl slipping past her tight lips. The one consolation was that her mother looked beyond bored, and her father seemed terribly unimpressed with whatever the judge was saying.

Fanny moved closer to the doorway, wishing she could hear what the odious man was saying to her parents. Looking at that superior smile on his face, she felt rage burn beneath her skin.

Judge Greene might claim he wanted a relationship with Jonathon, but Fanny suspected ulterior motives. She would never forget he'd once considered his own son a mistake.

No child was a mistake, of course, but Jonathon truly believed his birth was an unwanted accident. The foul message had been given too often, with too much strength, when Jonathon had been too young to understand the nature of the lie.

To this day, regardless of proof to the contrary, he believed he wasn't capable of breaking free of his past, that he would always be…somehow…less.

The drive to prove otherwise had made him a huge success. At what cost?

How did she combat a lifetime of distorted thinking? How did she help Jonathon recognize he was a treasured child of God?

The answer blew through her mind like a stiff, unrelenting wind. *Love.*

Jonathon's healing started and ended with love. God's love reflected in her love for him. Yes, Fanny would lead Jonathon to the truth by loving him.

She would stand by his side, always, and do whatever she could to protect him from his father.

"Despicable, loathsome man," she growled under her breath. "I should have kicked him in the shin when I had the chance."

Jonathon laughed at her remark. The sound was strangled, and a bit rusty, but loud enough that several party guests took notice. Fanny ignored every one of them.

"He doesn't matter." Jonathon took one of her hands and brought it to his lips. "Thank you for agreeing to be my wife."

A collective sigh fell over the room, a sure sign they were not only being watched but also overheard.

"There is nowhere else I'd rather be than right here, next to you," she replied. Happiness flared to life and she let it fill her. "I can't wait to become your wife."

He set her hand on his heart, a gesture she was coming to think of as his silent pledge of devotion. "You make me want to be a better man."

"I like you just the way you are."

Slowly, he released her hand. "People are staring."

"Are they?"

"Shall we give them something to talk about?"

She laughed. This was not the way she'd planned to prove their engagement was real, and yet it was the most perfect moment of the night. "What did you have in mind?"

"Nothing too terribly shameless."

By the look in his eyes, she expected him to do something sweet. He did not disappoint. He kissed her hand again, this time lingering a moment beyond polite.

If only this was *real*, she thought. The familiar ache clutching at her throat was immediately followed by a jolt of rebellion.

Why can't it be real? If only for tonight?

Why not revel in the joy of knowing this man would soon be her husband? Decision made, she smiled up at him and let her feelings show in her eyes.

Mrs. Singletary chose that moment to insinuate herself into their private moment. "Our guests of honor have arrived at last."

The announcement was all it took to send the rest of the room into a flurry of activity. One minute, people were staring at them, watching them enjoy one another. The next, Fanny and Jonathon were surrounded by family and friends.

Everyone talked at once, creating a cacophony of congratulations and thoughtful well-wishes.

Almost immediately, Fanny lost track of Jonathon.

She circled her gaze around the room, found him conversing with Callie, Reese and Reese's father at a spot near the fireplace.

Jonathon's father had moved away from Fanny's parents and now held court on the opposite end of the room with one of Denver's most prominent couples, Alexander and Polly Ferguson.

Their daughters Penelope and Phoebe completed the group. It seemed fitting somehow that the women who'd started the gossip that had led to tonight's celebration would be in attendance.

They wore matching dresses in blue, with silver trim. One of them—did it matter which?—turned her big blue eyes toward Fanny and smiled at her as if they were dear, dear friends.

Fanny pointedly looked away.

Jonathon caught her eye and motioned her over. She moved in his direction, but then found herself being pulled into a pair of willowy, female arms. "Congratulations, my dear."

Another tight squeeze and then Laney Dupree stepped back to smile into Fanny's eyes. "You and Johnny make a wonderful couple."

Dressed in a pretty bronze-and-gold dress that complemented her mahogany hair, the woman who'd started Charity House looked serene, elegant and incredibly beautiful. "I can't think of anyone I'd rather Johnny marry than you."

Fanny's heart fluttered with pure happiness. She liked this woman and knew how important she was to Jonathon. "That's so very kind of you to say."

"Not kindness, truth. You make him happy, Fanny. I can't tell you how much relief that brings me."

Overcome with too many emotions to sort through at once, Fanny reached up and wiped at her eyes. "He makes me happy, too, more than I can put into words."

"I'm glad." Laney hugged her a second time.

The moment she let go, her husband swooped in for

his turn. His embrace was briefer than his wife's, but no less special. Marc Dupree had been more of a father to Jonathon than Judge Greene had. For that reason alone, Fanny adored the man.

Dark-haired, clean-shaven, he wore a red brocade vest and matching tie made of the finest material available, the kind a successful banker might choose for his clothing.

"As my wife so eloquently said, we couldn't be happier with Johnny's choice of brides. Welcome to the family, Fanny."

"Thank you," she choked out, pleased for Jonathon that these two considered him one of their own.

Though Fanny didn't know all the particulars, she knew that Marc had been a strong influence in her fiancé's life.

"I believe you'll make Johnny a fine wife," Marc added with a smile. "A very fine wife, indeed."

"Far better than I deserve." The familiar voice came from behind her. Before Fanny could look over her shoulder, Jonathon's arm came around her waist, securing her to his side.

Tucked in close, she swiveled her gaze up to his.

For reasons she didn't want to explore too deeply, Fanny could do nothing but stare in muted wonder at the expression in his eyes. The warmth looked real, not pretend real, but *real*.

Her stomach rolled. Her throat burned. Her heart pounded. And still she continued staring up at Jonathon. Even when he turned his attention to Marc and Laney, Fanny continued watching him. She adored his profile.

So strong.

So handsome.

She should not be this aware of her fiancé, not if she wanted to survive their marriage in name only.

Perhaps, she could convince Jonathon to change his mind on the matter.

But how?

The answer came to her again.

Love him.

Could it be that simple? Yes. *Her* love would conquer *his* doubts.

All she needed to do was trust God to heal Jonathon's heart. Enough to give him the courage to take a leap of faith, to trust that he could break free of his past.

If in the process Jonathon chose to make Fanny truly his wife, well, she would know that it all started here, now. With love.

Her love.

Chapter Fourteen

Even as Jonathon carried on a conversation with Marc and Laney—something to do with the renovations under way at Charity House—he was highly attuned to the woman next to him. He kept his arm wrapped around her waist, at one point pulling Fanny closer.

She didn't protest.

In fact, she settled against him as if she was determined to stay by his side the rest of the night. He felt Fanny's eyes on him, felt the warmth of her smile wash over him.

He tried not to betray his pleasure. Nonetheless, his lips lifted in secret satisfaction. Tonight was a glimpse into what his future would be like with Fanny as his wife.

Jonathon liked what lay ahead.

The evening was turning out to be surprisingly enjoyable, partly because he hadn't spoken to Judge Greene once all night, but also because of Fanny herself. He liked her, admired her, valued nearly everything about her.

An absurd notion encroached on his thoughts, one he couldn't seem to ignore no matter how hard he focused on the conversation with his friends. Jonathon's entire life, every mistake, every wrong turn, every good and wise decision, had led him to this one woman. Fanny Mitchell was his destiny, his future.

It felt as natural as breathing to pretend he had deep feelings for her. Probably, he realized, because he actually had deep feelings for Fanny.

This is going to be a problem.

He was a man, after all, and Fanny was a beautiful, mesmerizing woman. Soon, they would be married in the eyes of God. How was Jonathon supposed to spend a lifetime with Fanny without making her his wife the way the Lord intended?

You are not a mistake, Fanny had once said to him.

If Jonathon wasn't a mistake, if the Bible verse from Jeremiah was accurate, and the Lord had known him before he was formed in his mother's womb, then perhaps he *could* break free of his past. Perhaps future generations wouldn't suffer because of who Jonathon was and where he came from.

The thought barely had a chance to slide through his mind when the conversation shifted to the newest arrivals at Charity House, two brothers and a sister.

Not long after that, Fanny's parents joined their group and the discussion turned once again, this time to the exciting topic of the weather. Seizing the opportunity to move on, Jonathon pulled his fiancée away with the excuse of needing a moment alone with her.

It was true. He wanted to be alone with Fanny, if only for a few minutes.

"Jonathon," she said, laughing as she broke into a trot to keep up with his long strides. "Where are we going in such a rush?"

"Somewhere private." He slowed his pace to match hers, then leaned down so only she heard his words. "You have a problem with that?"

"Not at all." She laughed again. "It sounds quite promising."

"I like that you think so."

Her eyes sparkled with delight. "Well, then, take me away. I'm all yours, Mr. Hawkins."

She was wrong, of course. She would never be completely his, not really, not unless he reconsidered the parameters of their marriage.

Did he dare take the risk?

It was something he needed to ponder seriously before their wedding night.

Hand clasped with Fanny's, he drew her into the darkened hallway. They'd taken several steps when a masculine voice spoke his name.

Jonathon's footsteps came to an abrupt halt and a deep unease sliced through him. He didn't need to look over his shoulder to know it was Joshua Greene who spoke his name.

"You cannot avoid me all evening," the man added.

At the familiar sound of icy disapproval, knots formed at the back of Jonathon's neck. He was transported to another time, to the night he'd first confronted his father. Jonathon had laid his heart bare in the hope of saving his mother's life. He'd actually *begged* for Greene's help.

Jonathon attempted to release Fanny's hand. With a little hum of rebellion, she held on tight. Together they faced his father. Jonathon eyed the older man without an ounce of emotion in his heart.

Dressed in a hand-tailored suit, Joshua Greene looked every bit the distinguished Denver citizen most of the world thought him to be. The disguise was so well done that Jonathon nearly believed the pretense himself.

"Must we do this out here?" His posture stiff, his arrogance evident in every inch of his pinched face, Greene looked around them in disapproval. "I dislike lurking in darkened hallways."

"Then I shall make a habit of lurking in darkened hallways."

"There's no need to be snide, son."

Son. For half his life, Jonathon had waited to hear that word come out of this man's mouth. He'd spent the other half forging his place in the world on his own terms.

He'd endured loss and suffering, had survived poverty and the humiliation of illegitimacy. He no longer needed, or wanted, this man's acknowledgment. Not now. Not ever.

Aware that Fanny still held tightly to his hand, all but vibrating with suppressed emotion, Jonathon kept his response curt. "We already had this conversation in my office last week. We have nothing more to say to one another."

"Now see, that's where you're wrong." Something calculated flashed in Greene's eyes. "While I confess I have not handled matters well in the past, you must admit that I have recently shown my willingness to mend our relationship—"

"We have no relationship."

"An oversight I wish to rectify. I am fully prepared to accept my duty as your father."

Jonathon leaned forward and addressed the real reason for the judge's sudden interest in *duty*. "We both know this is about your run for the Senate. How do you think the truth of what you did to my mother will go over with the voters?"

With a snort and a flick of his wrist, Greene dismissed the question. "They will sympathize with my decisions, once they hear my side of the story."

"What will they think when they hear mine?"

The question seemed to give the man pause, but only briefly. "Who will they believe?" he asked. "Me, a law-abiding, God-fearing member of the judicial community? Or you, a former pickpocket and by-blow of a prostitute?"

Jonathon stood very still, in full control of every inch of his body, knowing the importance of revealing not one ounce of weakness to this man. "Tell your story to the world. But be prepared for me to tell mine."

"Very well." Greene spun around and moved toward the doorway of the blue parlor with quick, clipped strides. "There is no time like the present."

A bolt of alarm shot through Jonathon. "Do not do this here. Not tonight." *Not in front of Fanny.*

Greene ignored the request. "May I have everyone's attention?" Playing to his audience as if he were a sea-soned stage actor, he swept his hands in a wide, dramatic arc. "I have a very important announcement to make."

Conversations came to a stuttering halt and a roomful of curious stares turned in their direction.

Time seemed to shift, transporting Jonathon back to his childhood, to the boy who'd shivered and quaked in back alleys, who'd witnessed his mother's fall into despair, then illness, then ultimately death.

Anger and hurt, regret and desperation, so many ugly emotions warred within him. For a dangerous moment, those memories paralyzed him.

"Jonathon." He felt more than heard Fanny's voice, but he couldn't respond. His gaze was riveted on Judge Greene.

The man shot a benevolent smile over the crowd. "It is my honor to announce to everyone present that…" he paused for dramatic effect "…Jonathon Hawkins is my—"

"No!" Fanny rushed in front of the judge, her swift,

unexpected move rendering him momentarily speechless. "Judge Greene is only offering up a joke no one will find funny. Carry on with your conversations."

She glanced briefly at Jonathon. A tactical error.

With the swift, deadly movements of a jungle cat, Greene regained the room's attention.

"I wish to announce that Jonathon Hawkins is my son."

A blast of murmurs and gasps followed the statement, then came a highly palpable lurch of silence.

"I only recently discovered my connection to this successful man, whose rags-to-riches story I greatly admire. His mother, I'm afraid, kept his existence from me a secret."

And so began a bevy of lies as the esteemed judge wove his fictional tale of the past.

This was Jonathon's legacy, he realized, as his father blatantly revised history. Lies, half truths, rationalizations when they suited the moment. Jonathon himself had used similar methods in the past, at first to survive, then in a desperate attempt to run from his past, to separate himself from this man.

He'd come full circle. There was no more escaping the truth. He was this despicable man's son down to the bone.

Perhaps it was for the best that everyone knew.

But what of Fanny? How would this affect her? Icy numbness crept into Jonathon's veins. He could still protect her from suffering the repercussions of the judge's announcement.

He pulled her close, spoke words in her ear no one else could hear. "You may break our engagement, if you wish. I will not hold it against you."

"I will *not* abandon you," she said in a low, ferocious tone. "As you have stood by me, so I shall stand by you."

Her conviction was a golden, glimmering keepsake. "Fanny—"

"Jonathon. My loyalty is nothing if not total."

Greene smiled over at him. "I am unspeakably proud to publicly ally myself with this man, my son."

The easy charm was to be expected, of course. Joshua Greene was a natural politician. He knew how to impress an audience.

However, he'd misread the room.

The horrified silence coming from the wide-eyed guests wasn't directed at Jonathon, but at Greene.

Fanny tightened her grip on Jonathon's hand.

He glanced down at her, an apology on his tongue, but she wasn't looking at him. She was glaring at his father.

Before Jonathon knew what she was about, she suddenly yanked her hand free and marched over to Judge Greene.

"Quiet," she snapped, fists jammed on her hips.

Greene blinked in mute astonishment.

"Judge Greene is shamelessly retelling the past. Do not be fooled. He has known about Jonathon since the day he was born."

Laney confirmed this to be true, as did Marc.

The expected outrage on Jonathon's behalf erupted like a spark to dynamite.

Greene attempted to explain himself, using phrases such as *youthful indiscretion* and *deep regret* and *mistakes that can still be corrected*. Once again, he miscalculated his audience.

The more he tried to rationalize away his behavior, the angrier the crowd grew. Jonathon half expected pitchforks and torches to materialize inside clenched fists.

Mrs. Singletary ended the spectacle by stepping firmly into the fray. "Enough."

In her no-nonsense tone, she asked the judge to leave her home at once.

Smart enough to recognize the need for retreat, he did as she requested. Before exiting the room, however, he stopped beside Fanny. "I find your interference in this matter most distressing."

She gave him her sweetest smile. "I cannot tell you how much it pleases me to hear that."

Greene left in a huff.

In the silence that followed his father's departure, Jonathon ran a hand across his brow, left it there for several seconds. Saying nothing, Fanny simply touched his arm. Her silent show of support was exactly what he needed.

He momentarily closed his hand over hers. "Thank you."

To his surprise, the party guests made the pilgrimage to where they stood. One by one, they expressed their support and their hope that his marriage to Fanny would erase the pain of his past. Even the Ferguson sisters had kind words for him.

Jonathon did not doubt their sincerity or that of the others. Yet his father's words continued echoing in his mind. *Jonathon Hawkins is my son.*

No matter how much he tried to distance himself from the man, one truth remained. Jonathon would be forever connected to Joshua Greene by blood.

Depressing thought.

The room eventually emptied out, leaving only Fanny's parents and the Duprees.

"It's going to be all right, Johnny." Laney made the promise in much the same voice she'd used when he was a boy. "In time, everyone will know the truth. They will have every reason to side with you."

There was no way of knowing how the rest of Denver

would take Greene's announcement. Unlike the people here tonight, mostly family and friends, many in town would believe the judge's version. *His word against mine.*

"Jonathon." Mrs. Mitchell gripped his forearm.

Fearing how the drama of the evening might have affected her, he swiveled his gaze to hers. Her brow was creased in concern, but her breathing appeared normal.

"Take heart," she said. "You are not alone in this."

"That's right, my boy." Cyrus Mitchell clapped him on the back. "By marrying Fanny, you inherit the entire brood. That's a total of nine Mitchells, their assorted spouses and various herds of children, all for the price of one slip of a girl."

He winked at his daughter.

The comment had the intended effect. Jonathon laughed.

He appreciated knowing that these good, solid people considered him part of their family. But right now all he wanted was to be alone with Fanny.

He endured another ten minutes, then made his and Fanny's excuses.

"We have an early morning" was all he said. It was enough. Not a single argument prevented their departure. Minutes later, and with great relief, he climbed inside the hired coach with Fanny and closed the door behind them.

He made an attempt to sit across from her.

She shook her head. "Oh, no, you don't."

With great deliberation, she settled on the seat beside him and leaned her head against his shoulder. In the calm following the dramatic events of the evening, he liked having her close. He braided their fingers together and breathed in the scent of her. They sat that way for nearly twenty minutes.

Only when the carriage pulled to a stop outside the

hotel did she smile up at him with a mischievous light in her eyes. "Well, I'd say tonight went quite well. Wouldn't you agree, Jonathon?"

Like an echo from the past, his responding bark of laughter was equal parts pain and tempered hope. "I adore you."

Still smiling up at Jonathon, Fanny let his beautiful words settle over her. He'd been quiet during the carriage ride back to the hotel. She'd honored as long as humanly possible his wish to remain silent.

Now, with their gazes locked and their fingers entwined, she felt his sorrow as though it were her own.

He reached for the door handle. She stopped him with a tug on their joined hands.

"Before we head inside, I want to say—"

She broke off, suddenly at a loss for words. What could she say that would make his pain disappear?

Her heart broke for this wonderful, giving man. Tonight had been difficult for him. Joshua Greene had claimed Jonathon as his son and in the process killed whatever chance there'd been for reconciliation.

Any hope his father would prove himself an honorable man was dead. Now, Jonathon clearly grieved. Fanny saw the sense of loss in his eyes.

"You can't pretend you're not hurting over what happened tonight, and I can't pretend not to hurt for you."

The smile he gave her was full of sadness, the depth of which she'd never seen in him before. "Fanny, you realize tonight was merely a trial run for the days ahead."

"I'm not sure what you mean."

"The truth is out, if somewhat skewed. By tomorrow morning everyone will know I am Joshua Greene's son and that my mother never told him about me."

"That's a lie. Not everyone will accept his word as truth." But she knew that wasn't entirely possible. Though she'd like to think the whole of Denver would believe Jonathon's version over his father's lies, Fanny wasn't that naive.

As if reading her mind, Jonathon voiced her concerns aloud. "Some will believe his tale, Fanny. They may even think I conspired with my mother for years and am now extorting Greene with this information for my own purposes."

"That's absurd."

"The gossip will turn toward you. Your reputation will suffer yet another blow. I can't let that happen."

Something in the way he spoke, with such resolve and a complete lack of emotion, terrified her. "What…what are you saying?"

"You don't have to go through with our wedding. I'd understand if you are having second thoughts."

"Are *you* having second thoughts?"

"Yes, I am," he admitted. "I won't marry you if a connection to me further jeopardizes your reputation. That would defeat the entire purpose."

Fanny thought she'd been afraid before. But now, at the determination she heard in Jonathon's words, she grew terrified he would break off their engagement.

She could not lose him, not like this.

Words tumbled quickly out of her mouth. "Judge Greene might be arrogant enough to think people will believe he is without fault. But he shamelessly committed adultery. That point cannot be denied. The people in this city will not be as forgiving as he claims."

For a long, tense moment Jonathon stared at her. Then finally, thankfully, his mouth lifted in a smile. "Is that your way of saying I'm stuck with you?"

Relief made her shoulders slump forward. "That's absolutely what I'm saying. In one week from today, in front of a hundred witnesses and God Himself, I will proudly become your wife."

Jonathon's eyebrows lifted. "Proudly?"

She leaned toward him. "You caught that part, did you?"

"You're the finest woman I know, Fanny Mitchell." He cupped her face in his hand.

"We'll get through this, Jonathon." She placed a kiss on his palm. "With all the practice we've had lately, we're masters at facing down gossip. We could teach classes on the subject."

He angled his head, searched her face as if looking for a hint of remorse or doubt. He would find none.

Being the good man that he was, he gave her one last chance to change her mind. "You can still back out."

"Yes, yes, so you've said. Can we be through with the discussion now?"

He moved his head close to hers, paused when their faces were inches from touching. A shift on either of their parts and their mouths would unite. "I'll take the full blame, Fanny. Your reputation won't have to suffer, and would perhaps be enhanced if you—"

"Are you going to continue blathering, or kiss me?"

One corner of his mouth lifted and a very masculine light shone in his eyes. "You want me to kiss you?"

"Yes, please."

He seemed to need no more encouragement, and pressed his lips to hers. Silent promises were made by each of them, promises Fanny prayed they both would keep.

Far too soon, he set her away from him.

This time when he reached for the door handle she

didn't stop him. As he escorted her to her room, they spoke about nothing of substance, a nice change from all the emotion of the evening.

At her door, he paused. "Good night, Fanny."

"Good night, Jonathon."

He lightly kissed her forehead, her temple and then her nose. There was such tenderness in each brush of his lips. Her eyes filled with tears.

One last touch of his lips to hers and he stepped back. "I pray you have sweet dreams."

"I know I will." With the memory of his kisses warming every corner of her heart, how could she not?

Chapter Fifteen

Fanny woke the morning of her wedding to the pleasant sound of birdsong outside her window. She stretched beneath the warm, downy comforter and looked around the luxurious room Jonathon had insisted she move into three days ago.

Snuggling deeper under the covers, she let out a jaw-cracking yawn, the result of too little sleep. Callie had spent the night with her, claiming it was one of her duties as the matron of honor. They'd stayed up late, giggling and sharing secrets as they'd so often done as young girls on the ranch.

Fanny hadn't realized how much she'd missed her sister. Ever since Callie had married Reese, Fanny had intentionally avoided spending too much time with her. The newlyweds deserved a chance to build their relationship without any distractions. An ex-fiancée—who also happened to be the bride's younger sister—definitely qualified as a distraction.

When Callie had announced she was going to have a baby, Fanny had created even more distance, this time for selfish reasons. She'd been fearful that her jealousy and yearning for her own child would put a permanent wedge between her and Callie.

She'd been wrong to worry. Last night, she'd felt only happiness for her sister.

Fanny attributed her change in perspective to her growing relationship with Jonathon. She'd never felt more treasured, more special, than when she was in his company. Not because of the few stolen kisses they'd shared under the stars, but because of Jonathon's tenderness toward her, his attentiveness and—all right, yes—his kisses.

More importantly, they'd faced down, as a couple, the gossip over his connection to Judge Greene, and had grown closer for the experience.

Society hadn't sided with Greene, or even Jonathon, but with the judge's poor, deceived wife. Fanny hadn't foreseen that particular result, but lauded the gossips for rallying around Mrs. Greene. Fanny almost felt sorry for Jonathon's father. *Almost*, but not quite, especially since he was still arrogantly sticking to his version of the story, as if *he* was the injured party.

Fanny banished all unpleasant thoughts from her mind. Today was a day for joy.

She stretched her arms overhead, and once again hooked her gaze on the ceiling. For this one moment, when Callie was off who-knew-where, and Fanny was completely alone, with no one watching her, no one asking her questions about the future, she let herself…dream.

In a matter of hours, she would become Mrs. Jonathon Hawkins. Anticipation hummed in her veins. They would have a good marriage, a happy, long—

Her door swung open with a bang.

Callie rushed into the room, jumped on the bed, then

proceeded to bounce up and down on her knees. "You're getting married in a few hours."

"Oh." Fanny pretended to yawn. "Is that today?"

"You know it is." Still bouncing, eyes lit with a teasing light, Callie pointed a finger at her. "No begging off this time."

"Ha-ha, very funny."

Fanny scooted to her right, as much to avoid getting mauled by her sister's enthusiasm as to make room for Callie on the bed.

Still laughing at her own joke, Callie collapsed backward, wiggled around a bit, then set her head on the pillow and studied the ceiling with narrowed eyes. "Will you look at that? Even the plaster is beautiful in this hotel."

Fanny eyed the swirling rosettes set inside a four-by-four square pattern. "When it comes to his hotels, Jonathon is a stickler for detail."

"So I gathered." Her gaze running from the center of the ceiling to the crown molding, Callie laughed again. Then stopped abruptly and swiveled her head on the pillow. "Are you happy, Fanny? Truly?"

"Oh, Cal, yes, *yes*, I am." Fanny smiled over at her. "I am so very, very happy."

"I knew you would end up with Mr. Hawkins." Her sister's voice held a decidedly smug note. "In fact, I have known for some time now, almost a full year."

Fanny very much doubted that. "You can't possibly have known for that long. Besides, I was in Chicago a year ago."

"I stand by my assessment." Callie held her stare without flinching. "I am very wise about these sorts of things."

"Are you?" Fanny rolled her eyes. "Might I remind you, oh wise one, how for weeks after I broke my engagement with Reese you pushed me to change my mind? And when I left town, you all but threatened to bodily drag me back to Denver so I could make amends?"

Callie opened her mouth, closed it, sighed heavily. "I find in cases such as these that a dreadful memory is most helpful, as is a swift change in subject."

"Indeed."

"Back to what I was saying." She lifted up on one elbow. "I've known Mr. Hawkins has had feelings for you ever since I worked as Mrs. Singletary's companion."

How could Callie possibly have known such a thing? Fanny and Jonathon had been veritable strangers at the time Callie had lived under Mrs. Singletary's roof.

"I detect your doubt, but remember, Mr. Hawkins was a frequent guest at the widow's house," Callie told her. "Whenever your name came up, he sang your praises."

Something warm and wonderful spread through Fanny. "Truly?"

"Oh, yes. He made a point of telling me that you were *thriving* in Chicago. At the time, I was very upset with him, so the news didn't sit well." Callie sank back onto the pillow. "I blamed him for helping you leave town."

"If he hadn't given me a job, I would have found another route of escape."

Callie sighed. "I know that now."

"Come on, Cal, you must admit." Fanny nudged her sister's shoulder. "Things worked out pretty well for you. You are married to a wonderful man and have a baby on the way."

Callie turned her head, her gaze full of gratitude. "If I haven't said it enough already, thank you, Fanny, thank you for breaking your engagement to Reese."

"You're most welcome."

They fell silent, each lost in her own thoughts.

Callie shifted, rose up on her elbow again. "I confess, I didn't know for certain that Mr. Hawkins was besotted with you until Mrs. Singletary's charity ball."

Fanny thought of the moment on the hotel terrace when she'd kissed Jonathon. "I have a confession of my own to make."

"That sounds interesting." Callie poked her in the ribs. "Do tell."

"I…" Fanny sighed. "I was the one who initiated our first kiss. If I'd known the Ferguson sisters were watching, I would have never—"

"Wait, stop, go back. I wasn't talking about Mrs. Singletary's charity ball this year. I was talking about the one she held last year."

"*Last* year?"

"I saw the way he looked at you. It's the same way Reese looks at me. But what really gave Mr. Hawkins away was how he capitulated to your every request for your current position. He adores you, Fanny, and has for some time."

Could it be true? Fanny barely dared to hope.

If Jonathon had feelings for her, feelings that had been building for over a year now, surely he would want to have a real marriage with her.

"Enough lazing about." Callie hopped off the bed and dragged Fanny with her. "It is my duty to ensure the bride has a hearty breakfast. I will not shirk my responsibilities."

Fanny hugged her sister. "I love you."

"Love you, too. Now," Callie clapped her hands together in a gesture that reminded Fanny of Beatrix Singletary. "You require sustenance and I shall see you get some."

"I think…" Fanny pressed a hand to her churning stomach. "I'm too nervous to eat."

"There's nothing to be nervous about." Callie presented her best big-sister smile. "It's going to be a good day, Fanny."

A ridiculously pleasant flutter went through her heart. "No, Callie, it's going to be a *great* day."

Later that same morning, huddled inside his heavy coat, Jonathon made the journey to Charity House on foot. In just over an hour, he would pledge his life to Fanny's at the church connected with the orphanage. It was one of the many things they'd agreed upon about their wedding.

He'd enjoyed the planning process. He and Fanny made a good team. Their easy working relationship at the hotel had seamlessly translated into a personal one.

Fanny was purity and light, so little of life's tragedies had truly touched her. Jonathon didn't want that to change because of him. He wanted to be a good husband, but he was a little fuzzy on what that actually entailed.

Surely Marc Dupree would have pearls of wisdom to share on the matter. The man had been happily married for over sixteen years.

Jonathon would like to think he'd played a role, albeit small, in Marc and Laney's romance. Had he not picked Marc's pocket that fine spring day, been caught in the act and then been marched back home to Charity House, the two may never have met.

Smiling at the memory, Jonathon unlatched the gate and sauntered up the front walkway, his gaze on Charity House. Not much had changed since he'd lived here. The three-story structure was as regal and imposing as he remembered.

The red bricks, black shutters and whitewashed porch rail fit in with every other mansion on the street. The difference being, of course, that forty boys and girls slept under this roof, rather than one family and a host of servants.

The familiar sound of children at play wafted from the backyard. Smiling at last, Jonathon conquered the front steps two at a time and entered the house.

The front parlor was empty, as was expected. The children weren't allowed in this area of the house without adult supervision. "Anybody home?"

"We're in Marc's office." Laney's muffled response came from the back of the house.

Jonathon worked his way through the labyrinth of hallways and corridors, then pushed through the door that led to Marc's office.

Warmth. Acceptance. Unconditional love.

They were all here for him, in this room, with these two people, the man and woman who'd taken on the role of his parents for four years.

"There's the groom." Laney rushed over and yanked him into a motherly hug. After nearly squeezing all the breath out of him, she stepped back and straightened the lapels of his morning suit. "Aren't you handsome? Your bride is going to swoon when she sees you."

He grinned at the absurd image her words created. "Keep complimenting me like that, Laney Dupree, and I might have to steal you away from your husband."

He winked at Marc, then swooped the petite woman into his arms and dipped her low to the ground.

She came up gasping and laughing.

"Oh, you." She playfully slapped his arm. "You always did have quick moves and too much charm for your own good."

"Which," Marc said, "if I remember correctly—and of course, I do—those quick moves got our boy into more than a few scuffles. One in particular comes to mind, involving my wallet."

"If *I* remember correctly," Jonathon countered, "had I not picked your pocket, you would have never found out about Charity House. The way I see it, you owe me a debt of gratitude."

"No argument there." Chuckling, Marc circled around his desk and, ignoring Jonathon's offered hand, pulled him into a quick, back-slapping hug. "You ready for today?"

He nodded. "Thank you, again, for agreeing to stand up with me."

"It's my honor and privilege." Sincerity sounded in Marc's words and shone in his eyes.

Jonathon's throat tightened.

This was the man he'd spent his entire adult life attempting to emulate.

"We have a while before we're due at the church. I thought you and I might take a few minutes to talk before we head over."

"That's my husband's polite way of telling me to leave the room." Laney rose onto her toes and kissed Jonathon's cheek. "I'm proud of you, Johnny. You're going to make your lovely bride a superior husband."

Jonathon wanted to agree with her, but found he could only manage a noncommittal shrug.

"Talk to Marc. You'll feel better once you do." She patted his arm, then quit the room without another word.

Typical Laney, he thought, as he stared at her retreating back. The woman was both perceptive and kind.

Still, dread slid down Jonathon's spine. He would never hurt Fanny, that was a given. He would provide for her and protect her from harm. Would it be enough? The world she came from was vastly different from the world he'd once inhabited. They certainly didn't have the same definition of family. Misunderstandings were sure to arise. Would they navigate them well, or would seemingly small matters grow into issues too big to overcome?

"Take a seat, Johnny, before you fall over."

"I'm good standing." But he wasn't. So he did as Marc suggested and sank in an overstuffed chair covered in brown leather worn to a fine patina.

Marc sat in the chair beside him. "I know that look in your eyes. It's called panic."

Not bothering to argue about the accurate assessment, Jonathon rubbed a hand over his face. "I don't want to hurt Fanny."

"Then don't."

"It's not that simple."

"It should be."

Too agitated to sit, Jonathon hopped to his feet and paced over to the bookshelf, ran his hand across several of the bindings. "My situation with Fanny isn't conventional."

"Perhaps your engagement didn't start out like most, but that's not to say your marriage won't bring you both great joy. I've seen you two together. You're good for each other."

Jonathon wasn't nearly as confident as his mentor. "You know where I come from, *who* I come from."

For several long seconds, Marc eyed him in stone-cold silence. "The question isn't if I know who you are. It's whether or not you do."

The look in Marc's eyes gave Jonathon pause. If he didn't know better he'd think he'd insulted the man. That hadn't been his intention. "I'm the product of an alliance between a woman of questionable virtue and an adulterer. *That's* where I come from. My blood is forever tainted."

"Your background is no different than my wife's." Marc leaned his elbows on his knees. "Is Laney's blood tainted?"

"You're missing my point."

"Am I?"

Heart grim, Jonathon told Marc about his half brother's recent antics, about the money he'd given Josh to set up his latest mistress in her own house, where she would raise their illegitimate child in secret. "The sins of my father have carried over into one of his sons."

Marc pressed the tips of his fingers together, brought them to rest beneath his chin. "You believe you'll turn out like your father and brother."

Unable to deny it, Jonathon merely nodded.

"What about my influence in your life?" Marc asked, his tone giving away nothing of his thoughts.

And yet Jonathon knew exactly what his mentor was thinking. By hanging on to his connection to Joshua Greene, Jonathon was denying his link to this man.

Breaking eye contract, Marc stood, stepped around his desk and rummaged through the top drawer. He pulled out what looked to be a faded photograph, and handed it to Jonathon.

The image of the first Hotel Dupree stared back at him. The brick building had boasted nine impressive stories, and large, wrought-iron balconies on every floor. Jonathon had copied Marc's original design, all the way down to the blue-and-white striped awning over the entrance.

"You once told me," Marc began, "that you kept my name on your hotels because you wanted your legacy tied directly with mine."

Jonathon continued staring at the photograph, the word *legacy* ratcheting around in his mind. "I remember."

Marc laid a hand on his shoulder. "Not only did you go into the hotel business because of me, but you have carried on my tradition of hiring employees who need a second chance. Men and women with little skill or talent, who may have made mistakes in the past but want to change their lives for good."

Jonathon looked up from the picture.

"The future stands before you, Johnny. You can either continue focusing on the fact that you are the son of an adulterer and a prostitute, or you can accept that you've overcome a difficult past to make something more of yourself. It's up to you."

Jonathon lowered his head and studied the image of the original Hotel Dupree, built by the man he most admired in this world. The backs of his eyes stung.

He swallowed hard, attempted to return the picture.

"Keep it," Marc told him. "As a reminder of where you really come from."

Unable to speak, he tucked the picture in an inner pocket of his jacket. "Thank you."

"I've had the privilege of watching you grow from a troubled youth to a good, solid, godly man. You'll make Fanny a proper husband. Don't let anyone ever tell you otherwise, including yourself."

If there was any good in him, it was because of this man's influence. The Lord had blessed Jonathon with a surrogate father a thousand times better than his real one. Part of him would always be defined by his past, but he didn't have to make the same mistakes the men who shared his blood had made.

Marc squeezed his shoulder. "Let's get you married."

They made the trek out to the backyard, which spilled onto the church's property. With plenty of time before the ceremony, Jonathon took a few minutes to toss a ball around with a couple of the older boys. The activity was simple, a game he'd played hundreds of times in this yard.

A reminder of where you really come from.

A half hour later, with Marc standing on his left and Laney perched in the front pew beside Fanny's mother, Jonathon took his place at the front of the church.

Reverend Beauregard O'Toole moved in on his right. The rebel preacher opened his church to the lost, the broken and the hurting. Jonathon had found God thanks to Beau's guidance. It mattered that he was the one to officiate this next step in his life.

Beau nodded to the woman at the piano and the short processional began.

Fanny's sister entered the church first and made the brief journey down the aisle. Callie's gaze was stuck on her husband sitting in the second pew. Reese Bennett Jr. winked at her. She blushed. He winked again.

Feeling as if he was intruding on their private moment, Jonathon looked away.

Still smiling, Callie drew to a stop on the other side of Beau, then turned to face the back of the church.

The music changed.

The wedding guests collectively rose to their feet.

And then…

Fanny appeared at the end of the aisle, her arm linked through her father's.

Jonathon's breath caught in his throat and all he could do was stare in wonder at the vision she made.

Dressed in cream-colored lace from head to toe, Fanny was the very picture of a beautiful bride. She'd pulled her blond curls into a fancy, complicated style atop her head. Little sprigs of wildflowers were scattered throughout, giving her beauty an ethereal quality.

His heart pounding with rib-cracking intensity, Jonathon knew he would forever treasure this moment when his bride stood in the doorway, arm in arm with her father, poised to begin her march down the aisle.

She was too far away for him to read her expression accurately, but he could feel her run her gaze over his face, each sweep a soft caress.

Minutes from now, she would be his wife.

She'd had little choice in the matter.

Jonathon braced his shoulders for the familiar guilt to slam through him. He experienced only a surge of joy.

His mind emptied of every thought but Fanny.

She was more than his business associate, more than his friend.

She was his future.

His bitter soul didn't deserve this woman, but now that he'd received her caring, experienced her generous spirit, he would never let her go.

Chapter Sixteen

Caught inside Jonathon's stare, Fanny's heart took a tumble. Now that the time had come to pledge her life to him, she couldn't be more ready.

She started down the aisle.

Her father pulled her to a stop. At the sight of the concentrated intensity on his face, she felt her stomach clutch. He had something important to say to her, something that he wasn't quite sure how to voice.

She waited, impatient for him to break his silence.

"Are you sure this is what you want?" he asked at last.

Fanny glanced to the front of the church, her gaze uniting with Jonathon's once again. His eyes were filled with promises, promises she knew he would do everything in his power to keep.

If she'd had any doubts before, they vanished beneath the silent assurances she caught pooled in his eyes.

There were no guarantees, Fanny knew, but she also knew that with her love, and God's guidance, Jonathon would one day give her his entire heart.

She had to believe he would fully commit to their marriage, and make their union real, preferably one day very soon.

Fanny wouldn't force his hand on the matter. She would not nag or cajole, but she wouldn't remain completely docile, either. Some things were worth fighting for, and her marriage to Jonathon lived at the top of that list.

For now, Fanny would take whatever he was willing to give her, and hope for the rest. "Yes, Daddy, I'm absolutely, positively sure this is what I want."

He tilted his head to the side and regarded her with a long, searching look.

"Truly," she added.

He nodded, obvious relief flickering along the edges of his gaze. "Then I wish you the same happiness I have with your mother."

Fanny remembered what her mother had said to her just this morning during the carriage ride over. *Where there is life, my dear, there is always hope.*

Hope. All Fanny needed was hope, which started with faith. One small leap of faith.

She lifted her foot to begin the march into her future with the man she loved. This time, her father didn't pull her back.

With a quick glance to the left, then to the right, Fanny took note of the people packed shoulder to shoulder in the pews. The majority of her family was here, Mrs. Singletary, of course, as well as friends and other close relatives.

She caught her mother's eye.

Mary Mitchell looked happy, healthy and—praise God—was breathing easily. Her asthma seemed to be improving by the day. For that reason alone, Fanny had been right to accept Jonathon's proposal.

Her gaze returned to the front of the church. Marc Dupree stood like a sentry by Jonathon's side.

Jonathon had gone through most of his life alone,

save for the four years he'd spent at Charity House. Four blessed years that had helped mold him into the man she loved. As she closed the final distance between them, Fanny made a silent promise to herself, and to Jonathon. She would spend the rest of her days making sure he knew he was loved.

The next few minutes passed in a blur. Pastor Beau asked who gave this woman away. Her father answered without pause, "Her mother and I."

Eyes shining, he kissed her cheek and then joined his wife in the front pew.

Jonathon took her father's place, reaching out his hand to her. Fanny placed her palm against his and let him draw her forward.

"Ready?" he whispered in her ear.

She smiled up at him. "I am more than ready."

Pastor Beau opened his Bible and began the ceremony.

"Dearly beloved, Jonathon Marc Hawkins and Francine Mary Mitchell have invited us to share in the celebration of their marriage." He paused to smile at Fanny, then Jonathon. "We, your family and friends, come together not to mark the start of your relationship, but to recognize the bond that already exists."

As the preacher continued, Fanny swiped surreptitiously at her eyes. Conflicting emotions rolled through her—joy and excitement, restlessness and anxiety. The combination made her stomach churn. She wasn't afraid, precisely, but…all right, yes, she was afraid, a little. What if Jonathon didn't come around to her way of thinking?

She didn't regret agreeing to marry him. She loved him. But what if she couldn't convince him to make their union real?

Fighting back a wave of panic, she swung her gaze

up to meet his. Her breath caught in her throat. He was watching her with tender affection.

The sweet expression helped allay her fears.

She gave in to a smile. Something quite wonderful passed between them, something that nearly stole her breath again.

Biting back a sigh, she quickly focused her gaze again to the front of the church. She really needed to pay attention to the words of the ceremony. Both she and Jonathon were about to make lifelong promises to one another.

Per the pastor's direction, her groom took her hand and repeated the first of their marriage vows. "I, Jonathon Marc Hawkins, take thee, Francine Mary Mitchell, to be my wife, to have and to hold from this day forward, for better, for worse, for richer, for poorer, in sickness and in health, to love and to cherish till death do us part."

His voice was strong, each word spoken with perfect diction. Fanny nearly believed he could love her.

She knew it would be unwise to allow her mind to wander toward something that could very well end in heartache.

Where there is life, my dear, there is always hope.

The preacher directed Fanny to repeat after him.

She did so with her chin high and her eyes locked with her groom's. "I, Francine Mary Mitchell, take thee, Jonathon Marc Hawkins, to be my husband, to have and to hold from this day forward, for better, for worse, for richer, for poorer, in sickness and in health, to love and to cherish till death do us part."

As she made each pledge, Fanny knew she would keep every word. She would stick by Jonathon through each and every trial, no matter what joy or suffering lay ahead. She would work through any challenge with him—even if they had a child together.

Pastor Beau's strong, steady voice broke through her thoughts. "Will you, Jonathon, have Fanny to be your wife? Will you love her, comfort and keep her, and forsaking all other, remain true to her as long as you both shall live?"

"I will."

Fanny detected the confidence in his voice, the seriousness behind his vows. She also noted how Jonathon's eyes gleamed with genuine affection. Surely, love was but a step away.

Pastor Beau shifted his stance and presented Fanny with the same questions he'd just asked of Jonathon.

She responded directly to her groom. "I will."

Jonathon clasped her hand and squeezed gently.

Her world instantly became brighter.

Only when he pulled his hand away did she become aware of the preacher's voice once again.

"Before this gathering, Jonathon and Fanny have professed their devotion. They will now give each other rings to wear as a sign of their deep commitment."

Jonathon stretched out his hand to Marc, who passed him a pretty gold band. Eyes dark and serious, Jonathon took her hand in his.

"Fanny, I give you this ring as a symbol of our vows, and with all that I am, and all that I have, I honor you." He slipped the gold band on her finger. "With this ring, I thee wed."

Fanny looked over her shoulder at Callie. At the sight of her sister's watery eyes, she felt her own fill. Firming her chin, she resolved to get through the rest of the ceremony without crying.

Callie handed over the ring Fanny had picked out for her groom weeks ago. She slipped it onto his finger and kept her hand over the band of gold.

"Jonathon, I give you this ring as a symbol of our vows, and with all that I am, and all that I have, I honor you. With this ring, I thee wed."

He smiled, then leaned so close to her she thought he was going to kiss her before given the go-ahead. Instead, he whispered in her ear. "I promise to do right by you, Fanny."

She treasured that final vow above all the others, because she knew he meant to keep his promise.

Everyone else faded away, leaving just the two of them.

"I'll never leave you," she whispered, not sure why she felt the need to say those words to him.

"Marriage is a gift from God," Pastor Beau said, straying slightly from the traditional service. "Fanny, Jonathon, through the sacredness of your vows you have become one with one another and God. I urge you to honor your commitment the way the Lord intended from the beginning. Be fruitful and multiply."

Be fruitful and multiply.

Prudent advice, straight out of the Word of God, and yet the words were like a dagger to Fanny's heart. Feeling like a fraud, she lowered her gaze. When she lifted her head again, Jonathon's eyes were different. He'd morphed into the stranger he'd once been, not the man she knew now.

The thought had barely materialized when the pastor continued with the ceremony.

"Let love rule your household," he said. "Hold fast to what is good and right and true. Outdo one another in showing love and mercy. And…" He paused, gave a self-deprecating laugh. "I think that's enough from this preacher for one day."

The gathered guests joined in his laughter.

Fanny and Jonathon simply stared at one another, neither moving, both caught in a suspended moment of shared consternation.

Unaware of the tension between them, the pastor placed his hands on their shoulders. "It is with great honor that I declare you husband and wife. Jonathon, you may kiss your bride."

Jonathon seemed to come back to himself at the pastor's instruction. Gaze somber, he placed a palm on Fanny's waist and drew her close.

Fanny wasn't sure what she saw in his dark, intense eyes. But when his lips pressed against hers, all her doubts and fears disappeared.

To Jonathon's way of thinking, this kiss with Fanny, their first as husband and wife, was filled with more emotion and feeling than all the others combined. He wanted to linger. Just a moment longer...

From a great distance, he heard Pastor Beau clear his throat, twice.

Slowly, reluctantly, Jonathon stepped back, away from Fanny, now his wife.

His wife.

By the sound of muffled snickering and actual hooting from a few of the Mitchell brothers, Jonathon figured he'd been a bit too enthusiastic with the obligatory kiss.

He gave Fanny an apologetic grimace.

She simply smiled. "Well done, Mr. Hawkins."

"Thank you, Mrs. Hawkins." He liked the sound of her new name rolling off his tongue.

Arm in arm, they turned and began their walk down the aisle.

Fanny's mother beamed at them from her perch on the front pew. Her father gave him a nod of approval.

Smiling at the people who were now his family, Jonathon continued guiding Fanny down the aisle. Each step pulled them toward an uncertain future, one they would face together as husband and wife.

Jonathon didn't know what awaited them in the days, weeks and years ahead, but he was determined to make their marriage a success.

At the back of the church, Fanny turned her face up to his.

She was so beautiful, so full of compassion and goodness. He wanted to believe all would turn out well.

But a sickening ball of dread knotted in the pit of his gut. He was going to let Fanny down, the truth of it as inevitable as snow falling in winter.

Smiling tenderly, Fanny touched his face. "I'm in this with you fully, Jonathon. I'm not walking away or letting you go, no matter what you say or do. I believe in you. I believe in us."

These were her real wedding vows, the ones that came straight from her heart. He had to blink to stop the tears in his eyes.

He wanted to be as confident as she, wanted to give her a similar pledge from the depth of his soul.

Overcome with emotion, and an unfamiliar surge of hope, he planted a tender kiss on the tip of her nose. "I'll do everything in my power to be the husband you deserve."

"I can't ask for more."

She should. She should ask for much more from him.

After a moment of basking in her goodness, her purity of heart, Jonathon looked out over the church still full of family and friends. "Please, everyone, join us back at the hotel and celebrate our marriage with us."

Taking Fanny's hand, he escorted her to the carriage

waiting for them outside the church. He climbed in behind her. The carriage dipped and swayed as he settled in the seat across from her.

He smiled at his beautiful bride. "And so begins our adventure as husband and wife."

"Not yet." She took his hand and yanked him onto the cushions beside her. Snuggling against him, she released a happy sigh. "*Now* the adventure begins."

Chapter Seventeen

The wedding reception lasted well into the evening hours. As they'd done for Mrs. Singletary's charity ball, many of the wedding guests had reserved rooms in the hotel. Jonathon predicted a long night.

He stood away from the main crowd gathered in the grand ballroom. Shoulder propped against the wall, he was content to watch the festivities from a distance.

His gaze followed Fanny as she wove from one group of guests to the next. She moved with natural grace, fresh and poised as a delicate flower that had found a way to bloom in the dead of winter. She'd worked her way past his defenses and had taken up residence in the darkest portions of his heart.

Despite their unconventional route to the altar, Jonathon couldn't say he was sorry to have Fanny for his wife. He felt more alive because of the vows he'd pledged to her, more awake, as if he were emerging from an unpleasant dream that had held him in its dark grip for far too long.

Already, after only a few hours with Fanny permanently united to him, the world made more sense. His footsteps were lighter, the air around him smelled sweeter and—

The air smelled sweeter?

Jonathon shook his head at the fanciful notion. Any more of this sappy introspection and he would find himself putting pen to paper in an effort to write verse in honor of his wife.

Him, a hardened street kid turned ruthless businessman, a worthy opponent in any fistfight, who'd maneuvered through every dark corner in the underbelly of Denver, had been reduced to poetic musings by a mere slip of a woman.

Then again, Fanny was no mere woman. She was confident and strong, bold and courageous, with a spine made of steel.

And now she was his wife.

Jonathon would share the rest of his life with Fanny Mitchell—no, Fanny *Hawkins*. By the grace of God, they would grow old together. An image of her in the distant future insinuated itself in his mind. She would be as beautiful to him in her dotage as she was to him now.

Jonathon would do anything—sacrifice everything— to make her happy. He adored her. He might even be in love with her.

Was he in love with Fanny?

It was too soon to tell. *Definitely* too soon.

Mouth tight, jaw clenched, he tried to calm his raging heartbeat. Sliding his gaze past Fanny helped.

The ballroom had a decidedly different feel for this party than the one hosted by Mrs. Singletary nearly a month ago. The atmosphere was more festive, while also being more relaxed.

Instead of elegantly dressed men and women twirling around the dance floor, people were gathered in small groups, talking, laughing and generally enjoying themselves.

But the most notable difference was the hordes of children in attendance. After a full day of being on their best behavior, many were growing tired of following the rules of decorum dictated by the adults. A few of the boys fidgeted, others tugged on their neck cloths. Some had already taken to poking each other.

Two of them began chasing a third boy in a circle; others soon joined them. A game of tag suddenly erupted in the center of the dance floor.

With a firm shake of his head, Jonathon alerted his hovering staff to let them play. The room was large enough to accommodate their antics without encroaching on the adult conversations.

Besides, the children's laughter was infectious. Jonathon would like nothing more than to join them. It had been far too long since he'd indulged in a rousing game of tag.

A smile tugged at his lips.

"Now that's the sight of a very happy groom. Does my heart good."

Mrs. Mitchell's pleased tone further improved his mood.

Smiling easier still, Jonathon pushed away from the wall. "How could I not be happy? I just married a woman nearly as beautiful as her mother."

Mrs. Mitchell's tinkle of laughter was its own reward.

"There is nothing I'd rather hear than flattery from a handsome young man, but my dear Mr. Hawkins—"

"Jonathon."

"Jonathon." She sent him a quick, lovely smile reminiscent of her daughter's. "Why are you hovering in the shadows instead of joining in the festivities?"

He decided to be truthful. "You have a large, extended family, Mrs. Mitchell, and I am bit—"

"Overwhelmed by the vast quantities of us?"

He laughed.

"It's not the numbers." He'd lived surrounded by hordes of boys and girls at Charity House. "It is more that I find myself besieged with too many people in one room who play very different roles in my life."

Her head tilted and she looked confused. "I'm not sure what you mean."

He expelled a breath. "I have known some of the people in this room since childhood. A few are new friends, many are old. And then there is…your family."

"Ah, now I understand."

"Do you?" He hardly understood himself what he was trying to say.

"But of course. You don't know where your new family fits into your very organized world. Everyone else has his or her place. The Mitchells do not. Adding to the confusion, there are…" she cast her gaze over the room "…quite a lot of us."

To his amazement she'd described the situation perfectly. "You are a very wise woman, Mrs. Mitchell. I have half a mind to put you in charge of my entire hotel empire."

"Tempting." She gave him a friendly nudge with her shoulder. "But keeping track of my grandchildren is more than enough work for me."

They shared a laugh, then turned as one to watch her grandchildren at play. One of Hunter's kids, the youngest boy—Christopher?—noticed them staring. He shot in their direction, a blur of shaggy blond hair and fast pumping legs in a tiny black suit.

Jonathon barely had time to scoop up the boy before he could slam into his grandmother. "Whoa, little man, what's the rush?"

Giggling, Christopher wiggled in his arms, then slapped Jonathon on the shoulder.

"Tag," the little boy shouted, loudly enough to be heard on the top floor of the hotel. "You're it."

Jonathon set him back on the ground, leaned over and tapped the boy's head. "Tag, *you're* it."

The kid blinked at him, once, twice, then a wide grin spread across his mouth.

"Okay." He sped off to find another victim, arms flaying, shouting, "I'm it. I'm it."

"You're good with children," Mrs. Mitchell noted.

Was he?

It'd been years since he'd spent any length of time around kids. Now that he thought about it, Jonathon decided he wasn't so much good with children as he understood them. They wanted very little from adults. A sense of safety. Authenticity. Honesty. Things Jonathon hadn't experienced himself until he'd moved into Charity House.

"You clearly like being around little ones."

Realizing he hadn't responded to Mrs. Mitchell's earlier comment, Jonathon nodded. "I suppose I do."

If he understood children, if he *liked* them, perhaps he wouldn't be such a terrible father, after all. Perhaps he might even make a decent one.

How would he ever know if he didn't take the risk?

"No frowning on your wedding day," Mrs. Mitchell scolded softly, patting his arm as Laney had done that morning. "The Mitchell brood isn't as daunting as we first appear. And for the record, we are pleased to call you one of us."

"Truly? But you hardly know me."

"You make Fanny happy. That goes a long way to softening even the most skeptical members of my family."

As if her words had the power to summon the "most

skeptical," Fanny's brothers sauntered toward them. They each wore a version of the same stern, determined expression.

"Ah," Mrs. Mitchell said, spotting the men mere seconds after Jonathon had. "Here come my three handsome boys."

With a show of amused indulgence, Mrs. Mitchell greeted her sons by presenting her cheek to each of them. They each gave her a loud, smacking kiss. Then they swung their attention to Jonathon.

Deciding to take the first shot, er...lighten the mood, he lifted his hands in mock surrender. "No need to kiss my cheek. A handshake will do."

All three men went stock-still for the length of a single eye blink. Hunter cracked a smile first, followed a half beat later by Logan and Garrett. Soon all three men were giving Jonathon hearty backslaps.

"Welcome to the family, Hawkins." Hunter gave his shoulder a hard squeeze. "You already fit right in."

Jonathon was surprised at how intensely pleased he was by the statement. He now had five brothers. These oldest three, plus the other two who were attending university back East.

Knowing how these men worked, having watched them interact with one another, Jonathon adopted a dry, ironic tone, and said, "Lucky me."

Again, it was the exact right thing to say. All three Mitchell brothers laughed.

"Well done, Hawkins." Logan gripped his shoulder as his brother had just done. "You are officially my second-favorite brother-in-law, Reese only barely nudging you out because he's been around longer."

Shaking her head, Mrs. Mitchell looked from her sons

to Jonathon and back again. "Yes, well, I'll leave you to your man talk."

Before she turned to go, she set her hand on Jonathon's shoulder and presented her cheek for him to kiss.

He did so without hesitation.

A whimsical smile crossed her lips as she wandered away.

The moment she was out of earshot, Hunter took on the role of family spokesman. "We actually came over for two reasons. The first is to welcome you into the family, the other to give you your wedding gift."

Wedding gift? The man couldn't have surprised Jonathon more if he'd called him out for a gunfight. "Fanny and I have everything we need."

"Everything you need, yes." Hunter gave him a meaningful look. "But not, I think, everything you want."

What Jonathon wanted was a wife he could not hurt, a wife he could not fail. Anything else, he could acquire on his own.

But then he remembered the land deal that had never come to pass. *Mitchell land stays in Mitchell hands.*

In the craziness of the day, he'd nearly forgotten his dream of creating a legacy for himself separate from his father.

The picture in his jacket pocket—*a reminder of where you really come from*—told Jonathon he was already forging his own legacy.

"I have everything I need *and* everything I want." It was nothing short of the truth.

"Not yet." Hunter hitched his chin at the youngest Mitchell brother.

Garrett reached into his jacket pocket and pulled out a familiar pack of papers. The contract Jonathon had

presented these three men the day before Mrs. Singletary's charity ball.

"Go ahead," Logan urged. "Take it."

With the brothers staring at him expectantly, he instinctively reached out.

"I predict you'll be pleased with the terms."

He flipped through the agreement, skimming the familiar words, taking in the changes, specifically the ridiculous price of *one dollar.* On the final page, the three
Mitchell names were scrolled across the bottom. All that
was missing was Jonathon's signature.

"The land is yours," Hunter said, eyes glinting with
good humor. "Assuming you can afford the asking price."

Before Jonathon could respond, Garrett added, "We'll
support whatever you want to do with the property."

Carte blanche. The Mitchell brothers were giving him
total freedom to develop the land however he wanted. Far
more than he'd expected.

The victory felt hollow, but he couldn't think why.

He'd been planning this project for an entire year, ever
since making the Denver Hotel Dupree his permanent
residence. But it was as if he'd somehow lost something
valuable, something he couldn't put a name to yet.

"I have a better idea." He thrust the contract back at
Garrett. "Put the land in Fanny's name."

Surprise registered on two of the three faces. Hunter,
however, simply nodded in approval. "Consider it done."

After the last guest left the ballroom, Fanny hid a
yawn behind her hand. Given the late night giggling with
Callie, coupled with the excitement of her wedding day,
she was worn to the bone. If she didn't sit down soon
she feared she would collapse in an embarrassing heap
at her husband's feet.

Jonathon's soothing voice washed over her in a low, rumbling, masculine purr. "Tired?"

She shot a smile at him. "Exhausted, actually."

"It's been a long day for both of us." He took her hand and drew her out of the ballroom. "Time to head upstairs."

The warmth in his gaze brought a rush of anticipation. Dare she hope her husband would make their marriage real? On their wedding night?

Most brides didn't have to wonder about such matters. After all, the Lord had created marriage for intimacy between a husband and his wife. There was no shame in that, she told herself, even as her cheeks heated.

Ever the gentleman, Jonathon escorted her into the elevator and told the attendant to take them to the top floor. With their very avid audience of one, they kept a respectable distance from each other.

Oh, but Fanny was tired of being polite. She wanted to be Jonathon's wife, in every sense of the word.

Out of the corner of her eye, she cast a surreptitious glance in his direction. He looked so handsome in his formal wedding attire, the gray of his jacket nearly the same color as his eyes in the darkened elevator.

Always, Jonathon lived easily in his skin, no matter what he was wearing or the situation in which he found himself. The impeccable clothing was merely drapery, elegant but inconsequential to the man beneath.

"Here we are," the attendant announced, releasing latches and sliding open the elevator door to the ninth floor, where Jonathon kept a suite of rooms.

Before exiting, Fanny made eye contact with the hotel employee. "Thank you, Harold."

"You're most welcome, Miss Mitchell, I mean..."

he cleared his throat, slid a worried glance at Jonathon
"...Mrs. Hawkins."

With Jonathon indicating she take the lead, Fanny
stepped into the hallway. But not before she caught him
handing Harold a bank note and then thanking him for
his hard work on behalf of the hotel.

Fanny's heart swelled with affection. Her husband was
such a generous man.

Her husband. She felt a rush of feminine pride that
this man was hers.

Would she ever grow used to being married to him?
She hoped not. She hoped she would always be full of
this same sense of wonder whenever she looked at him.

"This way." Jonathon settled his hand on Fanny's
lower back and escorted her to his—*their*—private suite
on the top floor of the hotel.

He opened the door with his key and again directed
her to take the lead.

She stepped inside the room.

For a moment, all she could do was blink in muted
astonishment. This was her first glimpse into Jonathon's
private world and it fell incredibly flat.

"I don't know what I expected but...*this*?" She
stretched out her hand. "Isn't it."

Jonathon followed the direction of her gaze, narrow-
ing his eyes as if trying to see his private domain from
her perspective. "Would you like a tour?"

"I suppose." But what would be the point?

Though the space was certainly luxurious and spectacular, especially compared to the single-bed rooms, there
was no sign of Jonathon anywhere. Gleaming woodwork
adorned the walls. The dark grain contrasted perfectly
with the rich burgundy and gold tones of the furniture

and draperies. The elegant chairs and settees were upholstered with a swirling brocade pattern.

Tasteful restraint ruled the first bedroom he showed her, the muted ivory and green hues a pleasant divergence from the vibrant colors in the common areas.

The more Fanny followed Jonathon from room to room, the bleaker her heart grew. The cold, impersonal decor was clear evidence that her husband hovered on the fringes of life, not really connecting, but instead remaining cool and distant.

She remembered what her sister-in-law had said about him as a boy. *He kept a part of himself separate from the other children. He was friendly, but he didn't have a lot of friends.*

Nothing had changed for Jonathon, despite his financial wealth and business success.

Fanny longed to wrap her arms around him and chase away the memories of his childhood. She longed to show him he was not alone and that he was loved.

If only he would let her.

In strained silence, he led her into another bedroom, this one done in soothing tones of various blues.

"I thought you would claim this room for yourself. It's the largest and most comfortable." His lips curved in a gentle smile. "You may, of course, redecorate to your specifications. I'm thinking the colors are a bit masculine, however—"

"This is *my* room?" It appalled her to feel hot tears of disappointment gathering in her eyes.

"Unless you would prefer one of the others I have already shown you." He compelled her with only his eyes. "I want you to feel comfortable here, Fanny."

Didn't her husband realize that sharing his room would

make her the happiest of all? That starting a family with him was what she wanted most in this world?

She'd seen him interacting with her nieces and nephews at various times throughout the day. He enjoyed children, more, she thought, than even he realized. He would be a good father. Fanny knew it. Annabeth knew it. It seemed everyone knew it except Jonathon himself.

Of course, now was not the time for that discussion.

"Where will you sleep?"

His eyebrows slammed together in masculine bafflement. "In my bedroom, of course."

"Which is where, precisely?" *Please don't say in another suite, or worse, on another floor. Anything but that.*

"My room is on the opposite side of the suite."

A moment of relief filled her. At least they would be living in close proximity. It was a start.

A very good start, indeed.

Summoning up her brightest smile, Fanny glanced around her new home and then back at her husband. "Thank you, Jonathon, this room will suit my needs perfectly."

For now.

Chapter Eighteen

Jonathon knew he was in trouble the moment Fanny turned docile and compliant. She was many things, but neither of those came to mind.

What was she up to?

He eyed her cautiously. "I'll have your belongings brought up from the other suite in the morning."

Her smile never wavered. "That'll be fine."

The overly polite response put him further on guard. "Is there anything else you'll want or need?"

"Not at the moment, no." She took a step toward him.

He took a step back and cleared his throat. "I thought we would share a late supper before we call it a night. I had room service deliver an assortment of cold meats and—"

"That sounds perfectly wonderful."

"I haven't finished telling you what I ordered for us."

Still smiling, she closed the distance between them and placed her hand on her chest. "I'm sure whatever the chef sent up will meet with my expectations."

Her low, accommodating voice poured warmth over the tense moment.

Jonathon quickly strode back to the main sitting area, where the staff had set up a small, intimate table for two.

An overabundance of meats, cheeses, breads and sugary confections were arranged in an artful display. Candlelight completed the romantic setting.

Fanny took her time examining the fare. She circled the table, running her fingertip along the edge of the pristine white linen cloth. Jonathon stood transfixed by her beauty. Her hair glimmered beneath the glow of the fire that snapped in the hearth.

"The setup is quite lovely, Jonathon."

Not nearly as lovely as Fanny was, swathed in golden firelight.

He cleared his throat again. "Would you prefer to eat here at the table? Or we could fill our plates and relax in the chairs over by the fireplace."

"I should think either option sufficient." The words sounded like cream in her soft, feminine voice.

Something inside him snapped. "Could you stop being so agreeable?"

Amusement entered her eyes. "You would wish me to be contrary instead?"

"Of course not." He drew in a sharp, impatient breath. "I wish…"

"You wish…?" she prompted, when he held his silence.

His breath stalled in his lungs.

What a picture she made, innocence and purity itself in her pretty wedding dress. He didn't regret marrying her, but he feared she would grow to regret marrying him. And that would be a tragic day, indeed. He felt as though he was seeing her for the first time, with the eyes of a husband.

He was in big trouble.

"Come here, Jonathon." With the faintest trace of nerves shadowing the move, she lifted her arms.

The emotion that swept through him when he pulled her into his embrace was like an unexpected thunderstorm that blew in out of nowhere, then was suddenly gone, leaving nothing but a sense of calm in its wake.

"Fanny." He buried his face in her hair, breathed in her scent of lilacs and mint.

Fanny belonged in his arms, in his life.

For a terrifying moment, he could hear nothing but the voice of his father on their first meeting. *You were a mistake never meant to happen.*

Jonathon knew it was a lie.

Fanny had taught him to see past the deception.

He kissed the top of her head, stroked her hair. When she pulled back to look at him, he lowered his mouth to hers.

The kiss started gentle, but it quickly got out of hand. He immediately set her away from him.

"Jonathon?" Confusion filled her eyes.

"Don't look at me like that."

"How am I looking at you?"

He put his back to her, speared a hand through his hair. It was easier to have this conversation without meeting her gaze. "You are looking at me as if you want the one thing I warned you I couldn't give."

"Oh, Jonathon, you're both right *and* wrong. I do want something from you." She threw her arms around his waist and pressed her cheek to his back. "I want you to know you aren't alone anymore. You'll *never* be alone again. I am here with you, always and forever."

Her words whipped through him like a balmy gust of wind. "I believe you."

He attempted to shift away from her.

Making a sound of protest deep in her throat, she worked her way around him until they were facing each other again.

No one had ever looked at him the way she regarded him now, as if she had every faith in him, as if he was the answer to all her hopes and dreams.

He had no armor against that look.

To keep from reaching out to her, he clenched his fists behind his back. He must not touch her. Not until they came to an understanding.

"You're tired." He saw the truth of it in the slight slump of her shoulders and the drooping of her eyelids. "Perhaps we should set aside any serious conversation until morning."

"No." She jammed her hands on her hips. "There's more to discuss."

She was quite spectacular glaring at him, her eyes full of purpose in the dazzling firelight.

He swallowed a grin. "All right, Fanny, have your say."

His agreement took all the iron out of her spine.

Sighing softly, she lowered her hands to her sides. "You are very good at keeping your distance from others, but it isn't necessary with me. One day you will know I speak the truth."

He knew it now and wondered why he continued fighting the inevitable. He could never have a marriage in name only with this woman.

As if coming to a similar conclusion, she whispered his name. "Will you do me the honor of making me your wife?"

His very soul wavered between battle and surrender.

If he did as she asked, if he made their marriage real, he feared he would eventually let her down. Maybe not today, or even tomorrow, but sometime in the future.

"Once we cross this line," he warned, "we can never go back."

"Jonathon, we crossed the proverbial line when we said our wedding vows. All that is left is making the commitment final."

A low rumble moved through his chest, sounded in his sharp intake of air.

"We have both had a long, tiring day," he said. One he didn't want to end anytime soon. But he needed to give her one last chance to retire to her own room. "You may still say good-night and I will let you alone."

In answer, she took his hand and smiled. "The tour of my new home is not yet complete. There is still one room you haven't shown me."

The only room he hadn't shown her was his bedroom. As the meaning of her words became clear, a slow grin spread across his lips.

Jonathon scooped his bride into his arms.

By morning, Fanny would be his wife in every sense of the word. For her sake, he prayed he wasn't making a terrible mistake.

The next three months were the happiest of Fanny's life. She was a blissfully married woman. Jonathon was turning out to be a very good husband. Their relationship grew stronger every day.

Now, as she sat behind her desk and reviewed next week's bookings at the hotel, Fanny allowed a smile to spread across her lips. She was completely, wonderfully in love with her husband.

She hadn't said the words out loud. Not yet, but soon, she told herself, when she felt Jonathon was ready to hear them. Perhaps once spring chased away the last of the winter chill Fanny would unveil the full contents of her heart.

For now, she showed her feelings for her husband in countless other ways. In the brush of her hand across his cheek before they fell asleep at night. In the notes she left on his desk beneath papers for him to find. Or simply wrapped in one of her smiles.

Though there were moments when she felt as though Jonathon still held a portion of himself back from her, she knew that tendency would go away in time.

Fanny had no doubt he cared for her. He might even love her. Like her, he displayed his affection in ways other than words. In the gentle way he spoke her name. In the unexpected moments he showed up at her office and whisked her away for one of their delightful walks.

There was one thing missing in her life with Jonathon, one thing that would make her joy complete. A child. Jonathon's child.

Fanny set down her pencil and placed her hand over her flat stomach. Would she ever feel a baby's kick against her palm?

Annabeth and Hunter had welcomed their newest family member three weeks after Fanny's wedding, a little boy named Sean, who had his mother's dark hair and his father's amber eyes.

Garrett and Molly's baby was due in another two months. Now that Mary Mitchell's asthma was under control, Fanny's parents planned to travel to Saint Louis for the birth. They would stay only two weeks, then head home in time to welcome Callie and Reese's child into the world.

It was baby season in the Mitchell clan. And Fanny couldn't help but yearn.

Her stomach performed a sickening roll. Suddenly,

She started to push around him.

He stepped directly in her path. "I need an heir."

"You have an heir."

"Joshua is a disappointment. I have tried to contain his excesses. I have forbidden him to carry on with his mistress, yet he continues and has even produced an illegitimate child. I will not encourage his willful disobedience any longer." A muscle worked in the judge's jaw. "I have cut him off, once and for all."

Fanny blinked at the vast amount of information the man had supplied. One point seemed painfully clear. "So now that your legitimate son has disappointed you, you think to make Jonathon your heir?"

"Of course not." Outrage filled every hard plane of the older man's face. "Your husband is the by-blow of a ostitute and therefore unfit to carry my name."

Appalled, Fanny treated the judge to a withering glare. is your son."

hat is true. More to the point, he made the very wise n to marry you, a woman of impeccable breeding rominent ranching family." His gaze dropped to ection. "I wish to name the first male child you official heir."

hand instinctively covered her stomach. "You my child as your heir over your own son." e horrified her. Just how many ways could Jonathon?

in the next generation. Josh's wife has is up to you, Mrs. Hawkins, to carry

stomach, she stumbled backward. t her balance did she realize Judge maneuvered her several feet down

her office felt small and overly hot. This wasn't the first time she'd felt the sensation. Over the past week, Fanny had battled bouts of queasiness at the oddest moments. Perhaps she was coming down with something. The flu had been making its rounds through the hotel staff.

Her head grew light. She needed to breathe in fresh air. Maybe she could entice Jonathon to join her for a brief stroll.

Swallowing back a wave of dizziness, she stood, left her office and made her way to Jonathon's. She found his assistant standing in the doorway, nose buried in the notepad he kept with him always.

"Is he in?" she inquired.

Burke Galloway looked up. "I'm sorry, Mrs. Hawkins, you just missed him. He had a meeting at Mr. Bennett's office across town."

"Oh, that's right." Before they'd left their suite this morning, Jonathon had mentioned having an appointment with Reese concerning a recent land acquisition.

"Was there anything I could do for you?"

"No, thank you, Mr. Galloway. I'll come back later."

Still feeling a bit light-headed, Fanny decided to take a short walk, anyway. After retrieving her coat and gloves, she left the hotel through the front doors and breathed in the cool air. Lifting her face to the sky, she concentrated on the glorious blue overhead. Her nausea almost immediately disappeared.

Just as she lowered her gaze, a masculine voice reached her ears. "Miss Mitchell, may I join you on your walk?"

A prickle of unease navigated up her spine. "I am Mrs. Hawkins now."

"Of course, my apologies. May I join you on your stroll…Mrs. Hawkins?" As he made his request a second time, Jonathon's father stood unmoving. The air around him crackled with arrogance.

Lowering her lashes to cover her surprise at his sudden appearance, Fanny couldn't help but wonder what Judge Greene wanted with her. Even acknowledging him made her feel as though she was betraying Jonathon.

But when she looked more closely, she saw the signs of strain on the judge's face. He looked older and somehow less sure of himself, despite the arrogant tilt of his head. From what Fanny had heard, he was still holding to his story that he'd only recently learned that Jonathon was his son.

It was on the tip of her tongue to tell him what she truly thought of him. But then she remembered the portion of the Bible she'd read just this morning during her daily quiet time. The Lord commanded His children to love their enemies.

She should at least give it a try. But, truly, it was times such as these that Fanny wished she didn't know Scripture quite so well.

Jaw tight, she gave a short nod. "You may have five minutes of my time."

"Thank you, my dear."

Love thy enemy, she reminded herself.

Her clenched jaw began to ache.

The judge gestured with his hand for her to continue walking. When she did, he fell into step beside her.

She could not fault his manners.

Gaze locked on the mountains in the distance, she expected him to speak. Surprising her yet again, he seemed content to walk beside her in silence.

She was not so patient.

Fanny stopped, waited for him to do the same, before saying, "State your business, Judge Greene."

"I have a request to make of you, Mrs. Hawkins."

She pursed her lips into what she hoped was a bored expression. "I'm listening."

"I wish to make amends with my son."

"What does that have to do with me?"

Stuffing his hands in his pockets, he lifted an elegantly clad shoulder. "He refuses to speak with me, no matter how many overtures I make. I have come to ask you to intercede for me."

Shocked by his colossal nerve, she stared at him. "You cannot be serious."

"I assure you, I am." He crowded her as he spoke, moving around her like a hawk circling its prey.

She backed up a step, and another, and then ___ more, until she found herself against a brick ___

"Even if I had the sort of influence on my ___ seem to think, I would never wield it in s___ am sorry, Judge Greene, you are on y___

"All I'm asking is that you dro___ behalf."

She dismissed his request ___ ask too much."

"It is but one small ki___

Did he not recog___ "Where was your ___ a boy and came ___

The judge ___ has told yo___

"Jona___ him no com___ for the very co___ realized that she c___ matter how hard she ___ you a good day."

"Your child will be my grandson. He will carry my blood." The odious man leaned over her, his sense of entitlement easy to read in his eyes, even in the shadows.

Joshua Greene was truly a selfish man, clinging to a twisted logic that made sense only to him. He would go after what he wanted, regardless of the people he hurt in the process.

Fanny jerked her chin at him. "I am not afraid of you."

But she *was* afraid. She was afraid for her husband, afraid for what this would do to Jonathon. His father would deny him his birthright in favor of his own son.

Lord, may we only have girls.

"Will you help me, Mrs. Hawkins? Will you encourage your husband to meet with me about this matter?"

A gasp flew from her mouth. She had no doubt this man would do everything in his power to make his desire a reality.

Fear held a tight grip on her, paralyzing her in place.

Now she understood the depth of Jonathon's pain and why he was so determined never to father a child. Fanny closed her eyes, her heart squeezing in sorrow, because a part of her agreed with his decision.

"What if Jonathon and I choose not to have children? What will you do then?"

Momentary fury flashed in the judge's gaze. "You arrogant, self-righteous chit."

"Name-calling will not soften me to the idea of— Oh!"

Without warning, she was swept into the strong, familiar arms of her husband. Relief made her heart beat faster. She'd never been happier to see Jonathon. She barely had time to catch her breath before he maneuvered her against the brick wall, then stood in front of her, using his body to protect hers.

"Are you all right?" An edge of danger burned in his narrowed eyes, in his too-calm voice. "Did he hurt you?"

"No, no. Jonathon, I am completely unharmed."

He lowered his gaze over her, searching, measuring. When his eyes met hers again, her stomach filled with spears of ice. She hardly recognized the man standing before her. He had a quiet, lethal edge she'd never seen in him.

This was the man who'd survived on the harsh streets of Denver by any means possible.

Hand shaking, Fanny reached up to cup his face, hoping to soothe away the rage simmering in his gaze. His eyes burned hotter still and she dropped her hand, regretting ever leaving the hotel.

Instead of making the situation better, Jonathon's arrival had made matters much, much worse.

Chapter Nineteen

Jonathon struggled to calm his breathing. Rage ran cold as ice in his veins, leaving an empty vacuum in his soul dark as the alley in which they stood. He'd never felt this vicious, territorial emotion before. But no one had ever threatened Fanny like this, either.

He widened his stance, wishing he could be on all sides of her. He continued searching for injury, relieved to find none.

When he'd caught sight of Greene pulling his wife into the alley, Jonathon had been all the way across the street. Too far. He'd broken into a run, petrified for his wife's safety.

"Jonathon." Fanny's voice washed over him, soft and soothing, a warm, unexpected breeze in the cold, harsh air. "Our business is concluded here. We can head back to the hotel now."

She took his hand and tugged him toward the busy street ahead, away from the dark alleyway, from the past, from everything he wanted to forget. For several steps, he let Fanny guide him along, wanting the light that defined her, needing it more than air.

The bright sunlight beckoned, washing over Fanny,

amplifying the blond streaks in her hair and displaying a dozen shades of gold.

"You are being overly dramatic." Greene's disapproving grunt hummed in the air. "The chit is perfectly fine."

With one fluid motion, Jonathon swung around, grabbed his father by the lapels and dragged him forward until their faces were inches apart. "Never come near my wife again. Do you understand?"

Greene's mouth went flat and hard, but he didn't struggle under Jonathon's hold. "There's no cause for violence. Your wife and I were having a pleasant conversation about the future."

"What did you say to her?"

"If you would unhand me, we could speak as civilized human beings rather than back-alley brutes."

The dig hit its mark, bringing up disturbing, dangerous images from his youth. Jonathon could feel his rage return, unraveling through him like a sticky spider web. But he was not the brute his father claimed. Not anymore. Violence was not a part of who he was now.

Filled with disgust for himself, as well as the man who'd sired him, he slowly, deliberately, released Green's coat and stepped back, palms raised in the air.

"Jonathon." Fanny's sweet, lyrical voice came from behind him. "Take me home. Please, I want to go home."

Over his shoulder, he looked at her, saw the plea in her gaze. But he wasn't through with his father.

"We will leave once the judge answers my question." He turned back around and repeated, "What did you say to my wife?"

He wanted to know, but sensed the truth would enrage him further. The only words he'd caught—*arrogant, self-righteous chit*—had been enough to unleash his fury.

Eyebrows lifted in condescension, Greene straightened his jacket, tugged his waistcoat in place, then finally deigned to give a response. "I merely told her my plans for your—"

"Jonathon, please." Fanny grabbed his arm. "It's not important what your father and I discussed. It means nothing."

The look of distress in her gaze told its own story. Now he *knew* he wasn't going to like what his father had said to Fanny.

Jonathon returned his attention to Greene. "Continue."

"I believe this conversation would be better served if we conduct it in a less unseemly environment. Let us follow your wife's suggestion." Green spoke in the tone of a man used to giving orders and having them obeyed. "And congregate inside the comfort of your hotel."

"We'll talk here."

"Very well, if that is what you wish."

"It is."

With a murmur of assent, Greene nodded. "I was hoping your wife would speak to you on my behalf."

"Why?"

For the first time the older man looked uneasy. "I wish to sit down and discuss the future of our family."

Feeling cold as ice and empty as a moonless night, Jonathon demanded, "What about it?"

His eyes shifting right, then left, Greene hesitated, as if to gather his thoughts. When he spoke, his voice came out smooth and confident. "It is my deepest desire to claim your firstborn son as my heir."

"No."

"I'm afraid it is already done. I had my will rewritten a month ago. Your son will carry on my legacy through future generations."

Legacy. The word ricocheted through Jonathon's mind

like a stray bullet. His skin burned beneath his clothes. This bland, lifeless emotion rolling through him was grief, grief for the life he and Fanny might have had if only Joshua Greene wasn't his father.

Jonathon knew what he had to do, had always known it would come to this. He'd fooled himself into believing otherwise.

"I vow, this very day, that your immoral, godless legacy will die with you." He made the proclamation softly, his tone so low the judge had to lean in closer to hear him. "You will have no heir from me."

"No." Fanny rushed to him. "No, Jonathon, do not say such a thing. Nothing has to be decided today."

The decision had been made long before he'd met his beautiful wife.

"Let us be done with this conversation." With her face leached of color, her brow creased in worry, she reached across the small divide between them and grabbed his hand, squeezing hard. "Come away with me now."

Greene continued talking, spouting off the grand plans he had for Jonathon's future son. Jonathon tuned out the words and, hand in hand with Fanny, stepped out of the darkness.

The bright, afternoon sunlight brought no warmth to his cold soul. He felt hollow inside, a shell of a man sleepwalking through life.

They made their way down the street in silence, their steps slow. People strolled past them, moving and living at a different speed.

Mind numb, Jonathon looked down at Fanny, then at their joined hands. His heart gave a quick, extra hard thump. Barely three months earlier he'd vowed to love, cherish and protect this woman. In the days since, she'd filled his life to completion. Her smiles, her voice, her laughter…he couldn't get enough of them.

In her presence, he'd come to believe he could overcome his past. But his past had caught up with him today. In the form of a selfish man who would do whatever necessary to forward his own agenda.

"Fanny." Hating that she'd witnessed the darker pieces of his soul, Jonathon released her hand. "What were you doing on the streets alone with my father?"

She lowered her head and sighed. "It was quite by accident, I assure you. I certainly never planned to run into him."

"I never thought otherwise."

She sighed again. "I wanted a bit of fresh air and so I went for a short walk. I'd barely left the hotel when he came up behind me." She lifted her gaze, her face pulled in a delicate frown. "He must have been waiting for me. Or you."

"I'm sorry he accosted you in public."

"It would have been equally reprehensible in private."

She released an unladylike sniff and increased her pace, all but stomping last night's snowfall into mush. "He looked rather terrible, as if he hasn't slept in weeks. Some dark part of my nature finds that quite heartening. But we won't discuss him anymore, at least not out here on the street."

Smoothly assuming control, Fanny gripped Jonathon's hand again and pulled him through the entrance of the hotel.

A group of guests passed, looking curiously at their clasped hands. Neither of them broke stride.

Halfway through the lobby, Jonathon took over the lead. "We'll talk upstairs, where we won't be interrupted."

"I was just about to suggest the same thing."

They were stopped several times by staff with questions and concerns. Jonathon brushed the bulk of them off with a promise that he would be back in his office within the hour.

Neither he nor Fanny spoke again until they were alone in their suite.

While she discarded her coat, hat and gloves, Jonathon looked around the room. Fanny was everywhere, her personal touch apparent in the homey details she'd added to make the suite their home.

Fresh flowers spilled out of crystal vases. Light, airy watercolors by local artists covered the walls. A spattering of hairpins had been left on a side table. The novel Fanny had been reading last night before they'd retired for the evening sat open on the overstuffed settee.

He and Fanny had fallen into a happy rhythm that included work and laughter and joy.

Neither had realized they'd been living on borrowed time.

Heavyhearted, Jonathon walked slowly to the empty hearth, lowered himself to his haunches and began laying a fire.

"That can wait."

His hands stilled over the logs, but he didn't rise to his feet.

With the grace that defined her, Fanny settled on the hearth rug beside him. She filled the moment with her scent, her soft smile. Her very presence wrapped around him like a warm hug.

"Talk to me, Jonathon."

He worked his response around in his mind, considered each word carefully. "I think it's safe to say we will never be rid of my father. He is determined to tie his legacy into mine."

Jonathon held Fanny's stare, willing her to understand the meaning behind his words.

She simply blinked at him.

"That is something that must never come to pass. Joshua Greene will not have the opportunity to poison another generation. I won't allow it."

His bone-deep sorrow was mirrored on Fanny's face. "What…what are you saying?" she asked.

"I will not, under any inducement, father a child."

Alarm shot through Fanny, making her head grow dizzy and her stomach churn. She was helpless when confronted with Jonathon's determined reasoning.

Joshua Greene will not have the opportunity to poison another generation.

She searched desperately for a compelling argument to change her husband's mind. She couldn't think of one. It was an impossible situation, because a part of her understood—and sympathized—with Jonathon's decision.

But it was a decision made in the heat of the moment, after a very tense encounter.

"My father taught me that decisions must always be made from a place of strength, not emotion. Thus, we shall table this conversation until we are both feeling a little less emotional."

Giving him no chance to argue, she hopped to her feet and brushed off her skirt. She managed to take one step, two. By the third, Jonathon's voice stopped her.

"I won't change my mind, Fanny. It is a decision I made long before I met you."

She slowly pivoted around to meet his gaze. She found herself staring at his chest. When had he risen to his feet?

Craning her neck, she attempted her brightest smile. "Perhaps, one day, you will change your mind. I can be quite persuasive."

It was the wrong thing to say.

His guard went up, the invisible wall between them as impenetrable as if constructed out of granite.

"I meant what I said. Judge Greene's wickedness will not influence another generation."

"We will deny him access to our children."

"He will find a way. Take, for example, today's sequence of events. He managed to get to you."

She had no ready response.

Jonathon pounced on her momentary silence. "The only way to ensure he doesn't get to our children would be for us to move our main residence to another city. Are you willing to leave your home, your family, *your mother* so that we can have a family of our own?"

His voice sounded so empty, so devoid of emotion.

"We can find a way. With God all things are possible. We cannot let your father win. We can—"

"Can we?"

Fanny's heart dropped to her toes. Her husband had become an immovable force. What else could she say to sway him?

Nothing. There was nothing that would change his mind.

Her stomach took a sickening roll, the nausea so profound she had to take several breaths to keep from being sick. "Do you not want a child with me?"

He blew out a frustrated hiss of air.

Fanny used his brief silence to firm her own resolve. "Jonathon. Do you not want to see a child created from the both of us? Half you, half me, a human being uniquely made from our union?"

Such grief washed across his face Fanny thought he would capitulate rather than give in to the loss.

Any moment now, he would agree their child—the one only they could create together—was worth every risk, including the risk of his father's interference in their lives.

"You're right, Fanny. We should table this discussion. I have work waiting for me downstairs."

Looking as miserable as she felt, he walked around her and headed to the foyer.

"Jonathon, wait."

He paused, hand on the doorknob.

"Will you at least think about what I said?"

"My mind is made up." Turning around slowly, he studied her with eyes she could not read. It had been months since he'd given her that impenetrable look.

"I will sire no children," he said. "I told you this before we married."

This time, Fanny didn't need to read his expression to know he wouldn't budge on the matter. She heard the stubborn resolve in his voice.

Well, she was a Mitchell. Stubbornness was a hereditary trait that came part and parcel with the name. "How will you prevent me from conceiving a child? Will you—"

He never let her finish. Moving with lightning speed, he closed the distance between them. She scarcely had time to breathe before she found herself enfolded in her husband's arms.

"I want a child with you, Fanny. I want an entire houseful. I want a family and a lifetime of happiness, but I *cannot* risk the possibility of Greene's poisonous influence on another generation."

Hope burst in her heart.

She knew what to say. She *finally* knew exactly what

to say. "You keep speaking of your father's influence. But he's had no bearing on who you've become. I have seen you in every situation imaginable. I know who you are when you're tired and pushed to the limit. I know who you are when you are feeling lighthearted and amused. I even know who you are when your family is threatened. I saw it today in that alley."

His arms tightened around her.

She pressed her advantage. "The only power your father holds over us is what we surrender to him. I beg you, do not let him win."

Jonathon set her away from him. His throat working, he swallowed several times. "I have to go."

"Will you at least think about what I said?" she asked again.

He tilted his head as if considering her words. "Yes."

Striding away from her, he didn't speak again. A heartbeat later, the door shut behind him with a firm click.

Just like that, he was gone. With nothing between them solved.

Fanny's mouth trembled and she sobbed, just once.

"I love you," she whispered to the empty room, wishing she'd had the courage to say the words to Jonathon's face.

Would it have made a difference?

She would never know.

Her husband must come around to her way of thinking on his own, or not at all, and certainly not because she'd manipulated him with tender words of love.

A wave of heat lifted up from her stomach, making her head spin. She had to reach out and steady herself on a nearby table, or else give in to the nausea that had plagued her on and off all week.

She and Jonathon were at an impasse, with each of

them set on their own course for the future and no hope of changing the other's mind.

Could their marriage survive?

Could Fanny survive?

Jonathon's nearness, without his full commitment to their marriage, would tear her apart bit by bit. To see him, to speak to him, but never to be close to him again would prove torture.

And what would happen to him?

He would pull away from her and distance himself completely, first physically, then emotionally. Joshua Greene's legacy would live on in the worst possible way imaginable.

Fanny hurt for her husband. *Lord, what do I do?*

She sank to her knees and did the only thing she could. She prayed.

Chapter Twenty

Jonathon charged into his office and slammed the door behind him with a wood-splintering crack. He moved around his desk, his mind still upstairs with Fanny. If he were a less cynical man he would say his wife had looked at him moments ago with love in her eyes.

Maybe it was wrong, or even selfish of him to wish it were true, but if Fanny loved him, there must be more good in him than bad. More Marc Dupree than Joshua Greene.

Fanny had claimed his father had no bearing on who'd he become. Jonathon wanted to believe her. He wanted the promise of long, happy years as her husband. He wanted to love her with everything inside him, as a man loved his woman.

It was true, then. He loved Fanny. He loved his wife.

So many impulses flooded him. He wanted to rush back upstairs and profess his feelings.

He'd told her the truth just now. He desperately wanted to know the wonder of having a child with her, of staring into the face of a precious baby, equally comprised of them both. Which actually made his point for him.

Jonathon was the product of the people who'd made him, half his mother and half his father.

You are also the Lord's child.

The thought swept through him with such strength he collapsed onto the chair behind his desk.

He wasn't an accident. He wasn't a mistake. He'd come to grips with that, in his heart and in his head. But he couldn't run from his past, couldn't deny that any child he created with Fanny would also be Joshua Greene's grandchild.

Fanny claimed his father could wield only the power they surrendered to him. Perhaps she was right.

Perhaps it was time for Jonathon to put the past behind him once and for all. He needed to speak with Greene, set a few things straight. He would do so now.

Just as he stood, a knock came at his door.

"Enter."

His assistant quickly pushed into the room, a harried expression on his face. "An urgent telegram has arrived for you from San Francisco."

Jonathon read the short missive, felt his stomach drop. A main water pipe had broken, flooding the entire first floor. "I'll need to leave at once."

"I'll make the arrangements." Burke paused at the door, tilted his head as if studying a difficult puzzle. "Will you be traveling alone, Mr. Hawkins, or will your wife be accompanying you on the journey to California?"

The question took him by surprise. Jonathon hadn't thought to have Fanny accompany him. Now that idea was in his head, he rolled it around. Once they took care of the problem at the hotel, he and Fanny could stay a few extra days in the city.

Jonathon could show his wife San Francisco, the city he'd found fascinating enough to build his fourth hotel there. He could take Fanny to all his favorite places. They could eat at five-star restaurants and walk hand in hand on the shores of the bay. He would fall in love with her all over again. When they retired for the evening, he wouldn't be able to keep his distance from the woman he loved with all his heart.

But the matter of children wasn't yet settled. There could be no more marital relations until final decisions were made.

Perhaps it was best to leave Fanny at home. Time away might actually help the situation.

"I will be traveling alone," he told his assistant, who stood patiently waiting for his response.

"Very good, Mr. Hawkins."

"Once you make the arrangements for my trip, alert Mrs. Singletary of the problem at the San Francisco Hotel Dupree." The widow owned one-quarter of his hotel empire. This situation affected her as much as Jonathon.

"I'll head to her house this afternoon and give her the news myself."

"I'm sure she'll appreciate that." Jonathon didn't need to give further instructions to his assistant. Burke Galloway already knew what to do in his absence.

When he was alone once more, Jonathon gathered the necessary papers and other accoutrements he would need to conduct business in San Francisco for the next several weeks.

All that was left was to go upstairs and pack his clothes.

Fanny was just coming out of the washroom when he stepped inside their suite. She'd restyled her hair and her features looked clean and bright, as if she'd recently splashed water on her face.

Jonathon had always thought his wife beautiful, but

right now she glowed. In the way spring chased away winter, she'd chased away his loneliness and had brought light into his life. He didn't want to lose her.

"Oh, Jonathon." She ran to him and flung her arms around his waist. "I knew you'd come back."

She sounded as if he'd been gone for months, when in reality it had been just shy of a half hour.

"There's a problem at the San Francisco Hotel Dupree." He set her away from him and briefly explained the situation with the water pipe. "I have to leave town immediately."

"Of course you do. Something this major requires your personal attention."

She was so understanding, so calm, his love for her swelled in his chest. He wanted to hold her close, to make promises, to tell her that he could be the man she needed, and she could have the life she'd always dreamed of—with him. Only him.

But there was still too much uncertainty and darkness inside his bitter soul, none of which he could allow to spill onto her.

"Would you…" Studying the runner at her feet, she dug her toe into the swirling pattern. "Would you like me to help you pack?"

"No." Emotion coiled in his muscles, tightened in his stomach. He speared a hand through his hair, shocked at the raw, shattered tone of his own voice.

Her head lifted, revealing the hurt in her eyes.

"Oh." She looked away. "All right. I will leave you to it, then."

She turned toward the door, but he caught her by the hand. "I don't need help packing, but I would very much like you to keep me company."

Her smile came lightning fast. "I would like that, too."

* * *

Fanny stood at the threshold of Jonathon's dressing room and silently watched him pack. His movements were stiff and impatient as he filled a medium-sized valise with various articles of clothing and personal items.

She knew he was still upset, but he'd erected a hard exterior to hide behind. The one he'd once worn as naturally as a medieval knight wore his suit of armor.

Was the cause of her husband's distance their conversation about children? Or was the problem with the San Francisco hotel the source?

Perhaps it was a little of both.

The thought of him leaving her with the tension still so strong between them was breaking her heart. She feared if he left Denver now, their marriage might never be able to recover.

Surely, he must be struggling with similar thoughts. And yet he hadn't asked her to join him on this trip. Fanny fought to remain outwardly calm, even as terror slid an icy chill down her spine.

"Why are you letting your father win?"

"I'm not leaving town because of my father. I told you why I have to go."

Her heart began to thump fast and hard and her stomach twisted in another sickening knot of dread. She thought she might be ill, right here, in her husband's dressing room.

She pulled in several tight breaths until the terrible sensation passed.

"Take me with you." She spoke so softly she wondered if he heard her.

Her doubts were dispelled when he looked up, his hand hovering over the contents of his luggage. "That wouldn't be wise."

"Why not?"

With a quick sweep of his hand, he shut the valise. "We need this time apart." Face expressionless, he secured the buckles. "To decide, individually, what we want from our marriage."

How could they decide such a thing individually? Marriage was a partnership, with two people making decisions together.

He was leaving her. Nothing else explained his refusal to take her with him.

Something bleak and angry rose up from her soul. The depths of the emotion would shock everyone who knew her, perhaps even Jonathon himself. It certainly shocked her. Enough that she again thought she might be sick.

She swallowed back the nausea. "You mean *you* need time away from *me* to decide what you want for your future. I already know what I want. Take me with you."

He moved past her and set the suitcase on the floor in the hallway. Then, eyes grim, he made the short trek back to where she stood. "There is only one thing that would induce me to ask you to join me."

"Name it."

"You come with me as my business associate, not my wife."

Sucking in a shocked breath, Fanny reared back. "You can't mean—"

But he did. She saw it in his cold, distant expression.

Casting aside all pride, she lunged herself at her husband.

As if expecting the move, he caught her against his chest. Her pleasure at being near him trumped the terrible pain swirling in her stomach. She was all feeling at that moment, her emotions closer to the surface than she wished to show her husband.

Recklessly, she pressed her mouth to his. His hold tightened around her and he kissed her back.

I love you. I love you. I love you. Her mind silently screamed the words in her head, over and over and over again. Then came the more desperate plea. *Don't leave me.*

Did she have the courage to make the humiliating request?

It was some time before Jonathon eventually set her away from him. Heavy emotion weighed heavy between them.

They both gasped for breath and stared at one another, wide-eyed.

Fanny's heart was full of love for her husband and she knew he loved her in return. She saw it in his tortured expression, in the rapid rise and fall of his chest.

"Take me with you," she repeated, "as your wife."

"You know my terms."

She couldn't go with him as only a business associate. But she feared if he went to San Francisco without her, he might never return. Not the man she married, at any rate. A stranger would appear in his place, and then nothing would ever be the same. "And you know mine."

He nodded. "We'll talk more when I get back." He brushed a brief kiss to her forehead. "I'll return as quickly as I can, I promise you that."

She thought she might weep.

He picked up the valise and maneuvered around her. "I will send a telegraph alerting you to the date of my return."

She made no sound, made no attempt to respond. She was too stunned that he would give up on her, *on them*, like this. She was cold to the bone. No amount of rubbing her arms warmed them.

Dimly, she heard Jonathon's footsteps move down the hallway, through the parlor, then into the foyer. The door opened and closed with a soft click. That was it.

Her husband was gone.

Only then, when she was completely alone, did Fanny acknowledge the nausea roiling in her stomach. She rushed into the washroom and gave in to the churning illness.

At least Jonathon wasn't here to see her brought low.

As the first week of Jonathon's absence turned into two, and he still didn't return or send a telegram, Fanny's sickness grew worse. She found herself wanting to sleep all the time. The sight of food made her ill. The only thing that seemed to settle her stomach was weak tea and a few bites of toast.

This is what grief feels like, she thought, wishing Jonathon would come home soon. They couldn't heal their rift if he wasn't here.

In the meantime, she put on a brave face. It proved quite a feat to swallow her nausea this morning, but Fanny eventually managed to get herself dressed for the day. She made it down to her office, and even managed to get some work done.

Not more than an hour into reviewing next month's employee schedules, she found the names and numbers beginning to blur. Though it was barely past ten o'clock, Fanny decided she needed to retreat to her room for a quick lie down.

She'd barely set down her quill when Callie poked her head into the office. "I've come to unchain you from your desk."

Fanny sat back in her chair and studied her sister.

"You have remarkable timing. I was just contemplating the wisdom of a short break."

"Then I'm not disturbing you."

"Not at all." She stood, but moved too fast and nearly lost her balance. Leaning on her desk, she calmed her spinning head with a few deep breaths.

She forced a smile for her sister.

Smiling back, Callie glided into the room, her tiny, slightly rounded belly tenting her dress in a most becoming way. She was nearly six months along, but didn't look more than three.

"You are looking quite well," Fanny told her sister, dropping her gaze over Callie's emerald-green dress with the pretty ivory trim.

"Oh, Fanny, I am feeling very well, indeed, especially now that the horrible morning sickness is behind me." She made a face that reminded Fanny of the time when they were children and she'd dared Callie to eat an entire lemon.

"Was it really so terrible, those first few months?" Fanny would give anything to experience morning sickness, knowing it heralded the reward of giving birth to Jonathon's child.

"Horrible doesn't begin to describe it. For months I could keep nothing down but weak tea and toast. But now…" She twirled in a happy, laughing circle, her joy as rich as if she'd just been freed from a prison. "I have more energy than ever before and the terrible bouts of dizziness are completely gone."

Fanny's mind latched on to several words, her heart filling with the ache of desperate fear. Weak tea and toast? Lack of energy? Dizziness?

Her hand flew to her stomach. Could she be…was it even possible…

Of course it was possible.

Fear, hope, anger, joy, too many emotions to count tumbled through her. She wanted to laugh. She wanted to cry. She wanted to give in to every emotion all at once, and then start over again.

She was carrying Jonathon's child.

Just for a moment, she let herself revel in the wonder of it. Her eyes filled with tears. She'd been doing that a lot lately, getting overly emotional over the tiniest things.

A baby is not a tiny thing.

No, a child was a blessing straight from God.

How would Jonathon take the news? Would he think she'd done this on purpose, to trap him?

The first tendril of anguish twined through her happiness.

"...and it's such a beautiful spring day." Callie's voice came at Fanny as if from a great distance. "Let's head outdoors and enjoy the living harmony of—"

She broke off and rushed to Fanny.

"What's wrong? You've grown pale as chalk."

"I...I need to sit down."

Callie guided her to the chair behind her desk. "I'll get you some water."

"No." Fanny stopped her. "I just need a moment to catch my breath. While I do, would you describe again what you experienced during the early months after you realized you were carrying Reese's child?"

"Are you..." Callie's hand flew to your mouth. "Fanny, do you think you're—"

"You said you were tired a lot? And could stomach only weak tea and toast."

Eyes wide with mounting excitement, Callie nodded. "There were other symptoms, as well."

"Such as...?"

Blushing furiously, she explained about the physical changes in her body, changes Fanny had experienced but had thought were due to the strain of her husband's extended absence.

"Oh, Callie. I...I think I'm going to have Jonathon's baby."

"Why, that's wonderful news." Her sister hopped to her feet and pulled her into a fierce hug.

Tears of joy, of fear, of wonder formed in Fanny's eyes and spilled over in a choking sob.

"Do you know what this means?" Callie twirled away from her. "Our children will grow up together. They will be as close as siblings."

"That..." Fanny snuffled into a handkerchief "...sounds perfectly delightful."

She only hoped Jonathon agreed.

Chapter Twenty-One

Jonathon arrived back at the Denver Hotel Dupree in the middle of the night. He'd been gone fifteen and a half days, which by his estimation was fifteen days too many. It had taken the cleanup crews longer to repair the damage to the hotel than he'd have liked. But construction was finally back on schedule, putting them only two weeks behind their original opening date.

The consequences of the water pipe bursting could have been worse, he knew, and could have kept him away from Fanny for months. But he was home now, home being wherever his beautiful wife laid her head. He'd meant to send her a wire warning of his arrival, just as he'd promised. But he'd been too eager to get home to stop at the telegraph office in San Francisco.

Jonathon let himself quietly into the suite, keeping his movements light, quick and methodical, so as not to wake Fanny.

Fanny.

His wife. His love.

His heart.

He needed her in his life. The days away from her had been torture.

Would he eventually destroy her? Or could he find a way to be a blessing in her life, as she was in his?

Unsure of the reception he would receive, especially at this hour, he went into his dressing room and took his time unpacking his valise. He could easily afford to hire someone to do these types of menial tasks, but he never wanted to forget his humble roots. Ironic, since he'd nearly allowed himself to forget the most important influences in his life.

Reaching inside his jacket, he pulled out the photograph of the original Hotel Dupree that Marc had given him on the morning of his wedding. *A reminder of where you really come from.*

Jonathon came from poverty. His mother had been a prostitute, his father an adulterer. But their influence had only partly made him into the man he was today. Marc Dupree had influenced him, as well. He'd taught him that character was the sum total of choices and habits.

Jonathon had a big choice before him. He could break the cycle of sin rampant in his family, or he could succumb to fear and live half a life.

He needed to see Fanny.

Assuming she'd been upset enough to separate herself from him, he checked the bedroom he'd given her on their wedding night. She wasn't there.

Lord, let this be a good sign. Let her be in the room we've shared since our wedding night.

His confidence grew, but was immediately replaced with dread. He'd boarded the train to San Francisco with matters between them unsettled. *Badly done, Hawkins.*

If Fanny had moved out of their home, he had only himself to blame.

He couldn't let her go. If she wasn't in this suite, he would find her and bring her back.

He moved to his bedroom, paused in the doorway and found himself struggling for every breath. He knew this sensation. It was the feeling of a narrow escape.

Bathed in a ribbon of moonlight, Fanny slept in his bed—*their* bed—in the spot Jonathon usually occupied, as if she wanted to be close to him even in his absence.

His heart swelled.

Barely able to move under the weight of pleasure that gripped him, he entered the room slowly and stepped to the end of the bed.

For several long breaths, he merely watched his wife slumber. Her long hair was fanned out across the pillow beneath her head. The golden waves appeared silver in the pale moonlight.

She was curled up like a cat, her hand resting protectively over her stomach.

This is what she will look like carrying my child.

The thought slipped through his mind with quiet ease.

In that moment, Jonathon admitted how deeply in love he was with his wife. Fanny had changed everything. He wondered what his life would be like without her in it. The thought was too dismal to contemplate.

After the wedding ceremony, her father had taken Jonathon aside for some friendly marital advice. Cyrus Mitchell had told him that the measure of a happy marriage is what a husband is willing to give up for his wife.

At the time, Jonathon hadn't fully understood what his father-in-law meant. Now, he knew. Love called for sacrifice. In San Francisco, Jonathon had come to the realization the he was willing to sacrifice anything, everything, for Fanny.

She wanted a child, the child only they could create together. Could Jonathon sacrifice his doubts and fears in order to give her what she wanted?

If love called for sacrifice, then faith called for surrender. Did Jonathon have the courage to surrender his fears, his very will and release the future into God's hands?

He didn't know.

Rubbing his palm across his tired, gritty eyes, he decided now was not the time for deep thinking. He needed sleep.

No, he needed his wife.

He sat on the bed and brushed her hair off her face. "Fanny, my love, I'm home."

Slowly, she came awake.

"Jonathon?" Her sooty eyelashes blinked in confusion. "Is it really you?"

He leaned over and kissed her cheek. "Shh, go back to sleep."

As if he hadn't spoke at all, she sat up, scrubbed the sleep from her eyes. "What time is it?"

"Just past midnight."

"Oh." She hid a yawn behind her hand. "I... Did I know you were coming home tonight?"

She yawned again. It was then he noticed the purple shadows beneath her eyes, shadows that came from too many sleepless nights.

"Lie down." He set his hand on her shoulder and gently pushed her back down on the bed. "We'll talk in the morning."

She didn't argue, but settled her head atop the pillow. A little hum of pleasure rumbled in her throat.

"If this is only a dream," she mumbled, "and you really aren't here with me..." her eyelashes fluttered closed "...then don't wake me again."

Within seconds her breathing evened out.

Jonathon leaned over and kissed her again, on her forehead, her cheek, her lips.

"I love you," he said to her sleeping form, promising himself he would say the words again when she was fully awake.

Fanny awoke to a cold, empty bed. Remembering the events of the night before, she propped herself up on her elbows and looked around.

Jonathon had come home.

Or had he?

She searched the room, looking for signs of his presence. Quickly donning her robe, she searched the bedroom, then Jonathon's dressing room.

The smell of strong coffee and the crisp sound of newspaper pages turning had her padding barefoot into the main living area of the suite. She drew in a quick, happy sigh at the familiar scene.

Jonathon sat behind the *Denver Chronicle*, completely hidden from her view. Before him, the table was laden with a large tray of eggs and bacon, buttered croissants and all manner of pastries.

The combination of scents made her stomach churn.

Bracing herself against the door frame, Fanny placed a hand over her mouth and willed her stomach to calm.

Once she had the nausea under control, she slowly, carefully, lowered her hand. "Good morning, Jonathon."

The newspaper immediately dropped to the table. "Good morning."

For a long moment, she drank in the sight of her husband, already dressed impeccably for the day. He looked so handsome, his gaze more approachable than when he'd left town. She'd missed him terribly and couldn't think why she shouldn't tell him so. "I'm glad you're home."

"I missed you, Fanny."

That was all it took. Desperate for her husband, she

was across the room in a handful of steps. He was up on his feet in the time it took her to get to him.

And then they were embracing as if they'd been apart an entire year rather than a few weeks.

They talked over one another, alternating between apologies and kisses.

Laughing, they separated at last.

He cupped her face in his hands and simply gazed into her eyes. Love swelled in her heart and she felt her knees tremble. Then, to her horror, little spots played before her eyes.

She was going to faint. No, much worse, she was going to be sick. She swallowed, but the nauseating sensation only strengthened.

"Fanny. What's wrong?" Jonathon moved his hands to her shoulders. "Color is draining out of your face right before my eyes."

"I…feel…sick." She'd barely gotten the words out of her mouth before bile rose into her throat.

She rushed to the water basin.

Jonathon was by her side in an instant, rubbing her back and whispering soothing words. Her dignity hanging by a thread, she attempted to straighten.

"No, stay there a moment." Working quickly, as if he'd done this before, he dipped a linen napkin in a glass of water on the table and placed it over the back of her neck.

The cool relief brought tears to her eyes.

"There now," he soothed. "Let's get you seated."

With a gentle yet firm grip he guided her to a chair far too near the breakfast table. One inhalation and she was back at the basin again.

Again, Jonathon placed the cold, wet cloth on her neck.

"The food," she gasped. "Get it out of here. The smell is making me ill."

He gave her an odd look but did as she requested.

Once the room was empty of the offensive odors, Jonathon sat beside her and searched her face. "Are you still feeling sick?"

She nodded.

His expression filled with masculine concern.

"Don't worry." She tugged her bottom lip between her teeth. "It'll pass by early afternoon."

"How can you possibly know that?"

"I have been having bouts of queasiness every day since you left, but only in the mornings."

Her heart dropped as she watched understanding dawn on his face. "You are—"

" —with child. Yes, Jonathon, I am carrying your baby."

She saw the shock in his eyes, and then the fear. "You are certain?"

"Yes." She lowered her gaze and plucked at the lace trim on her sleeve. "Dr. Shane confirmed it last week."

"I have to go." Jonathon stood abruptly.

"Don't you want to discuss this? I just told you I'm with child, *your child.*"

"Believe me, Fanny, I want to discuss this at great length. But I have something I must take care of first."

Risking another bout of nausea, she jumped to her feet and laid her head on his chest.

He smoothed his hand across her hair, the stroke as gentle as a whisper. She felt weak from her last bout of sickness and so terribly desperate. She wanted to fight for Jonathon, for the future of their marriage, but she feared she would somehow push him away if she said too much.

But what if she didn't say enough?

Clutching at his shirt, she whispered the truth in her heart. "I love you."

His chest tensed beneath her cheek, but he didn't say the words back. He didn't say anything at all.

Terrified of what she would find, she carefully stepped back and looked into Jonathon's face.

Fear rose up to choke her. A stranger stood before her.

"Are you not happy with the news?"

"Of course I'm happy."

His closed expression belied his words. From the start of their acquaintance, he'd warned Fanny he didn't want children.

She'd ignored his wishes, thinking she could one day change his mind, and now, *now*, she'd trapped him with the very thing he least wanted in this world.

Her hand instinctively covered her stomach in a protective gesture. Jonathon's gaze followed the movement.

After releasing a slow exhale, he said, "I'll be back shortly."

Dread burned in her throat. "Where…where are you going?"

Jonathon set out across the room, wrenched open the door and then looked at her over his shoulder. "To my father's."

His father's? "But…but why?"

"I must ensure our child is protected from my past." The steel of his determination was threaded in his voice. "There is only one way."

"What are you going to do?" She was talking to an empty room, with nothing but the slam of the door reverberating off the walls.

Chapter Twenty-Two

Too agitated to sit inside a closed carriage, Jonathon covered the five blocks between the hotel and his father's residence on foot. He moved with ground-eating strides, propelled by urgency and a need to settle the future—by way of the past.

A cold mist hung in the morning air, mimicking the gloom in his heart. He hunched his shoulders against the chill and rounded the bend, putting the Hotel Dupree at his back. The nine-story building was the crown jewel in Jonathon's hotel empire. An empire he'd created with sweat, perseverance and a determination to prove he was better than the man who'd fathered him.

He crossed the street and increased his pace. At the end of the block, he caught sight of his reflection in the shop window on his right. It was only the dimmest of images. But it was enough to send shock waves quivering through him.

He saw his father. He saw his half brother. He saw his future, if he chose to cling to past wounds and the darkness that came with them. Frowning at his image, he touched his jaw. The same shape as his father's and his brother's, the three of them similar on the outside.

But on the inside, thanks to God's mercy, Jonathon was a new creation. And he was going to be a father.

Fanny was carrying his child. Fascinated at the wonder of it, he felt a smile touch his lips. Then it instantly fell away. He'd responded to the news badly. He would make it up to his wife, *after* he reconciled with his past.

A light dusting of snow covered the ground. If Fanny was with him she'd point out the sound of the crystals crunching under their feet.

Just thinking about his wife brought him a moment of calm.

Fanny had accepted him without question. No condemnation. No judgment. She'd believed in him from the very beginning and had never let the knowledge of his past color her feelings for him. She'd shown him grace and mercy, and he'd failed her, by always holding a portion of himself back, afraid the ugliness of his past would somehow rub off on her.

He would spend the rest of his life showing her and their children the same unconditional love she'd always shown him.

But first, he had to deal with his father.

After being admitted into the house by the judge's impassive butler, Jonathon was left cooling his heels in the foyer.

He glanced around, remembering the last time he'd stood in this cavernous hall, when he'd been a boy full of anguish and desperation and lost hope. For a moment, he disappeared in the memory. He'd come seeking help for his mother, but also secretly hoping for acceptance from the man who'd fathered him.

He'd left empty-handed on both accounts.

Ever since that day, Jonathon had been trying to prove he was nothing like Joshua Greene, and in the process, had nearly condemned himself to a lonely, loveless life. But then Fanny had come along.

She'd brought warmth into his life. She'd brought love and chased away the aching loneliness that had always been a part of him.

He wanted to leave this cold house, to return to his wife and tell her he was blissfully happy with the news of their child. He couldn't allow himself that luxury. He had unfinished business with his father.

A shadow oscillated over the marble floor, elongated and then formed into a man. The butler had returned.

Posture erect, he directed Jonathon to follow him to a long, empty corridor. "He is waiting for you in his private study."

Jonathon lifted a questioning eyebrow.

"It is the room at the end of the hallway on the left."

"Thank you." Minutes later, Jonathon stood before a pair of gleaming ebony doors.

He nearly changed his mind. What he was about to do would tie him to this man until one of them died. The irony was that he would be tied to him, anyway. They shared the same blood.

But they didn't have to share the same legacy.

Reaching into the pocket of his coat, Jonathon pulled out the photograph of the original Hotel Dupree. *A reminder of where you really come from.*

A rush of—*something*—skittered though him. Guilt, maybe? Regret? For most of his childhood he'd dreamed of having a real home, with a mother *and* a father to care for him. He'd found those things at Charity House, but had turned his back on them after his fateful visit to this house.

It still amazed him that neither Marc nor Laney held

his youthful rebellion against him. Today, he would do his best to honor them, as a child would honor his parents.

He entered Joshua Green's private sanctuary without knocking. The smell of expensive tobacco and freshly polished wood greeted him. His father did not.

The silver head bent over a stack of papers on the polished surface of the desk did not lift, not even when Jonathon cleared his throat.

"So you have decided to grace me with your presence." At last, Greene looked up, a sneer curling his lips. "Yet you stand there glaring at me in silence. Am I to guess at the reason for your visit?"

The question was typical Joshua Greene, part arrogant superiority, part condescension. If Jonathon hadn't been studying the hard planes of his father's face, he might have missed the wariness in the other man's eyes.

A part of him wanted to prolong this moment, to wield the power he held over a man who'd filled his youth with nothing but misery. He could even choose to leave, and prevent Greene from ever having what he most desired.

For years, Jonathon had carried the weight of his father's rejection inside him. But the Lord had gifted him with a remarkable woman as his wife. Because of Fanny, because of the child she would soon give him, Jonathon had surpassed the need for vengeance. All that was left was one final act of mercy.

"I have come to make a concession."

The judge's eyes narrowed. Clearly sensing a trick, he carefully pushed himself to his feet. "Very well, go ahead."

Now that the time had come, Jonathon needed a moment to gather the words in his head. He moved to stand by the stone hearth. A fire spit and snapped, spreading warmth and a pleasant, smoky aroma through the room.

He turned and looked once more at Judge Greene.

For his entire life, Jonathon had told himself he didn't care what this man thought of him. Finally, it was true. He *didn't* care. The past no longer held him captive.

He was free.

"I came to say I have no objection to you naming my firstborn son as your heir."

Proving the cold, cynical nature of his heart, Greene's eyes turned hard as flint. "I am assuming you have stipulations."

"No stipulations." Certainty laced Jonathon's words. "No conditions."

An invisible weight lifted from his heart.

The judge's grim expression did not change. "The last we spoke, you were determined to prevent this. Why the sudden change of heart?"

"I am not doing this for you, but for my wife." His marriage to Fanny would never be whole if Jonathon didn't release his anger and hatred for this man.

Forgiveness was hard, and came at a price, but the cost of bitterness was far steeper. "That's all I came to say."

With that, Jonathon left the room, strode down the empty hallway and out the front door.

Dressed for the day, and dreadfully worried for Jonathon's welfare, Fanny sat on the overstuffed settee, hugging her knees to her chest. She felt tears forming again. After an hour of crying she would have thought she was through, but obviously not. Weary in both mind and spirit, she felt sorrow tear through her.

She would never stop loving Jonathon, would never stop thinking of him as her husband and the great love of her life, but she would not force him to stay with her.

She would rather let him go than trap him in a marriage he didn't want.

He'd said he was happy about the news of their child, but he hadn't acted happy. In truth, he hadn't been able to leave the suite fast enough.

She had no idea what he was doing at his father's, and that scared her. Sobbing, she buried her face in her hands.

The sound of a key twisting in the lock had her on her feet in an instant. Not wanting him to know she'd been crying, she swiped furiously at her face. But then she realized there was no reason to hide her emotions from her husband.

He'd married her. He'd agreed to love her and cherish her through sickness and in health and, she amended silently in her head, at the sight of messy, unpleasant tears.

The door swung open and—one breath, two—Jonathon entered the foyer. Their eyes met across the room.

Pocketing the key, he crossed to her.

"Jonathon," she breathed.

He cupped her chin in his hands and kissed her on the mouth. "I love you, Fanny. I should have said it to you on our wedding day and every day thereafter."

The words sank past her anguish and settled into the depths of her soul. The pain and fear in her heart vanished.

"I love you, too." She pressed her face into his shoulder. "I'll never stop loving you."

They clung to each other for several minutes, basking in the joy of simply being together. At last, Jonathon guided her to the settee and sat beside her.

"There's so much I want to say, starting with I'm sorry. I hurt you, Fanny, and there's no excuse for that. If you'll let me, I'll spend the rest of my life making it up to you. And our child."

Hope blossomed in her heart. "What are you saying?"

He kissed the palm of her hand. "I deeply regret how I handled your announcement earlier." He leaned closer, until his lips brushed her ear. "Tell me the news again."

The happy light in his eyes when he sat back gave her the courage to speak with a strong, confident voice. "Jonathon, my love, we're going to have a baby."

He let out a hoot of delight, and then yanked her into his arms. "Praise the Lord. You've made me a very happy man, Francine Mary Mitchell Hawkins."

"You…you are truly pleased about this child?"

"Overjoyed." He kissed her tenderly on the lips.

She wrapped her arms around him and kissed him back, fiercely, gleefully, this man she loved with all her heart.

He pulled away first, only far enough to whisper in her ear once again. "I am here to stay, my precious Fanny. I wish to raise an entire brood of children with you."

She believed him. But one thing still needed saying.

"You're not your father." Of all the things she wanted her husband to know, this was the most important. She would keep saying the words, keep reminding him, every day for the rest of their lives if necessary, until he was convinced he was his own man. "You're nothing like him."

"No, I'm not."

There was something different in his voice, something she'd missed before this moment, a note she'd never heard before. He sounded freer, easier…liberated.

Fanny studied Jonathon's face. He looked as if a heavy burden had been lifted from his shoulders. "What exactly happened at Judge Greene's house this morning?"

"I'll tell you everything. But look outside—it's a beautiful, crisp morning with a light snowfall." He tugged her toward the door. "Come, my love, join me for a walk and I will reveal all."

Laughing, she grabbed her coat and hurried out of the suite with him.

They strolled through the morning streets of Denver as they had hundreds of times before. All around them, people went about their business. No one paid them any attention.

Jonathon directed her to the small park where he'd brought her the day after Mrs. Singletary's ball. That had been when he'd officially started courting her, though she hadn't realized it at the time.

As he'd done that day all those months ago, he brushed off the wrought-iron bench and then directed her to sit.

"I'm happy you came home, Jonathon. However—" she gave him her fiercest glower "—never, ever leave me behind like that again."

"No, never again. I'm sorry, Fanny."

The look of utter remorse turned her heart to mush. "You're forgiven."

"It's that simple?"

She quoted a portion of her favorite Bible verse. "'Love bears all things and endures all things.'" She smiled. "Of course I forgive you. I forgave you before you boarded the train to San Francisco."

"You're a good woman. You deserve a good man."

"I deserve *you*."

Chuckling, he settled in beside her, then pulled her back against his chest and rested his chin on the top of her head.

They sat that way for several minutes. Fanny broke the silence first. "Will you tell me what happened at Judge Greene's house this morning?"

Jonathon drew in a breath. "His power over me has

been strong all my life, perhaps stronger than I ever knew. But you taught me that love is stronger."

She gave his hand an encouraging squeeze, but said nothing.

"When you told me you were with child, I knew there was only one way to release his hold over me, over us and our future generations."

"What did you do?"

"I didn't do anything, precisely. I told him…" Jonathon took a deep inhale, blew it out slowly. "I said if he wanted to name our firstborn son as his heir, he would get no objection from me."

She gasped at the implication of her husband's words. Pushing away from him, she twisted on the seat to stare at him. "You really told him that?"

"I realize I should have run it by you first." He gave her a repentant grimace. "I would understand if you are angry."

"Angry? I'm not angry. I'm proud of you. There are so many ways you could have handled your father's desire to name our son his heir. But instead of denying him, or threatening him, you gave him exactly what he wanted. You showed him grace."

"It was the only way I could break from the past."

Tears of happiness formed in her eyes. "Now you are free."

"I am free."

She threw herself at him.

He enfolded her in his arms.

"I love you, Jonathon, now and forever and always."

Smiling, he kissed her on the tip of her nose. "I love you, too, Fanny. More than I can ever put into words."

The sun chose that moment to split through a seam in the clouds. Fanny lifted her face toward the warmth before glancing once again at her husband. "What do you say we head back to the hotel and begin the rest of our lives as the happily married couple that we are?"

The corners of his mouth twitched. "We're going to have a full, sometimes frantic, mostly happy life together, with at least a half-dozen children underfoot."

"Only six?"

"All right, seven." He placed his palm flat on her stomach. "But we'll focus our love on this special blessing first."

"Oh yes." She covered his hand with hers. "This one first."

Epilogue

In a state of barely subdued terror, Jonathon paced outside Fanny's childhood bedroom on the Flying M ranch. Only moments before, he'd been banished by her mother and the other two women in the room, something to do with his tendency toward overreaction.

Admittedly, barking at the three women on more than one occasion to make his wife's pain stop—*now*—may have played a role in his expulsion.

He could only wonder what was happening inside that torture chamber disguised as an innocuous bedroom. The walls were thin enough that Jonathon could hear every sharp groan that came from Fanny, could feel every birthing pain that made her cry out in agony.

He'd never experienced this level of helplessness in his life.

Although he'd known the trip to her family's spread—their fifth in so many months—had seemed ill-timed this late in Fanny's confinement, there was something synergistic about her birthing their first child in the same room where she'd been born.

A screech of feminine anguish ripped into the unnatural stillness of the hallway. The last shreds of Jonathon's control snapped.

He lunged for the door.

A hand grabbed him by the shirt collar and bodily yanked him back. "That's it, you're done."

Jonathon strained against the inflexible grip at his neck.

Hunter pressed his face inches from his. "The expectant father needs to head outside and take a breath of fresh air."

Jonathon dug in his heels. "I'm not leaving my wife."

"She's in good hands." Reese Bennett Jr. spoke the words in his calm, lawyerly voice, which had defused many heated arguments at the negotiation table. "The women know what they're doing."

"That's a fact." Cyrus Mitchell agreed with his son-in-law, his shoulder carelessly propped against the wall.

Jonathon snarled at his father-in-law. "How can you be so calm?"

"The women have been through this countless times before. They haven't lost a mother or child yet."

It was the *yet* that sent Jonathon breaking free of Hunter's hold and sailing back toward the door.

"Enough." Fanny's father took charge. "You're coming with us."

He motioned to Hunter and Reese.

Giving Jonathon no chance to argue, the two men he'd come to think of as brothers dragged him down the stairs and tossed him out into the front yard.

Jonathon washed out his tight lungs with big, long gulps of air, then attempted to look around. The scenery was breathtaking. The barns were well maintained, the corral well tended. The roaming horses and cattle added to the picture of a large, successful Colorado ranch, as did the Rocky Mountains in the distance.

No matter how beautiful the setting was, abject terror remained alive inside him, nipping at him like tiny rodent teeth.

He strode back toward the house.

Cyrus barred his way. "Cool off, son. You're no help to your wife in your current state."

Shaking with pent-up frustration, Jonathon speared a hand through his hair. "I can't stand seeing Fanny in this kind of pain."

"Understandable." Fanny's father clasped a commiserating hand on his shoulder. "But as tough as this is to hear, what's happening inside that room upstairs is the natural way of things."

So everyone kept telling him.

Jonathon remembered silently scoffing at how the Mitchell brothers had hovered over their expectant wives. Turns out he was the hovering sort, as well.

Women didn't always survive pregnancy or childbirth.

Too overcome with a renewed surge of panic to stand by and helplessly wring his hands, he attempted to pray. But he couldn't focus his mind properly, so he sent up silent groans and wordless pleas.

Surely the Lord knew what was happening in that birthing room. Surely He was protecting Fanny and their child.

Another scream from the second floor sliced through the air. Jonathon broke out in a run.

Hunter tackled him to the ground, then hopped to his feet lightning quick and pressed his boot on Jonathon's chest. "Stay down or I'll make sure you're out cold for the rest of the day."

Rolling free, Jonathon scrambled to a standing position and glared at his brother-in-law, who was poised on the balls of his feet. Hunter's determined gaze communicated a silent message Jonathon fully understood.

He wasn't getting past Fanny's brother.

Grimacing, he glanced up at the second-floor window. *Please, Lord, let this be over for her soon.*

God answered his prayer a half hour later. Annabeth burst out the front door, a wide smile on her face.

Relief nearly brought Jonathon to his knees. "How is my wife?"

"Tired, but fine. May all the future births in this family go so well." The woman glided over to him and patted his cheek with affection. "Now, it's time you went upstairs and met your daughter."

"A daughter? I have a daughter?"

"She's beautiful. She has your dark hair and her mother's beautiful face and—"

Jonathon didn't need to hear the rest. He darted into the house and up the stairs three at a time.

He surged through the open doorway and froze a moment to take in the sight of his wife and brand-new daughter. He nearly wept in relief. Fanny was sitting up in bed, smiling one of her secret smiles that always managed to reach inside his heart and grip hard.

Someone had helped her bathe and change into a fresh nightgown. In her arms, she held a small bundle swaddled in soft cotton.

"We'll leave you three alone," Mrs. Mitchell said as she and Callie retreated from the room.

"Don't just stand there," Fanny said. "Come over here and say hello to your new daughter."

He gingerly moved to the bed and sat beside his wife.

Eyes stinging, he kissed her softly on the lips, then glanced down at the child in her arms. The tears came then, tears of wonder and joy. Their daughter was perfectly formed, fair-skinned like her mother, with a remarkable quantity of coal-black hair.

"What should we name her?" Fanny asked.

He'd already given the question considerable thought. "Mary Amelia Hawkins, after your mother and mine."

Fanny gave a delighted laugh. "We are of one mind, except for a small variance. I'm thinking Amelia Mary Hawkins has a much nicer ring to it."

"Either version will do. I'll leave you the final decision, since bringing her into this world was completely up to you." He settled in beside her, ran a fingertip down the infant's cheek. "You did amazing, Mrs. Hawkins."

Fanny grinned up at him. "I did, didn't I?"

He smiled into his wife's eyes. She'd brought light into his life, and now the future stretched before them with endless possibilities.

"Are you happy, Jonathon?"

"Unashamedly so. I love you, Fanny." He dropped a tender kiss to her forehead. "May the Lord continue to favor our family with His many blessings, now and in the days to come."

"What a lovely prayer." Her eyelids drooped.

"Before you drift off to sleep, I have a gift for you."

"Oh, Jonathon, I have everything I need."

He reached inside his jacket and pulled out the document Reese had given him upon their arrival.

Her eyes widened. "What in the world is that?"

"It's a deed in your name to a piece of land just north of here."

"But what will I do with my own piece of land?"

"We'll talk more after you've rested a bit."

"I want to know now."

He smiled. He would give this woman anything she asked of him.

"There's a run-down train depot on the property." He explained his original reasons for wanting to build on the land. "I hope you'll join me in creating a train stop to rival all stops. It will be our legacy, together."

He paused, thought of his mother, of the desperation that had led her to make bad decisions out of terrible choices. "We'll pay our employees a fair wage, give them on-the-job training, as well as provide room and board for them *and* their children."

"You've put a lot of thought into this."

"We could name the stop Mitchellville."

"I like it." Her smile lit her face from within. "But I have just one question."

"Ask me anything."

"When can we break ground?"

The question signified what he'd already known. Fanny was his perfect match and of a like mind in nearly everything that mattered. They were going to have a good life together. "We'll start building as soon as possible."

"Nice." She snuggled against him.

He kissed her nose, moved to her cheek and then finally landed on her mouth, lingering there for several long heartbeats.

Fanny was the heart of him, his ideal mate, his savvy business partner and the mother of his precious daughter.

Jonathon hadn't wanted a wife, and definitely hadn't thought a baby would ever be in his future. Now, he had both.

He had the family he'd always wanted but never believed could be his. Not a happy ending, no, but a happy beginning.

A *very* happy beginning.

* * * * *

Dear Reader,

I can scarcely believe this is the ninth book in my Charity House series, a series that started with a simple question. What did women who made their living in brothels do when they found themselves in the *family way*? The answer to that question brought me to the sad reality of baby farms in the Old West. And so began a unique set of stories focused around an orphanage for unplanned and often unwanted children. I hope you've enjoyed each book in the series as much as I've enjoyed writing them.

I must confess. Some books are harder to write than others. This one fell into the "others" category. In many ways, Jonathon's story was *all* the children's story. I wanted to do right by him and give him the happily-ever-after he deserved. Who better for him to end up with than a woman with the last name Mitchell? Now Jonathon has five brothers, a brother-in-law and a sister. His and Fanny's future, as well as their children's, will be filled with vast amounts of faith, hope and love. That's what I call a happy ending.

We've come full circle with this book. Many of you have sent emails asking if there will be more stories to come. Keep checking my website www.reneeryan.com and Facebook page ReneeRyanBooks for updates.

In the meantime, happy reading!
Cheers!

Renee

REQUEST YOUR FREE BOOKS!

2 FREE INSPIRATIONAL NOVELS
PLUS 2 *FREE* MYSTERY GIFTS

Love Inspired ® HISTORICAL

YES! Please send me 2 FREE Love Inspired® Historical novels and my 2 FREE mystery gifts (gifts are worth about $10). After receiving them, if I don't wish to receive any more books, I can return the shipping statement marked "cancel." If I don't cancel, I will receive 4 brand-new novels every month and be billed just $4.99 per book in the U.S. or $5.49 per book in Canada. That's a saving of at least 17% off the cover price. It's quite a bargain! Shipping and handling is just 50¢ per book in the U.S. and 75¢ per book in Canada.* I understand that accepting the 2 free books and gifts places me under no obligation to buy anything. I can always return a shipment and cancel at any time. Even if I never buy another book, the two free books and gifts are mine to keep forever.

102/302 IDN GH6Z

Name _____ (PLEASE PRINT)

Address _____ Apt. #

City _____ State/Prov. _____ Zip/Postal Code

Signature (if under 18, a parent or guardian must sign)

Mail to the **Reader Service**:
IN U.S.A.: P.O. Box 1867, Buffalo, NY 14240-1867
IN CANADA: P.O. Box 609, Fort Erie, Ontario L2A 5X3

Want to try two free books from another series?
Call 1-800-873-8635 or visit www.ReaderService.com.

* Terms and prices subject to change without notice. Prices do not include applicable taxes. Sales tax applicable in N.Y. Canadian residents will be charged applicable taxes. Offer not valid in Quebec. This offer is limited to one order per household. Not valid for current subscribers to Love Inspired Historical books. All orders subject to credit approval. Credit or debit balances in a customer's account(s) may be offset by any other outstanding balance owed by or to the customer. Please allow 4 to 6 weeks for delivery. Offer available while quantities last.

Your Privacy—The Reader Service is committed to protecting your privacy. Our Privacy Policy is available online at www.ReaderService.com or upon request from the Reader Service.

We make a portion of our mailing list available to reputable third parties that offer products we believe may interest you. If you prefer that we not exchange your name with third parties, or if you wish to clarify or modify your communication preferences, please visit us at www.ReaderService.com/consumerchoice or write to us at Reader Service Preference Service, P.O. Box 9062, Buffalo, NY 14240-9062. Include your complete name and address.

LIH15

SPECIAL EXCERPT FROM

Love Inspired HISTORICAL

James Wallin's family is depending on him to find a schoolteacher for their frontier town. Alexandrina Fosgrave seems to be exactly what he needs to help fulfill his father's dream of building a new community. If only James could convince her to accept the position.

Enjoy this sneak peek at
FRONTIER ENGAGEMENT *by* **Regina Scott***, available in August 2015 from Love Inspired Historical!*

"Alexandrina," James said, guiding his magnificent horses up a muddy, rutted trail that hardly did them justice. "That's an unusual name. Does it run in your family?"

She couldn't tell him the fiction she'd grown up hearing, that it had been her great-grandmother's name. "I don't believe so. I'm not overly fond of it."

He nodded as if he accepted that. "Then why not shorten it? You could go by Alex."

She sniffed, ducking away from an encroaching branch on one of the towering firs that grew everywhere around Seattle. "Certainly not. Alex is far too masculine."

The branch swept his shoulder, sending a fresh shower of drops to darken the brown wool. "Ann, then."

She shook her head. "Too simple."

"Rina?" He glanced her way and smiled.

Yes, she definitely knew the power of that smile. She could learn to love it. No, no, not love it. She was not here to fall in love but to teach impressionable minds. And a smile did not make the man. She must look to character, convictions.

"Rina," she said, testing the name on her tongue. She felt a smile forming. It had a nice sound to it, short, uncompromising. It fit the way she wanted to feel—certain of herself and her future. "I like it."

He shook his head. "And you blame me for failing to warn you. You should have warned me, ma'am."

Rina—yes, she was going to think of herself that way—felt her smile slipping. "Forgive me, Mr. Wallin. What have I done that would require a warning?"

"Your smile," he said with another shake of his head. "It could make a man go all weak at the knees."

His teasing nearly had the same effect, and she was afraid that was his intention. He seemed determined to make her like him, as if afraid she'd run back to Seattle otherwise. She refused to tell him she'd accepted his offer more from desperation than a desire to know him better. And she certainly had no intention of succumbing to his charm.

Don't miss
FRONTIER ENGAGEMENT by Regina Scott,
available August 2015 wherever
Love Inspired® Historical books and ebooks are sold.

her office felt small and overly hot. This wasn't the first time she'd felt the sensation. Over the past week, Fanny had battled bouts of queasiness at the oddest moments. Perhaps she was coming down with something. The flu had been making its rounds through the hotel staff.

Her head grew light. She needed to breathe in fresh air. Maybe she could entice Jonathon to join her for a brief stroll.

Swallowing back a wave of dizziness, she stood, left her office and made her way to Jonathon's. She found his assistant standing in the doorway, nose buried in the notepad he kept with him always.

"Is he in?" she inquired.

Burke Galloway looked up. "I'm sorry, Mrs. Hawkins, you just missed him. He had a meeting at Mr. Bennett's office across town."

"Oh, that's right." Before they'd left their suite this morning, Jonathon had mentioned having an appointment with Reese concerning a recent land acquisition.

"Was there anything I could do for you?"

"No, thank you, Mr. Galloway. I'll come back later."

Still feeling a bit light-headed, Fanny decided to take a short walk, anyway. After retrieving her coat and gloves, she left the hotel through the front doors and breathed in the cool air. Lifting her face to the sky, she concentrated on the glorious blue overhead. Her nausea almost immediately disappeared.

Just as she lowered her gaze, a masculine voice reached her ears. "Miss Mitchell, may I join you on your walk?"

A prickle of unease navigated up her spine. "I am Mrs. Hawkins now."

"Of course, my apologies. May I join you on your stroll...Mrs. Hawkins?" As he made his request a second time, Jonathon's father stood unmoving. The air around him crackled with arrogance.

Lowering her lashes to cover her surprise at his sudden appearance, Fanny couldn't help but wonder what Judge Greene wanted with her. Even acknowledging him made her feel as though she was betraying Jonathon.

But when she looked more closely, she saw the signs of strain on the judge's face. He looked older and somehow less sure of himself, despite the arrogant tilt of his head. From what Fanny had heard, he was still holding to his story that he'd only recently learned that Jonathon was his son.

It was on the tip of her tongue to tell him what she truly thought of him. But then she remembered the portion of the Bible she'd read just this morning during her daily quiet time. The Lord commanded His children to love their enemies.

She should at least give it a try. But, truly, it was times such as these that Fanny wished she didn't know Scripture quite so well.

Jaw tight, she gave a short nod. "You may have five minutes of my time."

"Thank you, my dear."

Love thy enemy, she reminded herself.

Her clenched jaw began to ache.

The judge gestured with his hand for her to continue walking. When she did, he fell into step beside her.

She could not fault his manners.

Gaze locked on the mountains in the distance, she expected him to speak. Surprising her yet again, he seemed content to walk beside her in silence.

She was not so patient.

Fanny stopped, waited for him to do the same, before saying, "State your business, Judge Greene."

"I have a request to make of you, Mrs. Hawkins."

She pursed her lips into what she hoped was a bored expression. "I'm listening."

"I wish to make amends with my son."

"What does that have to do with me?"

Stuffing his hands in his pockets, he lifted an elegantly clad shoulder. "He refuses to speak with me, no matter how many overtures I make. I have come to ask you to intercede for me."

Shocked by his colossal nerve, she stared at him. "You cannot be serious."

"I assure you, I am." He crowded her as he spoke, moving around her like a hawk circling its prey.

She backed up a step, and another, and then several more, until she found herself against a brick wall.

"Even if I had the sort of influence on my husband you seem to think, I would never wield it in such a manner. I am sorry, Judge Greene, you are on your own."

"All I'm asking is that you drop a kind word on my behalf."

She dismissed his request with a delicate sniff. "You ask too much."

"It is but one small kindness."

Did he not recognize the hypocrisy in his words? "Where was your kindness to my husband when he was a boy and came to you for help?"

The judge quirked an eyebrow at her. "I see my son has told you much."

"Jonathon has told me enough to know you showed him no compassion when he was in need. Yet you ask me for the very consideration you refused to give him." She realized that she could not love this particular enemy, no matter how hard she tried. "We are through here. I wish you a good day."

She started to push around him.

He stepped directly in her path. "I need an heir."

"You have an heir."

"Joshua is a disappointment. I have tried to contain his excesses. I have forbidden him to carry on with his mistress, yet he continues and has even produced an illegitimate child. I will not encourage his willful disobedience any longer." A muscle worked in the judge's jaw. "I have cut him off, once and for all."

Fanny blinked at the vast amount of information the man had supplied. One point seemed painfully clear. "So now that your legitimate son has disappointed you, you think to make Jonathon your heir?"

"Of course not." Outrage filled every hard plane of the older man's face. "Your husband is the by-blow of a prostitute and therefore unfit to carry my name."

Appalled, Fanny treated the judge to a withering glare. "He is your son."

"That is true. More to the point, he made the very wise decision to marry you, a woman of impeccable breeding from a prominent ranching family." His gaze dropped to her midsection. "I wish to name the first male child you bear as my official heir."

Fanny's hand instinctively covered her stomach. "You cannot claim my child as your heir over your own son."

The injustice horrified her. Just how many ways could this man hurt Jonathon?

"My hope is in the next generation. Josh's wife has proved barren. It is up to you, Mrs. Hawkins, to carry on my legacy."

Hand still on her stomach, she stumbled backward. Only once she caught her balance did she realize Judge Greene had somehow maneuvered her several feet down a darkened alley.